The Message?

The Message?

A thinking thriller about change and choice.

Avam Hale

ISBN-13: 9781506188911
ISBN-10: 1506188915
Library of Congress Control Number: 2015901026
CreateSpace Independent Publishing Platform,
North Charleston, SC

This book is dedicated to Dr. Stephen Merrill, a dear friend, who has intellect, kindness, and courage in equal measure and who, more than anyone else in my life, stoked my curiosity to ask questions that few others felt worthy of the time and effort.

AUTHOR'S PREFACE:

This is a book that explores, through a thrilling tale of intrigue, power, and deceit, why we believe what we do. We see what we expect to see is the practical outcome of what psychologists call precognitive conclusion, which is a fancy term for the simple fact that our brains process a small fraction of the data our senses make available. That's why there is so much disagreement in the world.

It is also a book about social and political inertia and why things often change at a much slower pace than we perceive they do – or should. That's because the people who have the ability to bring about change are often those who have the least incentive to do so.

This is a book of fiction. My hope, therefore, is that you find it entertaining. The characters, of course, are all fictional. But the philosophy is well researched and I have attempted to be accurate to the philosophical subject matter in every way. Socrates did exist, of course. But so did David Hume and William Paley.

I define myself as a student of life – people, actually. I take no position on the over-arching issues of politics or religion. If you perceive I have I will have failed. My purpose is to make you think in an entertaining way. If I get even one "*hmmm*" out of you I will have succeeded.

Enjoy the journey. I'm pretty confident it will end in a different place than you expect.

CHAPTER 1

"**T**he next item on our agenda is the case of Leah Warner," noted Dr. Russell Thornton, Chairman of the Saint Mary's Community Hospital Adult Ethics Committee. The committee had 27 members appointed by the Office of Clinical Affairs, including hospital physicians and nurses, social workers, members of the clergy, a representative of the community at large, a professor of medical ethics, and the hospital's chief legal counsel. Its purpose was to give advice on moral questions in clinical care, educate the staff and public on issues relating to medical ethics, and develop appropriate policies relating to patient care.

"Dr. Marcus, as attending physician, has been asked to join us," continued Dr. Thornton. "Dr. Marcus."

Dr. David Marcus, a neurologist of international repute, was a 58-year-old devout Jew. He had short, curly grey hair and bushy grey eyebrows that many of his female patients secretly wished to trim. He eschewed the golf course, the yacht club, and the tennis court for his personal library, although he seldom read anything other than the Tanach, which he read in its original Hebrew, and dry medical journals relating to his work, one of which he had been reading at the table, as he was not a member of the committee and abhorred idle time.

He was sitting to the right of Dr. Thornton at the massive conference table. The meeting was taking place in the newest building on the sprawling hospital campus, a modern glass structure that contrasted sharply with the older brick buildings, the original of which dated back to 1890. The architect of this newest building had intended the juxtaposition of neoclassical and modern styles to symbolize the joining of the hospital's rich history and its state of the art technology. The reaction among staff and patients, however, was decidedly mixed.

"Yes, thank you, Russ," he began after clearing his throat. "The patient is Leah Warner, a 38-year-old Caucasian female. Mrs. Warner has traumatic brain injury, or TBI, as well as numerous lacerations, contusions, and broken bones. The etiology was an automobile accident- a head on collision- approximately two weeks ago. She was alone in the car and the driver of the other car involved, also alone, was pronounced dead at the scene by the Coroner's Office."

"Have the police assigned blame?" asked Whitney Sharpe, General Counsel of the hospital. Mr. Sharpe was sitting to the left of Dr. Thornton, facing the building's exterior wall of glass. A balding, overweight man prone to wearing brightly-decorated suspenders, he was, as a result of his position in the room and the bright sunshine of a beautiful afternoon, squinting, making him appear even more distrustful and manipulative than he was commonly thought to be.

"As I understand it," replied Dr. Marcus, "the other driver was under the influence of alcohol and crossed over the center line."

"That shouldn't be a consideration," Ruth French, professor of medical ethics at the University of Michigan School of Medicine, noted sharply. "The patient's responsibility for her condition should have no bearing on our treatment. We are not a court."

"I obviously understand that," responded Mr. Sharpe, rather intolerantly. "If she were guilty, however, you can rest assured that there would be lawsuits and our treatment of her while in our care would come under scrutiny vis a vis her future ability to earn income."

As this type of exchange was all too common between the ethicist and the lawyer, several people around the table rolled their eyes in response to it. Dr. Thornton frowned noticeably.

"Dr. Marcus, please continue," Dr. Thornton pleaded.

"Yes. Mrs. Warner suffered a closed head injury due to abrupt cranial deceleration. At the time of her arrival her Glasgow Coma Scale score was

3, indicating that she was unresponsive to stimuli at any level. The intracranial pressure, or ICP, was substantially elevated, and this ultimately led to herniation and respiratory arrest. The patient now breathes with the assistance of a mechanical ventilator."

"For the non-medical members of the committee," interjected Dr. Thornton, "one of the things that makes the brain a unique organ is that it is housed within a rigid and inelastic container – the skull. It's a tight fit. If the brain swells, as it typically does following TBI, the skull doesn't comply and the pressure within the skull increases dramatically."

"Yes, thank you, Russ," said Dr. Marcus. "In the typical adult, I might add, the brain itself takes up approximately 85-90% of the intracranial volume; intravascular cerebral blood occupies about 10%; and cerebrospinal fluid takes up the remainder."

"And could you explain herniation, doctor," asked Rebecca Huber, the community representative on the committee. She was the wife of the founder and CEO of a local software company that had gone on to national prominence. As a couple, they had donated $10 million toward the construction of the building in which Rebecca was sitting. A plaque commemorating the gift hung on the wall of the room next to the main door.

"Of course," replied Dr. Marcus. "Herniation is caused when the brain moves across fixed dural structures and is damaged. Dura is a fibrous membrane that lines the bone of the skull. In this case, the swelling brain was pushed in a way that put significant pressure on the brainstem, or, more specifically, the medulla oblongata, which connects the brain with the spinal cord and controls breathing and heartbeat."

"So, when the swelling goes down, will the patient be able to breathe on her own?" asked Professor French.

"Don't know at this point," replied Dr. Marcus. "My educated guess is that the damage is irreversible and that she will not be capable of breathing on her own. Unfortunately, positive change, in this type of case, is very difficult to achieve."

"Does the patient have any immediate family?" Nurse Rebecca Numari, the newest member of the committee, asked.

"Two boys," Dr. Marcus replied after consulting the file in front of him, "ages 11 and 13. Family Services has been brought in, but the boys are staying with the patient's sister."

"Father or husband?" asked Dr. Thornton.

"The patient's husband and children's father died last year of malignant melanoma."

"Any advance directives?" asked Mr. Sharpe. "Living will or durable power of attorney?"

"Not that we're aware of," replied Dr. Marcus.

"Has anyone come forward to suggest that she had ever expressed her wishes in the event of incompetence?" Mr. Sharpe added.

"No. Her sister claims they never discussed it."

Leaning forward and resting his elbows on the table, Dr. Thornton said, "This item is on the agenda for information purposes only at this point. We want to give each of you a chance to do your own research before we consider it, should we ultimately be required to. Dr. Marcus has asked for our counsel should he conclude that the cognitive function loss is permanent and irreversible."

"One last question, Russ, if you don't mind," interjected Dr. John Heidrich, Chief of Psychiatric Medicine and personal friend of Dr. Marcus.

"Of course, John."

"David, would you describe the patient's other injuries. I assume there were some."

"Yes. Multiple lacerations on the face and upper chest. Ten required sutures. The most extensive was one across her left cheek, about four inches in length, one inch below the eye." Dr. Marcus looked down to consult the file. "There was an abdominal penetration, just above the bowel, but we found no internal damage during exploratory surgery. There were also the expected number of broken bones – several ribs and compound fractures in the left humerus and right fibula. Her right calcaneus, or heal, was also crushed, as were the third, fourth, and fifth metacarpal bones of her right hand," Dr. Marcus concluded, pointing to the bones just beyond the knuckle on his own hand for illustration.

"Any other questions?" asked Dr. Thornton, surveying the table. "If not," he continued, having visually canvassed the committee members, "we'll let Dr. Marcus get back to his duties."

"Thank you," Dr. Marcus said, gathering his papers and standing up to leave.

"Wouldn't these cases be so much simpler, doctor, if God would just show his face and tell us what to do," quipped Mr. Sharpe.

"Some of us believe he already has," responded Larry Rataj, Senior Pastor of the Carbondale Community Church, leaning forward in his chair in order to look directly at the lawyer at the other end of the expansive table.

"No offense, Pastor, but I'd be more comfortable if the proof was a little more definitive," responded Mr. Sharpe.

"Would you believe it if it was?" countered Pastor Rataj.

Professor French grinned discreetly into her hand, apparently elated by the pastor's challenge.

———

Professor Steven Bradshaw stood at the podium in the well of the Davis Lecture Hall on the campus of Great Lakes University. A Distinguished Professor of Philosophy at the university, and widely considered one of the four or five most influential living philosophers, he was about to begin his twice-weekly class on the philosophical arguments for the existence of a monotheistic God and Creator. As usual, the hall was filled to capacity.

Davis Hall was named in honor of GLU alumnus, Henry Davis, who had moved to Texas after graduation and made a fortune in oil, a third of which he had bequeathed to his alma mater upon his death. The hall seated 120 students, more or less, in comfortable cloth chairs with small writing tables that swung out of the way when not in use. The seats were arranged in horseshoe-shaped rows that rose steeply on three sides from the floor of the darkly stained wooden well on which the podium and a large table, currently empty, sat.

Built in the 1950s, the building was designed in the Gothic Revival style common to many older university campuses. The walls were covered in dark paneling, but the small southern-facing windows along the top of the back wall of the hall illuminated the room on sunny days with stark beams of sunlight. Due to the positioning of the windows and height of the hall, however, the sun's rays seldom illuminated the audience or the speaker, giving both the impression on such occasions that they were resident in a dark hole in the ground.

In his early seventies, but in the physical shape of a much younger man, Professor Bradshaw was extremely popular on campus, both because of his wry wit and his contagious enthusiasm for his field of study. The grandson of William Bradshaw, a reticent and little known industrialist who acquired a massive fortune supplying coke to the steel mills around Pittsburgh, the professor was also a bit of an eccentric whose eccentricities stood out from the abundant eccentricities of his colleagues. He wore only polyester, for example, rather than wool or tweed, smoked filter-less Camel cigarettes, and drove a mint condition cherry red 1968 Dodge Charger equipped with the legendary 426 Hemi engine. When street-tuned, as his was, the Hemi put out close to 500 horsepower of pure automotive muscle. His Charger also sported a jacked up rear end, wide racing tires, and a chrome plated air scoop that stuck up through the hood. Its roar could be heard across the campus and he delighted in peeling out in front of colleagues he knew would be disgusted by his politically incorrect choice in transportation.

Walking out from behind the podium with his notes in hand, Professor Bradshaw began. "Socrates was the father of philosophy, best known for his dedication to critical reasoning, which gave rise to what is commonly called the Socratic Method. Can anyone tell me what that is?"

A dozen hands shot up.

"Yes, the girl in the yellow sweater," he said, pointing to one of the students with raised hand. He never bothered to learn the names of his students, or anyone else for that matter. He considered it to be an unproductive use of mental capacity.

"It's a system of negative and positive questioning designed to expose truth," she stated in a loud, confident voice.

"Yes. And why do we need to expose the truth. Why isn't it obvious?"

"The truth can be complex," a young man in the back shouted out.

"It can be," Professor Bradshaw answered. "But even simple truths are rarely obvious. Why not?"

The room was silent.

"Because," Professor Bradshaw boomed, "we're all idiots."

Laughter erupted.

"Socrates said, 'Wisdom is knowing how little we know.'" A pause. "The problem is that most people don't know how little they know. So they draw false conclusions without realizing that they're false. By using the Socratic Method, we can break through our false assumptions to unveil the real truth that lies beneath." A pause. "What else did Socrates do?"

"Posed for a lot of busts?" a young man in the front row offered, generating laughter throughout the hall.

Professor Bradshaw laughed as well, saying, "Yes, he apparently did. Very good. A sense of humor. That's always helpful where philosophy is concerned. Nonetheless, I doubt Socrates would want that to be his legacy."

The professor paused as he moved across the floor, his free left hand clasping the wrist of his right hand behind his back.

"In addition to giving us the Socratic Method, Socrates formulated an argument for the existence of God that subsequently became known as the Teleological Argument. The name is derived from the Greek word *telos*, which is translated either end or purpose. And what is the major premise of this argument?" he asked, looking up at the class.

Several dozen hands went up.

"Yes, you, with the cap on backwards. By the way, do you know what wearing your cap backwards says about you?"

"No," the young man answered sheepishly.

"I don't either. I was just curious. Continue."

After the laughter had subsided, the young man explained, "The major premise of the Teleological Argument is, 'Whatever exists for a useful purpose must be the work of an intelligence.'"

"Precisely," responded the professor, thrusting his hand, forefinger extended, into the air for emphasis. "It is often described as an argument from design. The world is simply too complex not to have been designed by a Creator."

———

At precisely 5:17 a.m., the electronic alarm of the central patient monitoring system in the Saint Mary's Hospital Critical Care Unit came to life with an unnerving wail. The patient in room 384 was in cardiac arrest.

The alarm shattered the din of fluorescent humming, the soft clatter of a computer keyboard, the muffled sound of a distant television, and the gentle whir of the air conditioning system. Nurse Valerie Noosum, sitting alone at the nurses' station entering patient data into the computer, leapt from her chair and was already coming out from behind the desk as she looked back at the wall-mounted monitor to determine which patient was in the throes of death. She was immediately joined by Nurse Gail Harmon, the shift supervisor, who was returning from her break.

Gail had been a nurse at Saint Mary's for more than 30 years. That seniority would easily have allowed her to be assigned to the day shift, but she preferred working nights for the freedom it gave her to work in her beloved flower garden during the day in the summer. She had two grown children; one boy and one girl. The latter currently lived in Chicago with her husband and two infant sons. The former lived alone in Seattle.

Gail had raised her children largely on her own. She had married a stone mason while still in nursing school in response to an unintended pregnancy. The marriage dissolved a few years later, however, when her husband left town with another woman and vanished into a new life.

While not outwardly bitter about her circumstances, Gail gave her children little religious education. Her church was the temple of nature, where she could touch, hear, and smell the beauty of the flowers and the birds.

The two nurses sprinted down the short hallway of the CCU side by side, their rubber-soled shoes squeaking with urgency on the polished floor as they ran. Arriving at the doorway to room 384, Valerie slowed to allow Gail to enter first. Bursting through the door, however, Gail stopped abruptly just two steps into the room, causing Valerie to nearly run into her. Both women stood silently.

The lone patient in the private room was Leah Warner. She was sitting on the side of the bed, illuminated by the harsh shaft of light that entered the otherwise dark room through the doorway. Her hands were clasped in front of her and she was praying quietly, her head bowed and her eyes closed.

Leah was five feet, three inches in height, with straight brown hair of shoulder length parted in the middle. Her face was plain, but pleasant in appearance, and she never wore more than a modicum of makeup.

Leah had a quiet, reserved demeanor that bordered on meek. She frequently struggled to find the self-confidence and force of will to stand up for herself, a trait that had largely defined her life to that point.

After several seconds of frozen time, Leah opened her eyes slowly, looked up at the new arrivals, and laid her hands, palms flat, on the bed beside her. Her large brown eyes were clear and bright, almost sparkling, and her face was blemish-free and radiant.

Recovering from the shock of finding Leah Warner sitting on the side of her hospital bed, the two nurses entered the room tentatively, as if they were viewing an apparition that might dissipate into thin air in response to sudden movement or noise.

Gail spoke first. "Leah?" she asked softly as she reached over to turn on the overhead lights.

"Yes?" Leah replied in a soft, but clear voice.

The two nurses paused briefly in reaction to the response, exchanging brief glances of incredulity. They then continued to move cautiously toward the bed with outstretched hands, as if Leah might suddenly fall to the floor.

"I'm all right," Leah assured them.

"We don't want to take any chances," Gail replied. "Let's lie back in bed. You've been in a terrible accident."

"Yes, I know."

Experienced professionals, the nurses both realized immediately that the bruises and contusions on Leah's face had largely disappeared. As is often the case when one encounters the inexplicable, however, neither said anything aloud. They each filed the information away in their memories for future consideration without accepting or denying its veracity.

Valerie went around the bed and reached up to the patient monitor console mounted above the head of the bed. She pushed a button, silencing the alarm that had continued to shriek at the nurses' station.

"You have several broken bones as a result of the accident," noted Gail, as she helped Leah lie down in the bed. "Do you feel any pain?"

"No," replied Leah. "None. I feel fine."

Once Leah was prone, both nurses reached down and pulled the white blanket and sheet up over Leah's chest.

"Leah," asked Gail, "do you know where you are?"

"Yes," Leah replied without hesitation. "I'm in the Critical Care Unit of Saint Mary's Hospital in Waterford, Michigan."

The nurses again exchanged startled glances. The patient had been unconscious since her arrival, and since she had been transferred more than sixty miles to Saint Mary's because of its nationally recognized neurology department, it was doubtful that she had ever been admitted to the institution before.

Looking across the bed at Valerie, Gail said, "Dr. Singh is the neurologist on duty tonight, but Dr. Marcus will want to know about this immediately. Please page Dr. Singh and call Dr. Marcus at home."

Valerie nodded, looked at Leah one last time, and left the room.

Looking at Gail in a way that a mother would look at a child who appeared anxious or sad, Leah asked gently, "Are you all right? You appear upset."

"No doubt," Gail replied anxiously.

Working quickly and deliberately, Gail went around the end of the bed and picked up the wires from the patient monitor, which Leah had apparently removed on her own. Reapplying them, she pushed a few buttons on the wall display to reset the device and waited for it to resume its duties. She didn't bother to reinsert the ventilator tube although she knew that protocol would normally require a nurse to do so, barring a doctor's directive not to. It was obvious that the patient didn't require it, however, as baffling as that was.

"Do you feel dizzy or nauseous?" asked Gail, removing a pen and small note pad from the pocket of her uniform. Looking up at the monitor, she began to write down the various readings, including heart beat rate and rhythm, blood pressure, and oxygenation, which the system was again providing.

"No. I feel fine. Blessed, actually."

"I can understand that," chuckled Gail. "I've been doing this for more than 30 years and I've witnessed a lot of mysterious things. This has to take the cake, though."

"It is miraculous, isn't it," Leah noted in innocent excitement.

"It is that," Gail agreed.

"Of all the people in the world, God chose me to be a messenger," Leah said in a voice of combined disbelief and awe.

Gail's eyes quickly darted from the monitor to Leah's face, while she unconsciously cocked her head and wrinkled her brow. She concluded that she must have misheard Leah's last comment, however, and soon returned her gaze to the multi-parameter monitor.

At that moment, Dr. Singh rushed into the room. Even with the advantage of having been told what to expect, he, too, came up short at the sight of Leah Warner lying in bed, eyes open, face flush with healthy color.

Dr. Singh quickly regained his composure, nonetheless, and moved to Leah's side, where he instinctively took her left hand in his own.

"Vitals?" he asked.

"BP is 122 over 75. Pulse is 80. Temp is normal."

"How do you feel?" he asked in a soft clinical voice with a slight remnant of a Filipino accent.

"I feel fine," Leah replied. "I'm quite confident that you will find nothing wrong with me, doctor."

He ignored her comment. "How about your head? Do you have a headache?"

"No."

"And your vision? Can you see clearly?"

"Yes."

Placing the ear inserts of the stethoscope around his neck into his ears, the doctor placed the metal medallion on Leah's chest. "And your breathing? Is it difficult to breathe?"

"No."

"She removed the ventilator tube on her own before we got here," Gail noted.

Dr. Singh moved the chest medallion to several locations, stopping each time to listen. "Let's roll her over," he subsequently directed Gail.

Gail immediately reached down to roll the patient over, but Leah had already begun the process on her own, apparently in little or no discomfort.

Dr. Singh then listened through his stethoscope at several locations on Leah's upper back.

"Her breathing appears normal," he finally reported to no one in particular.

The doctor then removed an Ophthalmoscope from a rack on the wall over the bed and shone its bright light into each of Leah's eyes. Afterward, he removed an Ottoscope from the same rack and used it to look deep into each of Leah's ears.

Straightening up and returning the Ottoscope to its place on the rack, Dr. Singh let out a deep sigh. Looking toward Gail, he asked, "Who is the attending physician?"

"Dr. Marcus," she replied. "He's been called at home."

"Yes, I'm sure he will want to be informed."

Doctor Singh looked up at the monitor display to view the latest blood pressure reading. It was 125 over 72.

"The other nurse said that the cardiac arrest alarm went off."

"Yes," replied Gail. "We came immediately. When we arrived she was sitting up in bed and had apparently removed the monitor wires."

Dr. Singh looked directly at Gail. "Are you sure it wasn't the disconnect alarm?"

"Yes. They are very different. I can check the system log, but I'm quite sure."

"That would suggest that the cardiac arrest occurred first, before she removed the wires," observed Dr. Singh, wrinkling his face slightly as if experiencing discomfort from the knowledge.

"Doctor," continued Gail, "Mrs. Warner also said that she has no pain from any of her fractures."

"Is that true?" Dr. Singh asked, looking down at Leah.

"Yes. I don't feel the slightest amount of pain," Leah replied.

"Do you have a high tolerance for pain that you are aware of?" asked Dr. Singh.

"I can assure you not," Leah chuckled.

Looking up at Gail, Dr. Singh asked, "Would you mind getting her file from the desk?"

"Not at all," she replied, and left the room.

Doctor Singh continued his examination of Leah in silence, working purposefully and efficiently. Gail returned shortly and handed Leah's file across the bed to the doctor. He opened it and began to read. As he continued to read, he muttered in astonishment, "This can't be right."

"Doctor," Leah said, "I have been with God."

Dr. Singh looked up quickly, startled by the comment.

"Is that right?"

"I have a message. God asked me – me of all people - to deliver it to the world."

Dr. Singh remained silent.

"It is a message of love. God loves us and wants us to love each other in the same way. God wants us to embrace humility and selflessness instead of acquisition and achievement."

Dr. Singh remained silent and returned to reading the folder, as if Leah had said nothing at all. Finally, he looked up at Gail and said, "The patient had numerous lacerations and contusions, including a large contusion on her forehead in the frontal lobe area and multiple sutures below her left eye."

"Yes. And when I made my rounds earlier this evening, they were very obvious."

Dr. Singh bent over to look more closely at Leah's face. His own face was grave, as if everything he had ever learned or come to believe was being challenged by what he saw. He squinted to focus as his eyes rapidly scanned Leah's face. He slowly raised his slightly trembling hand and brushed the backs of his fingers lightly over Leah's cheeks and forehead. Her skin was smooth, soft, and radiant.

CHAPTER 2

Professor Bradshaw paused before walking across the floor of the well. Stopping on the other side, he paused before looking up at the audience and continuing his lecture.

"Socrates, it appears," he began, "also believed in eternal life, although that is impossible to know for sure. Why not?"

"He never wrote anything down," answered a young woman in the middle of the hall.

"That's correct. Virtually all of our knowledge of what Socrates did and did not believe comes from his contemporaries, such as Xenophon and Aritophanes, and his pupils, particularly Plato.

"One thing we do know for sure," he continued, "is that Socrates challenged the established order. That's always a dangerous undertaking. The status quo is frequently anchored by sheer momentum, largely because the people who have the most to lose, should it be challenged, are the ones who have the most power.

"Socrates, nonetheless, would not be silenced, so the establishment of the day, which desperately wanted to maintain the status quo for obvious personal reasons, ultimately dragged him into court and sentenced him to death. It is impossible to kill an ideal, however, and Socrates' teachings, even though he never wrote anything down, have survived to this day."

The professor paused as he put his right index finger to his lips.

"Socrates was philosophical until the end. In Plato's *Apology*," he continued, "we are told that Socrates had this to say to the judges who ultimately sentenced him to death for his theological and political transgressions: 'To fear death, gentlemen, is no other than to think oneself wise when one is not, to think one knows what one does not know. No one knows whether death may not be the greatest of all blessings for a man, yet men fear it as if they knew that it is the greatest of evils. And surely it is the most blame-worthy ignorance to believe that one knows what one does not know.'"

After pausing momentarily, Professor Bradshaw looked up at the class and asked, "What do you take from that?"

A hand went up. "Yes," Professor Bradshaw replied, pointing at the student.

"That he didn't fear death, but was unsure of what came after?"

"It certainly suggests that he was unafraid of death. I don't know many people who would be so poised and combative under the circumstances. And taken in isolation, this one quote might suggest that Socrates had doubts about his religious beliefs. Based on other accounts, however, most Socratic scholars believe that he did, in fact, believe that the soul survives the body."

The professor paused as he once again paced back across the floor.

"Here's what I take from this quote," he said quickly, again thrusting his right index finger into the air. "Socrates is essentially arguing that sim-ply because we don't know for sure that God exists – i.e., we can't prove it – doesn't mean it isn't true. In other words, an inability to prove the positive does not prove the negative. At the end of the day, we simply don't know, so neither side of the argument over God's existence can claim logi-cal superiority.

"But let's move on in time," Professor Bradshaw continued, gesturing casually as if he was waving someone on. "Despite its Socratic origins, the Teleological Argument is most commonly associated with William Paley, an Anglican priest, philosopher, and author who lived from 1743 to 1805. Paley built on the work of several previous philosophers and theologians, including John Ray, who lived from 1628 to 1705 and is widely considered the father of natural history in Great Britain.

"Ray was a devout Christian, who believed that God was best under-stood through study of his creation, the world of nature. He wrote, 'There is for a free man no occupation more worthy and delightful than to contemplate the beauteous works of nature and honour the infinite wisdom and goodness of God.'

"Paley took Ray's belief one step further when he wrote, in *Natural Theology*, in 1802: 'There cannot be design without a designer; contrivance without a contriver; order without choice; arrangement without anything capable of arranging; subserviency and relation to purpose without that which could intend a purpose; means suitable to an end, and executing their office in accomplishing that end, without the end ever having been contemplated or the means accommodated to it. Arrangement, disposition of parts, subserviency of means to an end, relation of instruments to a use imply the presence of intelligence and mind.'

"To make his case, Paley introduced one of the most famous metaphors in the philosophy of science. What was it?"

"A watch," a young woman shouted.

"Correct. He likened the complexities of nature to the complexities of a watch. When we look at the precise and elaborate mechanism within a traditional mechanical watch, he argued, we know that there must have been a watchmaker who made the watch. We know, without the slightest doubt, that it didn't make itself. And since nature is infinitely more complex than a watch, we can similarly assume that God must exist and was the Creator.

"Paley attended Christ's College, in Cambridge. Can anyone tell me who else attended Christ's College?"

The room was silent.

"None other than Charles Darwin. In fact, Darwin, who was born seven years after the publication of Paley's *Natural Theology*, was forced to read Paley's work in order to graduate."

There were snickers among the students.

"Ahhh," the professor said in response, wagging his finger in jest, "Socrates would not be proud. You are assuming that Darwin and Paley were philosophical opposites. As it turns out, Darwin was a huge fan of Paley. In his autobiography, Darwin wrote that the logic of Paley gave him as much delight as did the logic of Euclid. Darwin, in fact, credits his belief in adaptation, the foundation of evolutionary science, to Paley, even though Darwin ultimately extrapolated their common belief into a very different conclusion.

"As a result of Darwin's drastically different conclusions, however," the professor continued, "Darwin did influence the modern Teleological Argument. Can anyone tell me how?"

"He discredited it?" posed one of the students.

"For some. But not for all," replied the professor.

"He forced creationists to turn to Intelligent Design?" ventured a young man on the side.

"True, to a point, but that doesn't directly address the issue of the Teleological Argument. No, the change has to do with the focus of the argument. Paley was fascinated by the complexity of biological systems, such as the eyeball, and often referred to those biological systems in advancing the Teleological Argument. Darwin, of course, provided an alternative explanation. Modern Teleologicians, therefore, tend to use analogies relating to the complexity of the universe rather than the complexity of biological systems. They've taken the argument from design out of the realm of biology and into the realm of astrophysics.

"Can anyone tell me what famous astrophysicist provided a purely scientific explanation for the origin of the universe that many Teleologicians believe actually strengthens the argument from design?"

No response.

"Albert Einstein. Do you know why?"

"He was Jewish," a young man responded. "He believed in God."

"He was ethnically Jewish," Professor Bradshaw noted, "but it is unclear that his Jewish heritage played any significant role in his life. Einstein's parents were secular Jews and while he did frequently invoke the name of God, as in his famous quote, 'God does not play dice with the universe,' one of his many objections to the contemporary science of quantum physics, many students of Einstein have suggested that he merely used the term as a euphemism for the natural order. At any rate, to whatever extent

Einstein did believe in God, it does not appear that he accepted the kind of personal God that influences events and answers prayers." A pause. "What is Einstein best known for?"

"His hair," shouted the previous jokester in the front row.

Laughter again erupted.

"Why don't you sit out in the hall next time," the professor suggested, smiling. "What else?"

"The Theory of Relativity."

"Yes. And what about it?"

There was no reply.

"The Theory of Relativity implies that there was a beginning to the universe. That begs a question. How did the universe's expansion get started?"

"Hasn't that been explained by the Big Bang Theory?" offered a student in the back.

"Not really," the professor replied. "Astrophysicists generally agree that there is overwhelming evidence that the universe had a beginning. Before that beginning there was nothing – no space, no time, no matter, no energy. Then there was what scientists, including Big Bang theorists, call a singularity. No one really knows, however, what a singularity is or where it came from.

———

Lisa "Sunny" Clark was Leah's younger sister. Five years apart in age, the girls had never been particularly close growing up. Leah, who didn't believe that she could master the academic rigors of college, moved out of the house immediately upon graduating from high school and took a job as a press operator at an injection molding plant in Flint, about fifty miles away.

The sisters saw little of each other in the ensuing years. Sunny became the star of the school's field hockey team and maintained an active social calendar. Leah kept largely to herself and seldom visited her family.

Eventually, ever confident in her abilities, Sunny went off to college on a field hockey scholarship. Leah, for her part, met a young accountant, Greg Warner, through a mutual friend. They were married after a short courtship and Leah moved to Dearborn, anxious to start her own family.

Pretty and athletic, Sunny was rail thin and four inches taller than her sister. She wore her blonde hair in a short bob and dressed, more often than not, in dungarees, simple pastel-colored cotton shirts, and running shoes.

Thirty-three, Sunny had never married, although she had been engaged to a successful stock broker from the tony suburb of Birmingham before he developed a gambling addiction at one of the casinos that had been erected in downtown Detroit in an effort to resurrect the decayed inner city. Her fiancé was sentenced, just two months before the planned wedding, to three years in the state penitentiary for embezzling money from his clients in order to support his addiction. Deeply shaken, Sunny developed a deep sense of cynicism and distrust that had precluded any further meaningful relationships with men.

Instead, Sunny immersed herself in her work as a high school gym teacher and coach of the field hockey team. She did, however, following the breakup of her engagement, reach out to the older sister she hardly knew. At the time of Leah's accident, the sisters lived only five miles apart.

After an initial hesitation, Leah became receptive to Sunny's overtures and had found an unexpected sense of comfort in their growing intimacy. At times, however, Leah resented Sunny's tendency to act like the older sister, frequently telling Leah what to do and even scolding her for her tendency toward submissiveness. "You've got to learn to stand up for yourself," Sunny would frequently chide her.

Greg, whose temperament mirrored Leah's, had been supportive of Sunny's growing presence in their home and their life, although he frequently retired to his woodshop in the basement when she was at the house. Although Sunny was always pleasant to Greg, in part because she knew how much he worshipped her sister, her intense persona and proclivity for cynicism created in him a certain disquiet that bordered on anxiety.

Sunny was very close to her two nephews, Tyler, 13, and Ryan, 11, however, both of whom adored her. The boys often spent the night at Sunny's home, a practice that became even more common following Greg's diagnosis. He was often violently ill from chemotherapy, and in addition to requiring Leah's constant attention, he didn't want his sons to witness the full ravages of his disease.

The boys had been with Sunny on the night of Leah's terrible accident. When Leah didn't show up the following morning to take the boys to school, Sunny suspected the worst, eventually tracking Leah to Saint Mary's through the Oakland County Sheriff's Department, which had investigated the accident.

Being summertime, both Sunny and the boys were off from school. She was home, as a result, when the hospital called at nine o'clock to share the news of Leah's awakening. She shrieked with joy upon hearing the news, causing the two boys to run in from the den where they had been watching television.

Tears streaming down her face as she hung up the phone, she put her hands to her cheeks and turned to the boys. "Your mother is awake," she said excitedly, her hands beginning to tremble with excitement. "She came out of the coma."

The boys rushed to embrace their aunt, their pent up grief and anguish gushing up from within as they did. Having lost their father only a year before, they had naturally feared the worst.

While she had visited her sister daily, despite Leah's total lack of responsiveness, Sunny had only taken the boys to the hospital on one occasion. She could see in their eyes the distress that the sight of their bruised and battered mother caused them and, ever the protector, had decided to spare them further anguish.

When Ryan, the more effervescent and outgoing of the two brothers, asked if they could go see her right away, therefore, Sunny hesitated before answering. "Tell you what," she finally responded, still loosely hugging her nephews, "why don't you let me go check it out first. If your mother is up for it, I promise I'll come right back and get you. Deal?"

"Okay," Ryan answered in obvious disappointment. Tyler, as he often did, merely shook his head.

———

"Sunny," Leah shrieked gleefully, as her sister burst through the door, immediately sobbing tears of joy at the sight of Leah sitting up in bed. Embracing tightly, the two sisters just rocked silently back and forth for several minutes, each dampening the other's shoulder with her tears.

Still embraced, Sunny said, "I can't believe it. When they called and said that you were awake, I thought I must be dreaming. I mean," she sputtered, "I had no idea that you were really…awake."

Leah took Sunny by the shoulders and guided her backward far enough to see Leah's face. "Sunny, I didn't just awaken. Look at my face. The cuts and bruises are almost all gone. And my broken bones are all almost healed, too. They just took x-rays."

Sunny gasped as her mouth fell open in bewilderment. "Oh my God," was all she could manage to say in her shock.

Finally, her eyes still darting back and forth across Leah's face, Sunny said breathlessly, "How did that happen?"

Leah simply smiled.

"But that's impossible," Sunny observed.

"Exactly."

Sunny looked around the room. "I need to sit," she said, reaching for the chair beside Leah's bed and turning it to face Leah.

The sisters sat in silence while Sunny digested the incredible news. Finally, she asked, "So how do they explain it?"

"They don't," replied Leah. "But there's more."

"More?"

"Yes, and this will be an even greater shock." A pause. "While I was in the coma, Sunny, I was with God." She paused. "At least I think I was," Leah added, her voice trailing off.

Sunny just stared, her eyes narrowing as she fought to understand.

"It was incredible," Leah continued hesitantly, staring blankly at the wall opposite the bed.

Sunny sat motionless.

"I don't really know if God is a man or a woman. It somehow struck me that he, or she, or whatever, was both," Leah offered, shaking her head slowly in apparent confusion.

"What did God look like?" Sunny asked in a soft, restrained tone.

"I don't know," Leah replied, shrugging slightly. "I didn't see anything except white light, which seemed to be coming from everywhere at once." A pause. "And I heard a voice that kept saying, 'I love you, my child,' over and over and over again. Another pause. "Mostly, though, I felt a presence."

"What kind of presence?" Sunny asked, now fighting to conceal her skepticism.

Leah just shook her head from side to side. "Love," she finally muttered. "I felt the presence of love. I felt like love was just washing over me," she said with increasing excitement. "I felt totally and completely loved. I really don't know how to describe it. I only know that it was the most incredible sensation I've ever felt. I felt so safe. I felt so comforted. It was the kind of feeling a mother dreams that her baby feels when she holds it in her arms."

"Do you think you might just have been dreaming?" Sunny asked suggestively.

Leah turned to look directly at Sunny. "I don't know," Leah responded hesitantly, returning her gaze to the wall opposite her bed. "I really don't know." A long pause. "But there was more. God asked me to deliver a message to the world."

"What message?" Sunny asked with apparent incredulity, in an almost demanding tone.

"God asked me to tell everyone that he – or she - loves all of us, without exception, and God wants us to love each other in the same way. He wants us to come together in harmony and friendship. He wants us to stop serving ourselves and learn to serve each other."

"And how did God suggest we do that? By worshipping him – or her?"

"You're cynical," Leah observed, frowning. "I don't blame you." Another long pause. "God said that people are too pre-occupied with acquisition and achievement, which makes us self-centered. It's the reason, God says, for the great social and political divisions in the world today."

"So God wants everyone to learn to get along."

"God wants us to practice humility and selflessness. These, God says, are the essence of real love."

After a long pause, Sunny asked, "Have you told this to anyone else?"

"Everyone. My attending physician isn't here yet, but I told the doctor who was on duty when I awoke."

"And how did he react?"

"He didn't, really," Leah observed. "I'm not sure I can believe it. I don't know how anyone else could."

"I don't know, Leah," Sunny began after pausing. "You must have been dreaming."

"But wouldn't it be nice if it were true," Leah asked excitedly. "Wouldn't it be nice if God really existed and that he loved each of us, no matter who we are or what we've done?"

"Yes, of course," Sunny replied. "But how could it possibly be? Think about what you're saying, Leah. Nice is nice," she said testily, "but that doesn't make it true."

"Perhaps you're right," Leah conceded, sighing deeply.

After both women sat silently in thought for what seemed like several minutes, Leah suddenly snapped out of her reverie, as if the prior discussion had never occurred. "How are the boys?" she asked excitedly.

Sunny sat upright and shook her head slightly, as if trying to shake off drowsiness. "They're fine," she said. "They're at home. I left them with a neighbor. I decided to come alone first."

"And have they been with you the whole time?"

"Yes," replied Sunny. "When you didn't pick them up the next morning, I was obviously worried, so I called the police to see if there had been any accidents reported. They eventually told me you were here. I've been coming every day since."

"Thank you," Leah replied, smiling warmly.

"I only brought the boys once, though. I didn't see any point in it. And I didn't want to upset them any more than they already were. Leah, you were in terrible shape. It brought tears to my eyes every time I saw you."

CHAPTER 3

"There is, of course, a problem with the Teleological Argument," Professor Bradshaw continued. "Can anyone tell me what it is?"

"It's a theory," shouted a student.

"But why's it a theory?"

"It can't be proved," replied the same student.

"It can't be proved by deductive logic. It is an inductive argument. Rather than deducing a possible explanation of an observed conclusion, the argument from design uses an observation – i.e., that the universe is complex – to induce a conclusion – i.e., that God exists.

"Unlike deductive reasoning, inductive reasoning is not supported by the weight of measurable data. At some level, it relies on words. And words are, at worst, imprecise, and, at best, incomplete. Words, after all, are merely symbols that have been developed to allow for efficient communication.

"This creates a rather slippery slope, scientifically speaking. Scientists are generally hostile to inductive reasoning, although some systems of inductive logic have been proposed. The most well known is Bayesianism, named after Reverend Thomas Bayes, who, in the 1700s, proposed a theorem relating conditional and marginal probabilities.

"In the modern era, a staunch Bayesian, Edwin Jaynes, a distinguished physicist who taught at Washington University in St. Louis until the early 1990s, went on to argue that it is impossible to avoid subjectivity in *any* form of inference. To compensate for that, Jaynes developed the statistical principles of maximum entropy and transformation groups, tools that attempt to alleviate the subjectivity of assigning probabilities.

"Ironically, one of the biggest supporters of inductive logic was also one of the biggest critics of the Teleological Argument. Does anyone know who that is? I'll give you a clue: He was an influential Scottish philosopher."

"Hume?"

"Very good. Yes, David Hume, an 18th century philosopher and author of *Treatise of Human Nature*. Hume argued that we use inductive reasoning to reach reasonable conclusions all the time. In fact, he argued, our very existence depends on it. We eat bread, for example, because we know from experience that bread satisfies our hunger and keeps us alive. It's entirely possible, however, that we could eat bread at some point in the future that is, in fact, poisonous. Were we to demand deductively substantiated proof of its nutritional value before eating it, we would literally die of starvation.

"As far as the Teleological Argument goes, however, Hume argued that it relies too heavily on analogy and that the analogy, under any circumstances, isn't appropriate, since not all products of nature are complex.

"He's right, of course, although I prefer to characterize the objection a little differently. What's the problem with complexity?"

Only one student raised her hand.

"Yes," said the professor, raising his chin in anticipation of her answer.

"Complexity is in the eye of the beholder. What's complex to one is simple to another."

"Spoken like a true philosopher," he replied, causing the young woman to smile broadly. "It's all relative," he exclaimed, holding his arms out to emphasize the point. "What is complex? Is the human body complex?" A pause. "At one level, yes. Who's to say, however, that there isn't some other life form out there in a distant galaxy that is infinitely more complex? After all, you have to admit that we have our failings. We get sick. We break down. We die after what is, in astrophysical terms, the blink of an eye. The bottom line is that while the argument from design makes some philosophical sense, no one can say with certainty what level of complexity is complex enough to warrant a designer."

A student raised his hand.

"Yes."

"How do we know that even if there was a designer, that there was only one?"

"Excellent point. Another objection that Hume raised. Even if we do accept the argument from design, that doesn't prove the existence of any specific God, or the existence of a single God."

Returning his notes to the podium, Professor Bradshaw turned to the class and said, "We're obviously not going to settle this argument today, so let's stop here. At the next class we will discuss the argument from conscience. Please read the next three chapters in your text beforehand. And you," he concluded, pointing to the jokester in the front row, "Don't forget to sit in the hall. Good day, everyone," he concluded cheerfully.

———

The door to Leah's hospital room opened and a doctor walked briskly in.

"I'm Dr. Marcus, Leah, your attending physician. We obviously haven't had the chance to formally meet. I have, however, met your sister," he added, looking toward Sunny and smiling.

"Is this a dream, doctor?" Sunny asked.

"Not unless I'm sharing it," he replied. "I would, however, like to do a complete exam before attempting to explain it." His eyes were darting back and forth over Leah's face as an incredulous look came over his own face, causing his bushy eyebrows to somehow seem even fuller.

After a moment, Sunny said, "Why don't I get out of your way. Leah, I'll go home and pick up the boys." Standing up, she put the chair back in its original location against the wall.

"Thank you, Sunny. I can't wait to see them."

Dr. Marcus continued to visually examine his patient, oblivious to the exchange between Sunny and Leah. It was several minutes before he even realized that Sunny had left the room.

Thirty minutes later, Dr. Marcus returned the rubber-tipped hammer carried by all neurologists to the right-hand pocket of his white lab coat, sighing deeply.

"Leah," he finally said, compressing his lips, "I have examined you from head to toe and see nothing that I wouldn't expect to see in a healthy 38-year-old woman. The CT scan taken earlier didn't show anything either. Frankly, if I didn't know better, I'd say that you simply aren't the same patient that I've been treating for the last three weeks."

"Perhaps I'm not," Leah replied wistfully.

"Yes. Well, I've seen some pretty miraculous things in my day, but I can't begin to describe what's happened here."

"Dr. Marcus," Leah began hesitantly, "I believe that I was with God and that God asked me to deliver a message to the world. Could it be that God healed me for that purpose?"

The doctor compressed his lips again. "Yes," he slowly replied. "Dr. Singh told me of your perceived experience."

"It seems a little far-fetched, doesn't it?"

Dr. Marcus raised his eyebrows momentarily in a look of skeptical pensiveness. "At face value I'd have to say it does."

"So it could have been just a dream," Leah replied, unsure of whether or not she was disappointed in the possibility.

Taking a deep breath, Dr. Marcus explained, "Freud believed that the dream state is a mechanism for resolving the unresolved conflicts of the day." Lowering himself to the edge of the bed, he continued. "We do so by abandoning the discipline of linear logic for a less demanding from of logic known as paralogic. It's the same logic used by young children. In their case, it allows them to learn at a faster pace." A pause. "You mentioned a message. What was the message that God asked you to deliver?"

"God loves us, and wants us to love each other in the same way. God wants us to come together through selflessness and humility and to stop being so pre-occupied with material acquisition and hollow achievement."

"Sounds sensible enough to me," the doctor noted, cocking his head slightly.

"Sensible, maybe. But was it real?"

"For what it's worth," the doctor replied, clasping his hands in his lap, "I am a devout Jew. I believe wholeheartedly in God. I have witnessed, in my career, many medical miracles. And I honestly believe many were a result of God's intervention. That, however, is a conviction of faith. My agnostic colleagues have other explanations. None of these explanations, however, including my own, can be proven scientifically, because the results can't be replicated at will."

"So how would they explain my recovery?" Leah asked sheepishly.

"I think everyone would agree that your recovery is miraculous. The question is whether or not it was a divine miracle or a natural one. You see, as much as we've learned about the human body in recent decades, our medical knowledge remains elementary. There is far more that we don't know than we do know. It is entirely possible that medical miracles, therefore, are simply the result of insufficient knowledge and not divine intervention.

"Because of our relatively limited knowledge," the doctor continued, showing ever increasing interest in the conversation, "medicine is largely a process of elimination. Doctors don't so much determine what did happen as they eliminate what didn't happen. When a patient is ill, we determine the mostly likely cause based on our experience and knowledge. We then run tests to see if our thesis is correct. If it isn't, we test for something else. Eventually, we rule out the incorrect answers and are left with the correct one."

"But how do you rule out the answer that this is the work of God?" Leah posed.

"I don't. I can't prove or disprove any explanation." Standing, the doctor reached for the chair next to Leah's bed, arranged it facing the bed, and sat down. "Leah, do you know much about the Jewish religion?"

"Not really," Leah replied. "I know that you don't believe in Jesus Christ."

"We don't believe that Jesus was the Messiah, or Moshiach, as we refer to it. We do not believe that the Moshiach will be divine in the sense that Christians believe that Jesus was. Rather, we believe that he will be a charismatic political leader and invincible military commander who is very much a human being. And we believe that he will accomplish certain specific things relating to the redemption of the Jewish people, many of which Jesus did not accomplish.

"We also believe," Dr. Marcus continued, crossing his legs and resting his crossed arms on his thigh as if he might have some stomach discomfort, "that in every generation there is a person born with the potential to be the Moshiach, if the potential is right for the messianic age, or Olam Ha-Ba – the World to Come. In that sense, the idea that God would send a human messenger may, in fact, be more plausible to Jews than to Christians, although you would technically be disqualified from being the Moshiach on ancestral grounds."

"I'm sure that I'm not that person, doctor," Leah said.

"I understand." A long pause. "Leah, let's assume for a moment that what has happened to you is exactly what your mind tells you has happened. Why do you suppose God chose this point in time to communicate with us? And why you? Please don't take that the wrong way, but why didn't he choose some prominent religious leader? Wouldn't his message have been more credible? And, again, please don't take offense at that."

"None taken," Leah replied. "Frankly, I can't imagine a less likely candidate than me. I don't go to church. And I've never really believed in God in the same way that religious people do. I guess I never ruled it out, but I've never quite accepted it either."

"A fairly common perspective these days," Dr. Marcus noted.

"And me a messenger. I used to dread having to speak in front of my class as a kid. I can't imagine how I would ever be able to deliver a message to the world.

"Oh," she continued in forced exasperation, "I wish I had kept my big fat mouth shut about all of this. What am I going to do if somebody actually believes it?"

Dr. Marcus laughed gently. "Sadly, I think most people are too obsessed with their own stories to seriously consider anyone else's. And, in the end, people generally believe what they want to believe. They don't let the facts stand in the way."

"I hope you're right."

"Your story has a lot of pretty significant implications," Dr. Marcus added. "A lot of people don't like to think about what they don't like to think about."

They sat in contemplative silence for several moments, before Leah asked, "Can there be another explanation for what happened, doctor?"

"I don't know of one at the moment, but someone will come up with one, I'm sure." After pausing to collect a thought, and shift his weight, Dr. Marcus continued. "The average lay person doesn't understand that science is merely an attempt to explain reality. There is no such thing as a body of scientific knowledge. Science, as it were, is merely an approach to acquiring knowledge rather than knowledge itself. As a result, it is almost always possible to provide a scientific explanation for otherwise inexplicable events."

Dr. Marcus raised his semi-clenched hand to his mouth and thoughtfully tapped it against his lips. After a few moments of apparently conflicted consideration, he said, "Leah, I wonder if you wouldn't do me, and yourself, a favor and agree to speak to Dr. Heidrich. He heads up the department of psychiatry."

"You think I'm crazy?" Leah asked anxiously.

"No. No. Not at all. It's just that my expertise lies in the ways of the brain. And from everything I can see there is nothing whatsoever wrong with your brain. Dr. Heidrich's expertise is in the ways of the mind. Between the two of us, we might get a little closer to explaining what has happened — for your benefit. Medically, to be honest, my job is done. You are a healthy young woman. You are obviously quite unsettled by what's happened, however. I'd like to help you sort it out." Standing, he said reflectively, "Perhaps I'm afraid that you really are God's messenger and that he will judge me harshly if I don't embrace your message." The doctor smiled warmly, reaching out to touch her arm. "You see, there I go again, thinking only about how it affects me. We are a self-centered lot," he concluded, laughing warmly.

The doctor then turned to leave. As he opened the door to the hallway, however, Sunny, Tyler, and Ryan appeared.

"Are we interrupting?" Sunny asked.

"Not in the least," replied Dr. Marcus. "I was just leaving."

"Come here you two," Leah called out from her bed, leaning forward and extending her arms widely. The two boys quickly ran past Sunny and Dr. Marcus and eagerly surrendered to the embrace of their mother.

After watching the loving re-union momentarily, Sunny turned to Dr. Marcus, who was also smiling broadly at the warm scene. With her back to the room, she asked, in a quiet voice, "What did you find, Dr. Marcus?"

Looking at Sunny, he replied, "Your sister appears to be a perfectly healthy woman."

"And how do you explain that?" she asked impatiently.

"I don't."

"But there must be some explanation. What about the bruises and the broken bones?"

"I'm at a complete loss to explain any of it."

"Is this some kind of miracle?" Sunny asked, seemingly begging for an answer.

"Indeed," Dr. Marcus replied. "The only question is whether it is your everyday run of the mill medical miracle or whether there has been divine intervention."

"You can't be serious," Sunny said, almost sarcastically.

The doctor cocked his head in surprise, looking directly at Sunny. "I am indeed. I can't think of anything more wonderful. I'd be delighted to know, beyond faith, that there is a warm, loving God. And I have no doubt that such a God would want us all to get along. Social harmony, you must admit, is an enticing ideal."

Sunny grimaced. "I just don't want to see my sister make a fool of herself."

"Foolishness is in the eye of the beholder. Frankly, I would be more concerned that she doesn't have the courage to carry out her divine mission, should she, in fact, have one," Dr. Marcus concluded, turning to leave.

CHAPTER 4

"Are we born with a moral compass?" Professor Bradshaw asked from the podium of Davis Lecture Hall. "And if we are, where did it come from?

"Like the argument from design, the argument from conscience is an inductive and a posteriori argument for the existence of God. It is, in other words, an argument based on experience rather than pure reason. It is an argument wherein the premise of the argument – that there is a supreme morality – supports the conclusion – that our moral code was established by God – but does not guarantee it.

"Of all of the philosophical arguments made for the existence of God, the argument from conscience is either the strongest or the weakest argument for many people. It all comes down to whether or not you believe that deep down in every soul there is universal knowledge of absolute right and wrong. If you do, it's rather easy to make the leap to the belief that right and wrong must have been established by God. If you don't accept a universal and absolute morality, on the other hand, the argument is no argument at all.

"There is, of course, a very logical alternative explanation for the existence of a universal moral code that does not involve God. Can anyone tell me what it is?"

A young man with a silver ring in his nose raised his hand. "It allows society to function by providing a foundation for maintaining order."

"That is the alternative explanation for why there is a universal moral code," replied the professor. "But what is the explanation for how it developed?"

A woman with bright red streaks in her otherwise jet black hair answered, "It was a collective pact among the members of early tribes and clans that has been passed down through history."

"Correct. It was the result of voluntary agreement among members of society who understood the value of such a code to the society's smooth and predictable operation. The moral code, in other words, was devised by humankind to give legitimacy to the legal code, which provides for our safety and gives predictability to our actions. But why does the legal code need that legitimacy? Why aren't laws enough?"

An African-American man who appeared slightly older than the other students raised his hand. "Laws can't be enforced by force alone. There must be cooperation from the members of the society."

"Very good. Voluntary restraint is the only form of law enforcement that can maintain a lawful society. Throughout history it has been shown that if a majority of people do not accept the validity of a law, it will not be enforceable. It's a matter of math. You cannot possibly have enough police in enough places to enforce an unpopular law. And, as a practical matter, it is unlikely the police will have their hearts in it anyway, since they probably share the common view."

————

Leah was taken to Dr. Heidrich's office in a wheelchair by a nurse's aide that afternoon. His office was located on the fifth floor of the professional building that adjoined the main hospital.

Upon entering his office, she had the sense that she was no longer in the same building. The office was decorated and lit as if it were a warm Victorian parlor. All of the light was provided by floor and table lamps, and the furniture was all made of darkly-stained woods and plush, rich fabrics.

Dr. Heidrich had a dark complexion and dark hair that was tinged with grey, although the top of his head was bald. He had earned his M.D. as a lieutenant-colonel in the U.S. Army and had spent the early part of his career working with soldiers returning from Vietnam.

Unlike Dr. Marcus, Dr. Heidrich did have a hobby to which he devoted much of his free time – model railroading. When asked, he explained his fascination with trains on the basis that you always knew where a train was going to go. "Unlike many people, trains are very predictable," he'd point out. "They have to follow the tracks." Whatever the reason behind his interest, he built an elaborate train layout in the basement of the house that he shared with his wife of forty years.

The Heidrichs had no children and, in many respects, could not have been more different. She was an ardent entertainer and socialite. He, however, was seldom seen at any of the numerous parties and charity dinners hosted at their home. More often than not, he was working on his layout down in the basement, dressed in overalls and an engineer's cap, while the guests sipped champagne and nibbled on canapés upstairs. It was, nonetheless, an extremely successful marriage and no one who knew them doubted for a moment that the Heidrichs loved each other very much.

"Where would you like me to park her, doc?" the young African-American man who had brought Leah to Dr. Heidrich's office asked.

"Right in front of the desk is fine, thank you," he replied politely.

The aide nodded, pushed Leah into position, and leaned over to lock the wheels. "When would you like her picked up?" he asked.

"Let's say an hour," the doctor offered without looking up.

"Fine," replied the young man, who then turned and left.

Dr. Heidrich had Leah's medical file open on the desk in front of him. Holding his pointer finger in the air, he said to Leah, in a gentle and warm voice, "Please give me just a minute more."

After a pause of less than a minute, he looked up, peering over the top of his wire rim reading glasses and said, "Leah, I am Dr. Heidrich. Dr. Marcus asked me to talk with you. It seems that you've made a rather remarkable recovery and have an equally remarkable story to tell."

Leah simply nodded.

"I, as I'm sure Dr. Marcus told you, am a shrink. I head up the department of psychiatry here at the hospital."

"Yes," Leah replied hesitantly, almost fearfully. "He told me that."

Dr. Heidrich sat back in his chair, which squeaked loudly as he did. "It is a professional curse that shrinks make others uneasy. We seldom appear on anyone's party list, although that suits me just fine. Please be assured, however, that Dr. Marcus has not sent you here because he suspects any mental illness in the clinical sense. He's a good friend of mine and thought I might be able to help him – and you – sort out what's happened." A pause, while the doctor set his pen down on the desk. "Frankly, I don't know that I can be of much help. If I am to be, however, I will need you to be open and forthright with me."

"I'm sorry, doctor," Leah replied apologetically, looking down at her hands, which sat clasped in her lap. "I'm just very nervous. I know how ridiculous all of this sounds."

"That alone suggests that you aren't crazy," the doctor laughed, the lines at the corner of his eyes suggesting genuine kindness. "The real crazies have no such fears."

Dr. Heidrich leaned forward and to the side, extending his right leg and reaching down to rub his knee. "Sorry. My knee's a little sore today. I spent several hours crouched down under my train layout last night working on the wiring."

When he finished rubbing his knee, Dr. Heidrich leaned forward in his chair once again and laid his forearms flat on the desk, hands clasped. "So, let's talk a little about your story, if you don't mind. You claim that you were with God. Is that correct?"

Leah hesitated. "I'm not sure *claim* is the right word. When I first came out of the coma, that's what I thought. Now, however, I'm not so sure."

"A perfectly natural reaction, I'd say, given the implications of the story."

The doctor paused, apparently contemplating his next question.

"Are you a religious person, Leah?"

"No," Leah answered firmly. After looking to her side in contemplation, she looked back at the doctor and said, "I haven't exactly led a holy life."

"Neither has anyone else that I've ever met," replied Dr. Heidrich. "If God exists, he doesn't' live among us." A pause. "What is it that you think you need to be forgiven for?"

Leah exhaled audibly. "Oh, it's a long list."

"What's at the top?"

Leah thought for a moment before answering. "Most sins come down to selfishness, don't they? I guess that most of all I regret having been so selfish."

"How so?"

"I've let people down. I've never quite lived up to their expectations."

Dr. Heidrich leaned forward to again look at the file in front of him.

"Leah, you told Dr. Marcus that you were sent on a mission by God. That is why he cured you; to deliver a message to the world. Is that correct?"

"That's what I thought at the time."

"And what was that message, Leah?"

Before answering the doctor's question, Leah reached out to hold the armrest as she shifted her body weight. "Yes," she then said, without conviction, "a message of love. God loves us and wants us to love each other in the same selfless way."

"A message of love," Dr. Heidrich repeated.

"Yes."

Dr. Heidrich consulted the file. "And you say that God wants us to stop giving so much attention to acquisition and achievement and to develop humility and selflessness. Is that correct?"

"Yes."

"What do you mean by acquisition? Or, what do you think that God means, if that's the specific word God used?"

"I don't know," Leah answered, shaking her head from side to side in apparent confusion. "I suppose God meant stuff; like big houses, fancy cars, plasma TVs – that kind of thing."

"And achievement. Why would God be against achievement?"

"I don't know that either," Leah answered in exasperation. "I don't know anything, doctor." Tears began to well in Leah's eyes.

Dr. Heidrich leaned forward and picked up a box of tissue that sat on the side of his desk and handed it to Leah.

Leaning back, he said, "Sometimes we achieve to acquire. Sometimes we achieve to acquire more power, or more money, or more prestige. Our society honors achievement. In fact, we worship it. I see it every day."

Leah furrowed her brow, as if she was confused by the doctor's comments.

"A lot of very, very successful people have sat where you now sit, although for different reasons. They lead miserable, painful lives. They're filled with despair. Their success has not brought them the personal fulfillment they expected it to. And they don't understand why."

There was a lull in the conversation as Dr. Heidrich wrote notes on the pad in front of him. He stopped several times, as if he were having difficulty putting his thoughts into words.

Leah used the time to look more closely around the room. On one wall, there was a picture of a baby girl, perhaps a year old, with rather long curly blonde hair. She was naked and sitting in a large antique white porcelain washbowl holding a bright blue ribbon that contrasted sharply against her fair skin and the light background of the picture.

"Is that your daughter?"

Dr. Heidrich looked up from his writing to see where Leah was looking. Turning his head toward the picture, he said, "No. My wife and I tried to have children but we were born about twenty years too early. Fertility medicine was in its infancy. I actually don't know who the girl is. My wife bought that picture at an estate sale. The baby's expression is priceless. It's the best 'I'm not going to cooperate' pout I've ever seen. Look at that lower lip. You could set a cup of coffee on it. Makes me smile every time I look at it."

Setting down his pen and leaning back in his squeaking chair once again, Dr. Heidrich continued. "When confronted with their own mortality," Dr. Heidrich noted, "I've never known anyone to take much solace in their achievements or the things they have acquired. In the final moments of life, no one has ever said, 'Bring me my things.'"

After tapping his pen against his lips several times, Dr. Heidrich offered, "In many ways, Leah, shrinks are like spiritual advisors. We do treat cases of true mental illness, of course. A lot of the patients we deal with, however, are just people looking for answers."

"What kind of answers?"

"The meaning of life. Why are we here?"

"What do you tell them?"

"I tell them," Dr. Heidrich replied, "that I really don't know. I do know, however, that life is pretty empty without a life purpose. And, I tell them, making money and getting promoted are not legitimate life purposes. In the end, these things bring us little fulfillment."

"And what is a legitimate life purpose?" asked Leah.

"There are many. But they all have one thing in common. They all involve service to others," explained Dr. Heidrich, sitting back in his chair again.

"So, how does that apply to me?" Leah asked hesitantly.

"In two ways," the doctor answered. "First of all, it seems perfectly logical to me that if God were to send a messenger, the message would be one of selfless love."

"So you believe that God really has sent me on a mission?" Leah asked skeptically.

"I don't think that's for me to decide," he replied. "That's a question only you can ultimately answer."

"But how could it be true?" Leah asked, begging for understanding. "It doesn't make any sense."

Dr. Heidrich chortled. "There are few things about life that do."

Pausing to tent his hands in front of him, Dr. Heidrich asked, "Leah, are you familiar with the famous painter George Seurat?"

"I didn't go to college," she replied apologetically.

"Seurat founded the pointillist school of art in the late 1800s. It's a form of painting that uses only tiny dots of color. There are no brush strokes.

Seurat, nonetheless, was able to create marvelously detailed pictures. One of his more famous is a picture entitled, *Sunday Afternoon on the Island of La Grande Jatte.* I suspect you'd recognize it if you saw it."

Leah sat quietly with a puzzled expression on her face.

"If you were to extract, say, a hundred dots of paint from that picture and transfer them to a blank canvas, the new canvas would probably look like no more than a hundred dots of paint. There would be no discernible picture."

Leah remained silent.

"That doesn't change the fact, however, that each of those dots came from the original painting. Each of those dots, if you will, remain 'real.' If we think of those dots as components of a greater truth, a truth symbolized by the original picture, the fact that we do not recognize that greater truth does not disprove the validity of the smaller truths represented by the hundred dots."

"I'm afraid you've lost me, doctor," Leah noted.

"My point is that you shouldn't doubt the truths you do know simply because you can't discern the larger truth that they are part of. Just because you don't understand why God would pick you as a messenger, don't conclude, for that reason alone, that it didn't happen."

Leah again looked down at her hands and considered the doctor's comments for several moments.

"Doctor, is there any possible explanation of why I might have imagined this whole thing?"

"Psychologically? What might cause someone to think they carried a message from God when they didn't?"

"Yes."

"That's easy. And it's the second way in which the issue of life purpose applies here. That person, like the many successful people who lead painfully unhappy lives, may be searching for a life purpose. What greater life purpose can there be than to be a messenger of God?"

CHAPTER 5

Coming out from behind the podium, Professor Bradshaw began to pace the floor as he normally did, his notes in hand. He pointed toward a student. "Young lady in the cap," he said, "do you believe in absolute morality?"

"Sometimes," she replied tentatively.

"Sometimes you believe in absolute morality or there are some absolute moral truths?"

"I believe there are some moral truths that everyone should honor. I think others, however, should be left to the individual."

"Can you give me an example of each?" the professor asked, stopping to await the response.

The young woman thought for a minute, anxiously shifting her weight in her seat. After a few moments she said, "Well, I don't believe that it's ever moral to kill another human being."

"I happen to agree," replied Professor Bradshaw. "And a non-absolute moral truth?"

"Well," she said hesitantly, "I believe that when it comes to sexuality and a woman's body, I think it should be left to the individual."

"Okay. But who decides which behaviors are covered by universal and absolute morality and which are at the discretion of the individual?"

A young man in the back row raised his hand and immediately began to answer. "Morality is absolute when other people are affected by the behavior. When they're not, it should be up to the individual."

"No harm, no foul," the professor replied curtly. "So, I can't kill you, but I can't judge you either. The great morality of tolerance." A pause. "So we should do away with all sodomy laws, legalize all drugs, and make alcohol available to anyone with the money to buy it?"

A hand in the second row went up.

"Yes?"

"I think drugs are different," the young woman offered.

"How so?"

"You may not be affecting other people in the short term, but drugs lead to violence and crime, so the decision to use them or not shouldn't be left up to the individual."

"Okay. Would you make the same argument about pornography?"

"Yes," the young woman answered. "It degrades women."

"What about song lyrics which promote violence?" Professor Bradshaw continued.

"Nobody is being forced to listen," a young man responded with a note of scorn.

"Nobody's being forced to buy pornography, or to pose for it," the professor noted. "Look, my point is not to argue what your moral standards are or should be. I leave that up to your parents." Laughter. "My point is that most of us have moral standards. They may vary by individual, but the fact that we all have them, and that most of us feel deeply about them, argues that morality is something more than a collective social pact that we've adopted so that we can all get along with each other.

"And, in fact, there are certain moral standards that virtually everyone accepts. Everyone accepts that child molestation is immoral, for example."

The professor bowed his head briefly.

"But let's take the conversation in a different direction. Do you believe that it is ever moral to violate your own conscience? Let's see a show of hands. How many people believe that violating your own conscience is never the moral thing to do?"

Most of the hands went up.

"As I suspected," the professor said. "I agree. But let's think about this. If morality weren't absolute, why would it be immoral to violate your moral standards?" A long pause. "And if it's immoral to violate our conscience, what natural explanation could there be for such absolute morality?"

Walking across the room, Professor Bradshaw put his pointer finger to his lips. "Shifting gears again, I, as a philosopher, have one overwhelming problem with the idea that there is no universal and absolute morality and that however you want to behave is equally moral so long as you don't hurt anybody. Anyone care to guess what that problem is?"

Several hands went up.

"Yes, the lady in the cap again."

"It ignores intelligence?"

"Explain."

"Some people are more intelligent than others, so their moral standards should carry more weight."

"Elitist," a young man behind her said sarcastically.

"Here, here," the professor said reproachfully. "This is an open forum." After pausing, he said, "That's an interesting perspective, and I may share that perspective to a degree. But that's not my primary reservation. How about you, in the green shirt. What were you going to say?"

"Religious convictions?"

"Good guess," replied Professor Bradshaw. "But no." A pause. "My problem with the idea of no universal and absolute morality is that it's just too damned convenient." He paused for a long time as he scanned the room for reaction. "I am just naturally skeptical of any belief system that puts no demands on anyone. Without absolute morality, there is no personal accountability for our actions. We can always excuse our behavior. We can indulge in our pleasures without guilt. That is so *tempting* to believe that I must instinctively be skeptical of its validity."

45

When Leah was wheeled back into her room by the same young aide, Tyler and Ryan were leaning against the end of the bed, playing handheld electronic games that Sunny had purchased in the hospital gift shop. Sunny was standing on the near side of the bed talking with a young, professionally dressed woman of Asian descent.

"Hi," the woman said immediately, smiling broadly, as she walked briskly toward Leah with her hand extended. "I'm Rebecca Lee. I'm with the Community Affairs department of the hospital."

"It's nice to meet you," Leah responded hesitantly, accepting the woman's outstretched hand.

The aide pushed Leah to the side of the bed, removed the arm rest, and helped her get out of the chair and onto the bed. Returning the arm rest to its place, he nodded, smiled, and turned to leave.

"Thank you," Leah said.

"You're welcome m'am," the young man replied with obvious sincerity. "You have a nice day."

""The hospital got a call from the *Detroit Dispatch*," Sunny said, with a hint of foreboding in her voice. "They want to do an interview."

"Oh?" Leah responded, as she worked herself into a sitting position on the bed, fluffing up the pillow behind her. "They want to interview me?"

"Yes," Rebecca replied, before Sunny could continue the explanation. "It seems somebody made a call to the paper this morning and suggested they might want to check out your story."

"What story do they think that is?" Leah asked, feigning ignorance.

Rebecca looked to Sunny with a puzzled expression, but Sunny didn't meet her gaze.

Turning to Leah, Rebecca said, "The story of your miraculous recovery." After hesitating, she added, "And that you were with God while in your coma and that God asked you to deliver a message to the world."

"I'm not sure I'm ready to share that message with the world yet," Leah observed matter-of-factly.

"Oh?" Rebecca asked, obviously surprised, again looking to Sunny for some explanation. "It's certainly a touching story. Your recovery is a miracle. Now that the word is out, I've got to believe that there is going to be continued interest. I'm not sure it's realistic to think that people aren't going to learn about it. The hospital is abuzz with it already."

"What happened to patient privacy?" Sunny asked accusingly.

"I assure you that we take patient privacy very seriously. No one is going to discuss your sister's medical records. The fact that she is sitting up in bed with no signs of any injuries just three weeks after arriving in the shape she did, however, is going to be difficult to hide. People are going to want an explanation."

The room was silent except for the sounds coming from the boys' hand held video games. Leah watched her sons, while Sunny stared out the window, frowning. Rebecca looked back and forth between the two sisters, anxious for some explanation.

Finally, Leah said, "What do you think, guys? Should your mother do an interview with a newspaper reporter?"

Sunny's head snapped around in astonishment. "You can't be serious, Leah."

Leah didn't answer. Instead, she continued to look at her sons, awaiting an answer. Finally, Tyler stood up and turned to face his mother. "Are you going to tell them about God?" he asked quietly.

"Are you afraid that I will? Would that embarrass you?"

"Yeah, I guess so," Tyler shrugged. "People might laugh or something."

"I think you should do it," Ryan offered excitedly. "Maybe you'll become famous."

"I doubt that," Leah replied, smiling at her son's innocence. "Besides, I don't want to be famous. I just want to be your mother."

"And you won't be if they lock you up," Sunny said pointedly.

"Sunny," Leah reprimanded her sister, "don't scare the boys like that. I really don't think anyone's going to lock me up just because I claim to be a messenger of God."

"They used to burn suspected witches at the stake," Sunny observed.

"That's hardly the same."

Sunny didn't respond, but turned her head to again stare out the window, obviously discomforted by the fact that her sister was even thinking about doing an interview.

"Besides," Leah added. "I don't have to talk about the messenger part. I can leave that out. I think Rebecca's right. I'm not going to keep my recovery a secret. Why not just get it over with?"

"You know my position," Sunny replied tartly without looking back.

After several moments of tense silence, Rebecca asked cautiously, "So, do you want me to set it up?"

"When do they want to do it?" Leah asked.

"I believe there will be a reporter on the way as soon as I call them. A senior reporter by the name of Brad Frank will be conducting the interview, as I understand it."

"Okay," Leah finally conceded hesitantly. "I might as well get it over with. Hopefully people won't pay attention and we can all get back to our quiet lives."

———

Brad Frank arrived at three o'clock. In his late thirties to early forties, he was a little over six feet in height and reasonably handsome. His appearance, however, was greatly disheveled, as if getting dressed for the day was a perennial after-thought. On this day, he was wearing a badly wrinkled short sleeve plaid cotton shirt and dungarees. On his feet was a pair of scuffed cordovan Mephisto walking shoes, one of which had a broken lace that had been repaired by knotting the broken ends together.

Brad stood with a slouch and his arms hung to his side as if his brain had turned off all of the muscles within them. In one hand he carried an old cloth briefcase with a handle stretched so tight by the weight of the case's contents that it appeared as if it might snap at any moment.

"Hi. I'm Brad Frank," he offered as he entered the room. "I'm with the *Detroit Dispatch*."

"Hi, Brad. I'm Leah Warner. This is my sister, Sunny. And these are my sons, Tyler and Ryan."

Brad smiled at each as they were introduced, but did not offer to shake hands.

Sunny got up from the chair beside Leah's bed and suggested that Brad sit there. She spoke cordially, but without enthusiasm.

"Thank you," he said. Settling into the chair, he put his battered briefcase on his lap and unzipped the top. Removing a small tape recorder, he held it up to Leah and asked, "Do you mind if I record our conversation? It makes it easier to keep everything straight."

"I guess that'd be all right," Leah replied.

"Why don't I take the boys down to the cafeteria," Sunny offered.

"I'd rather you stayed," Leah replied, with a look of playful pleading.

"Fine," Sunny replied curtly, causing Brad to look up at her as she moved to sit on the windowsill.

Brad turned on the tape recorder and set it on the cabinet next to Leah's bed. He then removed a pad of yellow legal paper from his case and an inexpensive Bic pen from his shirt pocket. "Ready?" he asked, smiling at Leah.

"Fire away," Leah replied.

"Well, why don't we start by you telling me, in your own words, everything that's happened – the car accident, the coma, the awakening, everything that you can recall. The woman who called this morning gave us the rough details, but assume that I know nothing."

"Okay," Leah began, looking up at the top of the far wall, apparently collecting her thoughts. Slowly, Leah began telling her story. She began with a brief background of her life, stopping twice to ask Brad if she was going into too much detail. With his assurance that she was not, she continued.

When she finally got to the accident, she said, "On the night of the accident, I attended a Sephadora jewelry party being hosted by a friend in White Lake."

"I'm sorry," Brad interrupted, "what is that? Is that like a Tupperware kind of thing?"

"Exactly. Except it's sterling jewelry. It's beautiful stuff, but I really couldn't afford much. I went because the hostess was a mother of one of Ryan's friends from school. At any rate, the accident occurred when I was driving home that night. I really don't remember the accident itself, or anything that happened after that, until this morning." Pausing, she looked to Sunny and asked, "Can you fill in the blanks?"

Sunny got up from her perch on the windowsill and walked toward the far side of the bed. With her arms crossed in front of her she offered what she knew about the accident. "I was told by the police that a drunk driver crossed over the center line and hit Leah head on. He was killed in the crash."

"The accident was actually covered by the paper, although not by me," Brad noted. "I looked up the story. Turns out the guy had been convicted of DUI twice before and was driving on a suspended license."

"Do you know anything else about him?" Leah asked.

"Late thirties, I think," Brad responded, rubbing his chin in recollection of the details. "A plumber, if I'm not mistaken. No family. A pretty hard luck case, I guess."

"A hard luck case with a serious problem," Sunny noted caustically.

"Unfortunately," Brad opined, "there are a lot of them out there. As a society, we tend to overlook them until something like this happens."

"Well," Leah noted, "I'm not bitter. I feel sorry for him in a way."

"Easier said than done, I suspect," Brad observed.

"What's done is done," Leah responded. "We all make mistakes."

Turning to Sunny, Brad said, "Your sister obviously has no apparent cuts or bruises from the accident. From what I understand, however, she was pretty banged up before last night. What did you observe?"

"It was hard to look at her," Sunny replied. "If I didn't know it was her, I wouldn't have recognized her. Her face was all swollen and discolored."

"And they were all there as of yesterday?" Brad asked, with a slight hint of suspicion.

"Yes," Sunny explained. "When I left late yesterday afternoon, it didn't look like she had really healed at all. The doctor said that it would take months before her appearance returned to normal."

"And when she awoke from the coma early this morning, she looked like this?" Brad sought to confirm, gesturing toward Leah. "Perfectly healthy?"

"Yeah," Sunny replied, nodding.

"And were you here?"

"No. The nurses told me that it happened at around 5:30 this morning. I think the hospital called me at around nine.

"Were you at home or work?" Brad queried.

"Home. I'm a high school phys ed teacher, so I'm off for the summer."

"She's very athletic," Leah noted with obvious pride. "Went to college on an athletic scholarship."

"I'm sure," Brad said, smiling slightly.

Looking back to Leah, Brad asked, "So how do the doctors explain what happened?"

"They don't," Leah replied, shrugging. "My doctor says that he can't explain it."

"That's Dr. Marcus?" Brad asked, consulting his legal pad.

"Yes." A pause. "Met him for the first time this morning," Leah noted. "And here I am talking to you."

Brad had shown little reaction to Leah's story. Although he had a professional poker face, however, Leah suspected that he was somewhat skeptical. Still, there was something about him that suggested an inner gentleness that his professional cynicism apparently suppressed.

After looking at his notes, Brad looked up to Leah and offered, "If I'm not mistaken, for what it's worth, I think your doctor is fairly famous in medical circles. I'm pretty sure I've read things about him in the past."

"He seems very nice," Leah suggested.

"Good. Just a couple more questions, if you don't mind. So, you were in this terrible accident, relatively near death, it sounds like, and all of a sudden there's nothing wrong with you. And no one has any explanation whatsoever," he concluded.

Leah looked uneasily at Sunny.

"She talked to God," Ryan suddenly blurted, causing everyone to look at him in astonishment.

"I'm sorry," Brad said quickly. "Could you repeat that?"

"Yeah," Ryan answered, before Leah or Sunny had recovered enough to stop him. "God asked her to be a messenger."

Brad turned to Leah, patiently awaiting her reaction.

After an uneasy silence, Sunny said, "Ryan's always had an active imagination," hoping Leah would follow her lead.

"Sunny, I've worked hard to teach the boys not to lie. I don't think my doing it is going to help."

Brad's gaze darted quickly back and forth between Leah and Sunny, but he remained silent.

Finally, Leah began, "When I awoke from the coma, I thought that I had been with God and that God had healed me in order to deliver a message. I'm sure I was just dreaming."

"What was the message?" Brad asked.

Leah grimaced slightly. "That God loves us and wants us to love each other in the same way," Leah answered hesitantly.

"And what way is that? Can you be more specific?" Brad prodded.

"Selflessly," Leah replied. "He wants us to stop being so pre-occupied with trying to get ahead and acquire stuff and focus instead on becoming more humble and selfless."

"Is that it?" Brad asked.

"That's it," Leah answered. "I'm sure it never happened."

"Why?"

"Because it's a crazy idea and people will ridicule her if they hear it," Sunny said tersely.

"I don't know that it's so crazy," Brad offered. "I can't personally speak to the God part, but it sounds like a pretty cool message to me. There's no question we've become a materialistic society and that we are bitterly divided on almost every issue."

"Including God," Sunny added.

"True," Brad conceded. "A lot of the people who don't believe in God in a religious sense, however, might be the first to applaud the idea of social harmony. I don't think it would be as controversial as you think.

Besides, if there's one thing I've learned in this business it's that memories are short. Everyone will be on to something else by tomorrow." After hesitating momentarily, he added, while looking at Leah, "I'm sorry. I didn't mean that to sound disrespectful."

"No offense taken," Leah assured him. "In fact, I hope you're right. I was happy with my old life. I just want to get back to it."

"I understand," Brad said sympathetically. "Can you tell me any more about what it was like to talk with God?"

There was a long silence, as Leah struggled to decide if she should continue the conversation along its current path. "I don't remember it being a conversation," she finally offered. "I think of it more as having been in his presence."

"But you heard a voice?"

Leah grimaced again, pushing herself up off the bed to shift her weight. "It's difficult to describe, but it's more like I *felt* a voice. It's as if it wasn't just coming through my ears, but through my entire body. Still, it was a voice as we normally think of a voice, I guess."

"Man or woman?"

"Both, really. I couldn't say with certainty. It was unlike any voice I've ever heard before."

"How would you describe it?"

"Loving. It was a very loving voice. Very warm."

"And did you see anything?"

"Light. It was very bright. But I couldn't tell where the light was coming from," Leah explained, apparently attempting to recreate the scene in her mind. "It was like the light was coming from every direction at the same time."

The boys had stopped playing their games and were watching their mother and listening to the interview from the foot of the bed. Tyler looked to Sunny on two occasions.

"And the message?" Brad asked. "Could you repeat it again, please?"

"The voice said, 'Leah, my child, I love you.' It repeated it several times."

"How many? Do you remember?"

"Perhaps dozens. Maybe even hundreds. It's hard to remember because the words were so comforting." A pause. "I felt so safe. And so loved. It was blissful in a way that I've never known before."

"Relaxing? Euphoric?"

"Intimate," Leah responded after a pause, narrowing her eyes as she gazed into her memory. "There was an overwhelming sense of intimacy."

"With God?" Brad asked, looking briefly at the two sons for their reaction.

Leah came out of her reverie and looked directly at Brad. "With life."

There was a long pause in the conversation as Leah and Brad continued to look at each other appraisingly.

"What happened after the voice stopped saying that he – or she - loved you?" Brad finally asked.

"It said, 'I have a message that I want you to deliver to all the people of the world. I want you to tell them that I love them just as I love you. And it is because I love them that I want to warn them. They must learn to love each other. They must learn to love each other as I love them. Acquisition and achievement are not the foundation of love. Humility and selflessness are.'"

"Warn them? What do you suppose he meant by that?"

"I don't know."

"Do you think he's going to punish us if we don't learn to love one another?"

"I don't know. I leave that to the clergy."

"Fair enough," Brad replied, cocking his head slightly. "Did the voice say anything else?"

"It said not to be afraid."

Leah hesitated, causing Brad to ask, "Do you want to add to that thought?"

"Despite the assurances, however," Leah continued, looking past Brad at a spot on the wall behind him, "I remember thinking 'What if I fail?'"

"Did the voice respond to your fear?"

"Yes. It said 'You can never fail in love, my child.'"

"Those exact words?"

"Yes. And the next thing I knew I was awake in my hospital bed. I removed my ventilator and the monitor wires and sat up to pray, which I hadn't done since I was a child."

Both sat quietly in contemplation for several moments, Brad drumming his Bic pen unconsciously on the pad of paper.

"So, what do you guys think about your mom having talked to God?" he suddenly asked, looking toward Tyler and Ryan.

Tyler simply shrugged and looked at his mother.

"I think it's great," Ryan said excitedly.

"I guess it would be," Brad replied, a slight smile on his face.

Brad consulted his notes again. Looking up, he asked, "Do you believe that God has instilled you with any kind of holiness or divinity?"

"No. I'm the same person I always was. I just have a message," Leah replied.

"So you're not looking for people to worship you, or follow you in any way."

"I'd be horrified if they did," Leah assured him.

"And how do you plan to get your message out, in addition to doing newspaper interviews?"

"I honestly don't know. I'm still trying to get over the shock that this has all happened."

"Do you think it will be easy to get people to listen?" Brad asked.

"I don't know. What do you think?"

"People are pretty skeptical. If it were true, it would certainly shake things up. And that's always hard to do. Most people don't warm to change, particularly those who have a lot to lose. To play on a law of physics, it takes a lot to move the status quo. I've been frequently amazed at just how much."

Leah and Sunny exchanged looks.

"You'll be stepping on some pretty powerful toes, should people believe you," Brad added. "I think you can expect that there will be attempts to discredit you."

"Why?" Leah asked in alarm.

"The status quo thing. In my experience, people will do whatever they have to to protect their own interests."

"Do you believe me?" Leah asked.

"Honestly, no. I'm sorry, but it's just too out of sync with everything I've come to believe." After pausing, Brad added, "I have to admit, though, that I'd like to. It's a very reassuring story. I'd like to think that we could all get along better than we do, even though that would probably put me out of a job. What would there be to report on?" he concluded, smiling pleasantly.

CHAPTER 6

Professor Bradshaw looked up from his notes and said, in a loud clear voice that filled Davis Hall, "One of the most famous proponents of absolute morality was John Henry Newman, a 19th Century Englishman who converted to Roman Catholicism and was ultimately named to the College of Cardinals by Pope Leo XIII in the late 19th Century. That was, by the way, a hugely symbolic milestone in then-tattered relations between Anglican England and Catholic Rome.

"An Oxford scholar, Newman became part of the Oxford Movement, also referred to as the Tractarians. This was a group of Anglican clergy who sought to renew the declining Church of England by bringing back some of the Catholic doctrines and rituals which had been eliminated during the Reformation. Ultimately, however, his work for the Tractarians served to undermine his faith in Anglicanism and led him toward Catholicism, causing some critics to accuse him of dishonestly undermining the Anglican Church from within.

"In response, Newman wrote *Apologia Pro Vita Sua*, detailing his conversion to Catholicism." Pausing to again consult his notes, Professor Bradshaw continued. "In it, he wrote: 'As I have already said, there are but two alternatives, the way to Rome, and the way to Atheism: Anglicanism is the halfway house on the one side, and Liberalism is the halfway house on the other.'"

There was scattered laughter throughout the hall.

"In Newman's mind, the difference between atheism and Catholicism came down to inner conviction, or conscience. He believed strongly in the concept of subconscious reasoning, or implicit reasoning, as he called it, noting that the human mind, 'is unequal to its own power of apprehension; it embraces more than it can master.'" Looking up to the upper tiers of the auditorium, he asked, "What did he mean by that?"

"That there are some things that we're not smart enough to figure out on our own. We just know them," responded an Asian woman with a heavy accent.

"Correct. And morality, Newman believed, is one of them. Morality is not something that we acquire or deduce, he argued, but something that we simply know. And we know it, not because of some evolutionary process of passing thought from one generation to the next, but because God put it there.

"A generation prior to Newman, Prussian philosopher, Immanuel Kant, had used his 'Copernican Revolution,' as he called it, to argue for the existence of an absolute, universal morality that is part of the fabric of the universe. Morality, he argued, is not a hypothetical imperative, but a categorical one. Under Kant's Categorical Imperative philosophy, as it is now referred to, the correctness, or morality, of an action lies within the action itself, not in the consequences of the action, as Utilitarianists believe."

Accelerating his cadence, the professor asked, "Can anyone tell me what Utilitarianism is?"

A young man in a wheelchair, sitting at the end of the front row, raised his hand and spoke. "It's a theory of ethics based on quantitatively maximizing social good."

"Good. The greatest happiness for the greatest number. Who is the most famous Utilitarian philosopher?"

"John Stuart Mill," a young woman called out.

"Correct. Mill, however, stood out from his fellow Utilitarians, who typically equated good and pleasure or satisfaction. Mill, by contrast, argued that mere physical pleasure shouldn't carry the same weight as cultural or spiritual happiness.

"But back to Kant." A pause, during which Professor Bradshaw once again brought the pointer finger of his empty hand to his lips. "The key to

Kant's philosophy of religion is his argument that the human mind does more than collect and organize the data provided by the senses. The mind, he argued, actually creates experience. It is the representation of something, in other words, that makes the thing possible, not the other way around."

A hand went up.

"Please."

"Wasn't Kant an atheist?" a tall African-American woman asked.

"Kant was, at times, very critical of organized religion, leading some to conclude that he paved the way for the strong denial of God by Nietzsche and others. Kant was not against religion per se, however. Rather, he thought that the practice of religion should be limited to the practice of morality and should not involve ritual or promote superstition, as, he perceived, organized religion did."

Professor Bradshaw returned to the podium and deposited his notes there. Turning back to the class, he asked, "Anyone care to offer the classic philosophical argument against the argument from conscience?"

Several hands went up.

"It's inductive?" responded the first young woman called upon.

"True. What else? Yes, toward the back, in the blue sweater."

"Euthyphro's Dilemma?" the young man answered.

"Go on."

"Euthyphro's Dilemma was posited by Plato, and essentially asks, 'How does God determine what is good?' If God decides based on a universal moral code, then why do we need to follow God to be moral? And if God simply decides what is good, there can be no universal moral code."

"Excellent," responded Professor Bradshaw in a jubilant tone. "As usual, the argument on both sides is rather circuitous and begs many irresolvable philosophical questions which we're out of time to address today. At the next class, we will discuss the argument from universal consent. Please read the next five chapters in your text."

Audible groans arose in the lecture hall as the students stood to leave.

———

"So, is she a nut case?" asked Marvin Granger, managing editor of the *Detroit Dispatch*, at the daily meeting of reporters and editors to finalize the next morning's edition.

"Not of the obvious variety," responded Brad. "I wish my own mother seemed so normal." Everyone laughed.

"Except that she's on a mission from God," noted Harry Snyder, metropolitan editor.

"Except for that," conceded Brad, "although, as I said in the article, she herself doubts her own story. Frankly, I'll be surprised if she pursues the messenger role."

The meeting was held in Granger's office, although there was barely enough room, and certainly not enough chairs, for all of the attendees. The office sat in the middle of the otherwise open editorial floor and the upper half of all of the walls was glass. For some, that created a sense of openness, while for others, Granger included, it created an unsettling sense of being in a fish bowl.

Beth DeNazio, Chief Counsel for the *Dispatch*, asked, "And how did you come across this story?"

"Got a call from someone we believe to be on the staff at the hospital," Harry replied.

"Believe?" Beth asked.

"Yes," Harry answered. "They wouldn't give us a name. The hospital, of course, is pretty strict about medical privacy. We think the caller may have been concerned about getting into hot water. The attending physician has confirmed her story, however, regarding her general medical condition, anyway."

Looking down at the proof sheets laid out in front of him, Marvin said, "And the message that God has asked her to deliver, you say, is that God loves us and wants us to love each other in the same way. He thinks we're too focused on acquisition and achievement."

"Simple as that," replied Brad.

"That won't sell many newspapers," Marvin noted somewhat caustically. "Love never does, unless there are Hollywood celebrities involved or somebody gets killed."

"No, but controversy does," offered sports editor John Hannifan, "and there are few things more controversial than religion."

"That's true," agreed Brad. "And miracles tend to get people talking. This story has religion and miracles."

"Does it really past muster for a miracle?" asked Marvin. "I see you've got a quote to that effect from Dr. Marcus."

"It sure does for him. And it sure does for me," Brad replied. "Coming out of the coma may not have been that miraculous. It's happened before. A couple of years back, some guy in Arkansas suddenly came out of a coma after 19 years. It is unusual, however, according to Dr. Marcus. And the degree to which her other injuries have healed so quickly is extraordinary, he claims. He says he has no plausible medical explanation."

"Marcus is a good man, but very religious. I know him from the synagogue. I'm not sure he's an objective judge of the miraculous," Marvin offered.

"For what it's worth," added Lisa Sweeney, city reporter, "I covered that accident. I didn't get much of a look at her because they whisked her away pretty quickly, but from what I saw, she was one hurtin' lady. There was blood everywhere and the paramedics were pretty darn serious."

"I don't know," Marvin said. "We're not a tabloid. It seems to me that this story belongs at the grocery checkout counter."

"I think it's worth running," Harry responded. "It's a feel good story. It might soften our image a little. Besides, I haven't got much else to replace it. It's been a slow news day."

"Okay," agreed Marvin. "But let's put it on the back page of Metro, below the fold, and put the story about the two cousins attacked by the Pit Bull on page one."

"Got it," Harry replied.

———

Sunny stopped by a convenience store to pick up a copy of the *Detroit Dispatch* on her way to the hospital. When she arrived at the hospital, Leah was reading a copy of *People* magazine.

Entering Leah's room briskly, Sunny dramatically dropped the paper she had purchased on the bed next to Leah, saying, "I hope you're not going to regret this."

"Have you read it?"

"Yes," Sunny replied curtly. "Metro; back page."

Leah pulled out the Metro section, found the article and began to read. When she finished she folded the paper and returned it to the bed. Sunny was standing next to the window, her arms folded in front of her.

"I guess I sound kind of nutty in black and white," Leah finally offered.

"Loony-tunes, if you ask me," Sunny replied with emphasis.

"Well, Brad seemed very nice," Leah proclaimed. "And I think he kind of liked you," she said, making a plainly exaggerated attempt not to smile.

"What?" Sunny replied in exasperated disbelief.

"Just a hunch," Leah retorted. "Big sisters are often right about these things, however."

"That's ridiculous," Sunny concluded forcefully.

There was a soft knock at the door.

"Come in," Leah called out pleasantly.

The door opened and an elderly man using a walker stood in the doorway. Hunched over his walker, he appeared to be extremely frail. Indeed, as he started to move into the room he shuffled his feet only a few inches at a time.

It was difficult to judge the man's age. There were only a few wisps of white hair remaining on his head and his scalp was splotched with skin discolorations and lesions. He was dressed neatly, but casually, although he wore black wing tip shoes that would normally be reserved for a suit. And despite the summer heat outside, he was wearing a heavy cardigan sweater that he had incorrectly buttoned.

"Are you sure you have the right room?" Sunny asked as she moved toward the man.

The man didn't respond, but continued to shuffle toward the bed. Leah and Sunny exchanged puzzled glances, but it was apparent that the man posed no threat.

Finally arriving at Leah's bedside, the man looked up and said, in a soft, raspy voice, "I read about you in the newspaper this morning and had to come see for myself. Is it true? Is it true that you're a messenger of God?"

Leah was too startled to reply.

"Is there a heaven?" the man asked expectantly.

"I don't know," Leah answered hesitantly.

The man reached over the top of his walker to take Leah's hand. She reflexively pulled it back but then uneasily held it out for him to touch.

"Is Gladys there?" he asked hopefully.

"I don't know," Leah again replied, increasingly anxious.

"Is Gladys your wife?" Sunny asked brusquely.

"Yes," he replied ruefully, his gaze falling to the area just in front of him. "She died last year from pneumonia." A long pause. "We both thought that I'd go first."

"I'm sorry," Leah said kindly. Looking first to Sunny, Leah looked back at the man and said, "I'm sure she is with God." Hesitating to look again at Sunny, she meekly added, "He loves all of us."

"No matter what we've done?" the man asked skeptically, not bothering to raise his head.

"Yes, I think so," Leah replied in a soft whisper.

"I know Gladys is with him," the old man replied. "She deserves to be."

As a tear began to roll down the man's face, Sunny went to him and took him firmly by the elbow, saying, "I think we need to go now and let her rest. She's very tired."

The man didn't respond, but he did oblige, allowing Sunny to guide him slowly toward the door. When he was almost there, Sunny still holding his arm, he stopped and turned his head ever so slightly. "Will you pray for me?" he asked Leah over his shoulder. "My name is Bob."

"It's time to go," Sunny replied before Leah could answer.

Sunny and the old man continued their slow but deliberate procession out into the hall and toward the nurses' station. When a nurse came toward them, Sunny explained his unexpected arrival, as well his unknown identity and origin. The nurse took the man by the other elbow and moved him toward the elevator, while asking him, in a rather loud voice, how he had gotten there and where he needed to be.

Sunny returned to the room, where Leah was sitting pensively, considering the man's unexpected and bizarre visit.

"Talk about nuts," Sunny offered as she entered the room.

"I wonder where he came from, or how he got here," Leah responded absently.

"I don't know. The nurse is taking care of him. He's obviously not entirely right."

"I feel so sorry for old people," Leah said sadly. "It must be so difficult to watch your life and your health unravel like that."

As Leah spoke, a young woman entered the room holding a Bible. She was not particularly attractive and extremely overweight. Her hair was greasy, as if it hadn't been washed in some time, and she wore no jewelry or makeup. Without saying a word, she walked quickly to Leah's bed, knelt down beside it, and began to pray fervently, but incoherently.

"Can I help you?" Sunny demanded.

The young woman did not respond, but continued to clutch her Bible and chant in prayer, her eyes closed.

"I'm sorry," Sunny said firmly, "but what is it you want?"

Again, the young woman seemed oblivious to her surroundings.

Leah looked distraughtly at Sunny.

Finally, Sunny said, "Look, you're going to have to leave if you can't tell us who you are or why you're here."

The girl still didn't respond. Sunny, frowning, leaned over and pushed the call button clipped to Leah's bed.

"Can I help you?" a voice responded.

"Yeah," Sunny replied. "We have a woman in the room who just showed up out of nowhere and we have no idea who she is."

"I'll be right there," the nurse responded.

Soon, the same nurse who had led the old man off the floor came purposefully through the door. When she arrived next to the young woman, she bent over to see her face, her hands on her knees. Turning toward Leah and Sunny, but not rising from her stooped position, she asked, "You don't know her?"

"No," Leah replied, shaking her head in bewilderment.

Looking back at the woman and placing her hand on her back, the nurse asked, "Who are you, honey? Do you have a reason for being here?"

Again, the woman failed to respond. She simply continued her ritualistic prayer, muttering incomprehensively.

Finally, the nurse rose from her crouched position, went around the far side of the bed, and pushed the call button.

"Can I help you?" a voice responded.

"Pat, this is Jill. Can you call security and ask them to send someone up. We've got a non-family member in here who the patient doesn't even know. Unfortunately, the visitor is unresponsive."

"Will do," the voice replied.

A large African-American security guard arrived a few minutes later. The nurse explained the situation and the security guard knelt on one knee beside the young woman.

"M'am," he said gently, but firmly. "You're not supposed to be here. Do you know where you're supposed to be?"

No reply.

"Can you tell me your name?" he asked.

Still no reply.

Standing up, he bent over and gently placed his large hands loosely on her upper arms. "I'm sorry, m'am, but you're going to have to leave. This ward is restricted to family members only."

After a brief hesitation, the woman stood up on her own, although the guard kept his hands loosely on her upper arms. He then turned her around and led her toward the door.

"Thank you," the nurse said.

"You're welcome," the guard replied.

"Is there any way we can cordon off the ward? She's the second uninvited visitor this morning," the nurse noted.

"I'll call down and see if we can't post somebody at the elevator to check visitors in," he responded helpfully. Turning to Leah, he asked, "Are you the lady in the newspaper? God's messenger?"

"I guess so," Leah responded apprehensively.

He shook his head, smiled broadly, and said, "I'll be damned."

He left the room, still shaking his head while guiding the still-praying young woman.

———

Later that same morning Leah was lying in bed, deep in thought, when there was a soft knock at the door. Sunny had gone down to the cafeteria for a cup of coffee.

"Come in," Leah answered apprehensively.

The door opened and a tall man, nearly 6 feet 4 inches in stature, looked slowly around the door. He was casually dressed but carried himself with the stiff and deliberate demeanor of one accustomed to presiding over ceremonies.

"Mrs. Warner?"

"Yes?"

"I'm Larry Rataj. I'm the senior pastor at the Carbondale Community Church. I'm also a member of the Adult Ethics Committee here at Saint Mary's."

"Ethics Committee?"

"Yes," he replied entering the room and approaching Leah's bed. "We advise the hospital staff, patients, their families, and the community at large on issues of medical ethics. The council includes representatives of the medical staff, hospital administration, local clergy, medical ethicists, and the community. I'm one of the representatives from the local religious community."

In addition to being tall and slender, Larry Rataj had thin wispy hair that looked perpetually windblown and was almost orange in color. His exposed skin was excessively populated with freckles of a similar shade.

"Am I a medical ethics issue?"

"No," Pastor Rataj chuckled, interlocking his long, bony fingers at his waist. "You might have become one if you hadn't awakened from your coma. The committee was made aware of your case a week ago, by Dr. Marcus. It was strictly an informational discussion, however."

"Oh. Well, what can I do you for you, Pastor?"

"Please call me Larry," Mr. Rataj replied. "We're very informal at Carbondale. In fact, we like to think of ourselves as the non-church church, if you will." A pause. "As far as what brings me here, I thought, given your miraculous recovery and your subsequent explanation for it, which I read about in the paper this morning, that you might like to speak to someone in the clergy. Not knowing if you have any current church affiliation, I thought that I'd stop by to see if I could help in any way."

"Oh. Actually I don't belong to any church," she replied apologetically. "I guess that makes me a bad person," she added.

"The Lord will always forgive our mistakes. We only have to ask. It's never too late."

Leah remained silent and unconsciously looked away from the pastor to escape his intense gaze. Finally, she turned her head toward him, but did not raise her eyes. "What denomination is your church?" she asked, apparently embarrassed by her prior confession.

"We're independent, although we affiliate informally with thousands of community churches around the country that are Bible-based, but progressive in their style of worship. We're evangelical, although that has become a pejorative term in some quarters, so we don't often use it to describe ourselves to outsiders. Essentially, we believe that there are a few key ingredients to being a good Christian and that the majority of stuff that has historically divided the Christian community isn't important enough to declare sides over."

Leah sat quietly, her hands clasped on her stomach.

"Chief among those core beliefs is the acceptance of the Bible as the word of God. We also believe God is benevolent and will answer our prayers."

"I'm afraid that I have never been a religious person," Leah offered sheepishly.

"I see," Larry replied, raising his right had to rub his chin. "Is there a specific reason for that, if I might ask?"

"No. I mean, yes, you can ask. No, there is no specific reason," Leah stammered.

"Well, you're not alone. The goal of our church, and others like it, is to get people on – or back on, as the case may be - the road to Christ. These are people which traditional churches simply haven't met the spiritual needs of. Perhaps we can help you, too."

"Would you really want to after what I said to that reporter?" Leah asked.

"Say again?"

"Well," Leah continued self-consciously, "I'm sure you're offended that someone like me would claim to have a message from God. I didn't mean to say it, actually. My son accidentally spilled the beans, but that's no excuse. I should have refused to talk about it."

"But you did initially believe that you had been in God's presence and that he asked you to deliver a message to the world, did you not?"

Leah nodded as her eyes began to fill with tears.

Sunny entered the room as tears began to slide down Leah's cheeks. When she saw that Leah was crying, she rushed to her side and demanded of Pastor Rataj, "What's going on here?"

While Sunny reached for a box of tissues and put her arm protectively around Leah's shoulders, Larry replied, "I'm Larry Rataj, the pastor of the Carbondale Community Church. I do a lot of work here at the hospital. I simply stopped by to offer my services."

After casting the pastor a skeptical look, Sunny lowered her face to Leah's and asked, "What's wrong, Leah? What happened?'

"I'm all right," Leah replied as she fought to regain her composure. "I guess I was just feeling guilty for what I've been saying. It just struck me how preposterous it was for me to think that any of it could be true."

With a feeble attempt to smile, Leah looked up at Pastor Rataj and said, "I'm sorry. It wasn't your fault." Gesturing toward Sunny she added, "This is my sister, Sunny."

"No need for apologies," Larry reassured her. "It's a pleasure to meet you," he said with genuine sincerity to Sunny.

After a few moments, Sunny stood upright and said tersely, "My sister's been through a very trying time. In addition to this, she lost her husband a year ago. She's been under a lot of emotional stress."

"I understand. I'm sorry to hear of your loss."

"Hopefully," Sunny observed, "this will all clear up once she gets out of here and we can all get on with our lives. I hope you haven't gotten your hopes up that you can use her story to further your cause in some way."

Pastor Rataj exhaled audibly. "That's not why I'm here. In fact, I'm not sure I can embrace the idea of her being a messenger of God even if she were to stand by it."

Leah looked up abruptly.

"Why's that?" Sunny asked.

"Well," the pastor began, "there is no biblical mention of such an event, and, as I was telling your sister, I believe that the Bible is the one and only word of God."

"Perhaps God didn't anticipate the need," Leah posed cautiously.

"And the story does present some theological difficulties. You see, God did use prophets in the time period covered by the Old Testament. Jesus Christ, however, represented a new covenant between God and humanity that superseded the relationship between God and the prophets of old. Much of the book of Hebrews, in fact, is devoted to explaining that Jesus represented the ultimate manifestation of God to the world.

"As a result," the pastor continued, "We can only be with God through Jesus. 'I am the way and the truth and the life. No one comes to the Father except through me.' John 14:6. Jesus was the human embodiment of God himself, you see. Having appeared before us in the form of Christ, who lived the sinless life, God essentially eliminated the need for messengers or prophets."

"But people claim to speak to God all the time, through their prayers," Sunny retorted.

"They pray to God. And he does, I believe, answer our prayers. It is, however, a very personal communication. To suggest that he has chosen one individual to speak on his behalf is very problematic, I'm afraid."

Pursing his lips before speaking, the pastor continued. "Please don't be offended by the question, but how do you think the millions of devout Christians who have led holy lives will receive the news that God has chosen a messenger, who, by her own admission, has not devoted herself to Jesus Christ?"

"So, God's prejudiced? He won't speak to anyone that doesn't go to church regularly. I thought God believed in forgiveness," Sunny said with more than a hint of sarcasm. Aggressively coming to her sister's defense, she continued. "Or is this really about the church itself? Is that your worry? That your pews and your offering plate will be empty if people believe that they don't have to go to church to be loved by God?"

"Sunny!" Leah said accusingly. "That's blasphemous. I think you owe the pastor an apology."

The tension hung heavily in the air while Leah stared accusingly at her sister and Sunny fought to re-bottle her temper.

Finally, Sunny looked at the pastor and said, "I'm sorry if I offended you. My sister's a good person. I'm overly sensitive at the moment that someone is going to accuse her of being an opportunist or a nutcase or something."

"I understand," the pastor replied calmly.

"Before I leave," the pastor continued, looking down at his hands, "I feel obligated to warn you that there will be those who will readily believe that you are a messenger of God and who will attempt to attribute divinity to you."

"I assure you that I will set them straight," Leah replied.

"I'm sure. I do hope, however, that you will consider the interests of those who are already attempting to spread the word of God, should you decide to move ahead. To the extent that Christian doctrine is further fractured, it will only serve to dilute our efforts.

"And one last thing. It is politically correct today to suggest that all religions are equal; that all are essentially correct. That, I would point out, is heretical to many Christians. That could only be true if the Bible were a largely fictional document. If taken literally, the doctrines of most of the world's leading religions are, in essence, mutually exclusive. They can't, in other words, all be right.

"Thank you for your time, Mrs. Warner," he concluded politely. "I wish you the best. God bless."

Leah and Sunny remained silent as the pastor turned and left.

CHAPTER 7

"Can so many people be wrong?" began Professor Bradshaw, standing in front of his class at Great Lakes University. "Proponents of the argument from universal consent, which is a variation of the argument from absolute morality, suggest that the mere fact that so many people have believed in the existence of a Supreme Being for so long is more than confirmatory; it is itself proof of God's existence.

"The Greek philosopher and biographer, Mestrius Plutarch, traveled widely in his duties as priest and magistrate, representing his town of Chaeronea on many missions. He wrote, 'If you go round the world, you may find cities without walls, or literature, or kings, or houses, or wealth, or money, without gymnasia, or theatres. But no one ever saw a city without temples and gods, one which does not have recourse to prayers, or oaths, or oracles, which does not offer sacrifice to obtain blessings or celebrate rites to avert evil.' To this day, in fact, true atheists remain in an extreme minority around the world."

A young man seated in the middle of the lecture hall raised his hand.

"Yes?"

"Isn't it true, however, that isolated tribes have been discovered that had no religion and had never considered the existence of any Supreme Being?"

"Such observations have been attributed to some early explorers, such as da Verrazano and Amerigo Vespucci, both of whom lived in the early 16th Century. These have been disputed, however, in part because these explorers typically spent relatively little time with these tribes. Documenting tribal culture was not their primary mission.

"More recently, late 19ᵗʰ Century English naturalist, Sir John Lubbock, maintained, after concluding extensive scientific study, that such non-religious tribes did, in fact, exist. Other 19ᵗʰ Century scholars, however, such as German geographer, Oskar Peschel, disagreed.

"As a practical matter, I think we can say that most people today accept that the belief in a Supreme Being, or beings, is fairly universal and has been so throughout history.

"There are, of course, other possible explanations for this. Can anyone come up with one?"

A young woman in the back raised her hand.

"Yes."

"There is a universal need to overcome fear."

"Very good. Yes, the belief in God could be spontaneous; the easiest and most natural way to explain life and calm our fears of the unknown. Herbert Spencer, the famous British philosopher and sociologist of the Victorian era pointed out that the religion of primitive people is typically so primitive that it really doesn't even qualify as religion in the modern monotheistic sense.

"The Scholastic philosophers of the 19ᵗʰ Century, who believed, along with Thomas Aquinas, the father of modern Catholicism, that the Divine Essence is not comprehendible to the finite human mind, however, had an explanation for that. They believed that those tribes or nations had, in fact, corrupted an earlier, natural monotheism. While they weren't monotheists now, the argument goes, they had once been. It is perfectly logical, the Scholastics argued, that our natural monotheism is prone to deteriorate into Polytheism, Dualism, and Pantheism, particularly among primitive people."

———

"Steven?"

"Yes?"

"It's David Marcus."

"David, how are you. To what do I owe the pleasure of your call? If it's about the car, it's not for sale."

"Goodness, no," chortled David. "I wouldn't know what to do with it."

"You just drive around and pick up chicks. It's a magnet."

"I hope you're not serious."

"Oh, it is a magnet. When the young girls see who's driving, however, they giggle rather than fawn."

"Your life is much simpler as a result, I should think," Dr. Marcus noted.

"Couldn't be any simpler," Dr. Bradshaw grumbled.

"Well, perhaps I can help. Did you happen to read the *Detroit Dispatch* this morning?"

"About the messenger from God? Yes, I did see that. You're her physician I see."

"Yes," Dr. Marcus replied. "It's a rather extraordinary case. Frankly, I'm inclined to believe that she really is a messenger, even though she herself isn't so sure. I was wondering if we could chat about it. I thought your insight might help me to sort it all out in my own head."

"Philosophy, I'm afraid, is seldom helpful in helping anyone sort out reality, but I always enjoy our discussions and would be delighted to talk about it. Why don't you come out for lunch. I'll take you to the University Club and show you off to my colleagues. Afterward, we can drive around campus and lay some rubber."

"You're incorrigible, Steven. But, yes, that sounds lovely. Are you free today by chance?"

"I am indeed. What's a good time for the busy doctor?"

"Will one o'clock work?"

"I'll see you then, David."

Steven Bradshaw and David Marcus had known each other for several years. David had read one of Steven's first books on the philosophy of religion and become so intrigued that he contacted Professor Bradshaw and asked if he could monitor his philosophy of religion class.

Several years later, Dr. Marcus treated Professor Bradshaw's niece, who had suffered severe head injuries as the result of a diving accident. She made a full recovery. The two men had stayed in touch ever since, and although they saw each other seldom, both being rather averse to socializing, they always felt like old friends whenever they got together.

"I always feel like I'm going back in time when I come here," David offered as they sat down at the elegantly set table in the University Club's formal dining room.

"You are," Steven replied with flourish. "The bone china dates back to the Enlightenment; the sterling dates back to Paul Revere; and the glassware dates back to 16th Century Murano. Some of the members, I think, go back even further."

"Well, it's all very elegant. I hope I don't break anything," David said as he unfolded the cloth napkin in his lap.

"Professor Bradshaw," the elderly waiter said rather jovially as he ambled unsteadily over to their table. "We haven't seen you in here in some time."

"Well, it's just not like the old days, Gordy," Steven said affectionately. "Remember when everyone drank small vats of Scotch for lunch and the only choice on the menu was what cut of steak to have?"

"And don't forget the sliced tomato and onion salad," Gordy interjected.

"Drowning in Italian dressing. Yes, those were the days when men knew how to eat," Steven concluded.

Looking to David, Steven said, "You don't believe me, but it's true. Now if you order a glass of wine with your meal everyone looks at you with contempt. And the only thing on the menu is cous cous and range fed chicken breast."

David smiled broadly, glad to be with his old friend.

"So, Professor Bradshaw, can I offer you and your guest some nice raspberry iced tea or a glass of cranberry?" Gordy asked politely.

"I'll stick with water," Steven replied. "How about you, David?"

"Same here," David answered, smiling genuinely at Gordy.

"Very well," Gordy concluded. "I'll let you look at the menu and I'll be back in a few minutes to take your order."

As Gordy ambled away, David look about the dining room and observed, "Place isn't very busy. Professors must eat promptly at noon."

"They're lucky to eat," Steven replied. "The young professors don't like it here much. You seldom see anyone under the age of 60 in here."

"Why's that? Too formal?"

"That's part of it. There's a lot of competition in academics today. There's no fellowship among the young people. They're all out to cut each other's throats – or at least steal their grant money."

"I think that's true in every profession," David noted sadly. "I remember when doctors took Thursdays off to play golf together. I was never one of them, of course, but I'm not sure any of them do it anymore."

"Well, I spend most of my time with dead philosophers," Steven observed, "so my life has stayed pretty consistent over the years. That's just the way I like it. You never age that way; you just get older."

There was a short pause in the conversation while each man looked at the menu. When they had decided, Steven signaled to Gordy, the waiter, and they placed their lunch orders.

As Gordy departed with the menus in hand, Steven began, "So tell me about your patient, the messenger from God."

"Her name is Leah Warner; late thirties; stay-at-home mother of two."

"What's her husband do?"

"Deceased. Used to be an accountant at Ford, I believe. Died of malignant melanoma about a year ago."

"And she doesn't need to work?"

"Don't know the details," David replied. "She said he was a good saver and that she got enough from the insurance settlement to see her through until the boys are older. Sounds like she lives a very modest life.

"At any rate, she was driving home from a friend's house one evening a few weeks back and had a head on collision with a drunk driver. He was pronounced dead on the scene and she was taken to Saint Mary's in a Level 1 coma."

"That's not good, I assume," Steven observed dryly.

"As bad as it gets. No response to stimuli of any kind. The prognosis in such cases is always dire. Rarely do patients come out of it. And in the few cases they do, it takes months, if not years, for them to regain lucidity.

"In Mrs. Warner's case, however, she emerged from the coma fully lucid, almost instantly. When the nurses entered the room at five o'clock in the morning, she was sitting up on the side of the bed praying. And upon closer examination it became immediately obvious that her contusions and lacerations had healed to a degree that is inexplicable. Even her broken bones, we discovered with x-rays, had healed to a degree we wouldn't have expected to see for several months."

"A genuine miracle, in other words," Steven observed.

"To say the least," David agreed. "Frankly, I've never seen anything like it."

"And how does God fit into the picture?"

"Well, when she first awoke she said that she had been with God and that God had asked her to deliver a message. She was asked to tell the world that God loves each of us and that we should learn to love each other in the same way."

"Which way is that?"

"Selflessly. God told her to warn people that they were too pre-occupied with getting ahead and acquiring stuff and that they needed to be more humble and to spend more time serving each other rather than themselves."

"Sounds good to me," Steven replied, "as long as I get to keep my car, of course."

"I agree. It does sound good. And it's not personal."

"Go on," Steven responded, furrowing his brow in apparent anticipation of an ensuing clarification.

"Well, there's nothing about her story that really singles her out, other than being chosen by God to be a messenger. She claims no divinity or special powers. She's not out to start a church or to re-write any theology. She takes no position on which, if any, of the world's established religions is the correct one. She seems genuinely incredulous that anyone could ever think that she possibly knew."

"Sounds like a rather humble messenger."

"Indeed," David agreed. "I'd say reluctant, at best. But that's what causes me to think that she may, in fact, have had the experience she first described. There's really nothing in it for her. If she was just dreaming, her dream would typically relate to her in a much more significant way."

"All our dreams are personal," Steven observed. "Or so said Freud."

"Exactly."

"Is she strong-willed?" Steven asked.

"No, I don't think so. She seems quite timid, almost meek. Which is why, I think, she's starting to second-guess herself. I think she's convincing herself that it didn't happen."

"But you think it did."

David looked directly at Steven. "Yes. Yes, I do. I can't explain why, but I do."

"David, are you familiar with precognitive conclusion?"

"Yes, of course. We see what we expect to see."

"Yes. Our brains process very little of the data that is available to our senses. It's a matter of efficiency. We'd never get out of bed if we didn't skip over most of it. The price we pay for that efficiency, however, is the loss of objectivity. We become biased, even prejudiced. We develop a world view; a perspective, if you will. And that perspective often shields us from the truth. We come to think that we're smarter than we really are."

"Socrates," David interjected, smiling.

"Good for you. You've been studying. For my money, Socrates was the greatest philosopher of all time. And, between you and me, I've always had a suspicion that Socrates was, in fact, divine – a messenger from God, if you will. Of course, I'd never say that to my fellow philosophers. They'd have me fired, tenure or not. They couldn't tolerate the implications for their own insignificance.

"Think about it," Steven continued, obviously warming to the discussion. "If God exists, on the one hand that's great. On the other hand, however, he wins every contest – i.e., he'd be the smartest, the richest, and surely the best looking - hands down. There would be no big men on God's campus. We would all be, without exception, so inferior to God that any superiority we may have over each other would be irrelevant. Essentially, we'd all be the same. That would be a very hard reality for a lot of people to swallow. Their superiority – or what they perceive to be their superiority – is their identity. Take that away and they're just another face in the crowd."

"It is true, in my experience," David observed, "that people of deep faith are generally very gentle and not particularly competitive."

"The world of competition, on any front," Steven agreed, "is a world that turns on the individual. The world of faith turns on God. In the former, it's all about me. In the latter, it's all about Him."

"She's not the first, of course, who claims to have been with God or had a vision from God. What can we learn from her predecessors' example, Steven?"

"It's the argument from revelation. Unlike most of the arguments I deal with in the world of philosophy, it's experiential, not philosophical. It's not a logical argument, by which I mean it's not an argument built on a foundation of logic. As such, it's impossible to prove – or disprove. For the person who has the revelation, however, it is typically the strongest possible argument for God's existence. They know rather than conclude, so they're often quite confident in the reality of their experience."

"Which would argue against Mrs. Warner having experienced a true revelation from God," David noted.

"Maybe; maybe not. You can't ignore the individual personality. If she's a shy, humble person, it might just be a question of time before she accepts her experience as real."

As Steven concluded his comment, Gordy shuffled over to the table with their lunch entrees. Setting them down in their appropriate places, he inquired as to their need for further assistance, and having received polite assurances that they didn't require any, slowly departed for the kitchen.

The two men sat quietly for several minutes while they began to eat their meals and digest the discussion thus far. Finally, Steven laid down the fork full of food that he had been raising to his mouth and said, "I will tell you one thing that intrigues me about this case. It has no theological significance. None of the monotheistic religions is really discredited in any way. It is true that some Christian sects tend to think of God as more demanding than loving, but that's more an issue of emphasis. In nearly every case of past revelation that I can think of off the top of my head, the revelation has had theological significance."

"Does that really matter, though?"

"Don't know." After pausing to look directly at David, Steven said, "What I really don't know, however, is why you're so interested in this. I know you're a man of faith, but you've always struck me as being pretty pragmatic."

"Thank you; I think. To be completely honest, I don't know why I'm interested. I guess I'm thinking of helping her."

"How so?"

"I don't know that either. Maybe it's just a question of moral support; helping her to gain the confidence to decide what happened without the influence of fear."

"Whatever she does," Steven interjected, "fear – a lot of fear – is appropriate. You know that she'd be throwing herself to the wolves in much the same way Socrates and a long list of others have. Throughout history, society has seldom been kind to people who want to disrupt the status quo. Sure, if everybody's starving, as was the case prior to the French Revolution, the forces of change can be overwhelming. It still takes a lot of bloodshed, however. And, more often than not, the people who want to protect the status quo emerge victorious."

"I suppose you're right," David said with a hint of sadness. "Why do you suppose that is?"

"Simple," Steven responded brusquely, sitting upright in a gesture of incomprehension at the question. "The people who have the most to lose are the ones in power. The people who have the most to gain are typically on the outside looking in."

———

Late in the day, Dr. Marcus walked through the open doorway of Leah's hospital room. Sunny was sitting on the bed next to Leah and the two women were playing a card game.

"Who's winning?" he asked playfully.

"We're playing Spite & Malice," Leah replied, "so Sunny has a huge advantage. I'm better at Solitaire."

Sunny stuck out her tongue at her sister.

"Well, I'm not much good at *any* card game," Dr. Marcus observed.

After a short pause, he asked, "How are we feeling this afternoon?"

"Just fine," Leah replied nonchalantly.

"Any headaches? Blurred vision? Dizziness? Nausea?"

"No," Leah replied, shaking her head from side to side.

"How about pain? Are your fractures giving you any trouble?"

"No. I feel fine."

"How long do you think she'll have to stay in the hospital, doctor?" Sunny interjected.

Dr. Marcus folded his arms over his chest and brought his right hand to his chin. "A couple more days, I should think. There's not much I can do medically, of course, but I'd like to have her nearby in case her condition changes significantly. I'm not overly concerned that it will, but it seems prudent to be wary of what we can't explain."

Leah looked briefly at the doctor before looking away.

"You must have some theory by now," Sunny prodded.

"Medically? No. No, I don't," he replied. "To be honest, I'm increasingly convinced that Leah's initial explanation is the only logical one."

Both women looked at the doctor in astonishment, which, in Sunny's case, was coupled with retort, and, in Leah's case, fear.

"I can see from the look on your face that you've gone the other way," he said to Leah.

Leah remained silent as she looked down at the bed.

"You're serious," Sunny observed incredulously.

"Yes, I am indeed." Looking at the chair next to the bed, he asked politely, "Do you mind if I sit?"

"Of course," Leah replied softly, gesturing toward the chair.

The doctor pulled the chair from against the wall and turned it to face the bed and the two women.

"I'm the first to admit," he began after sitting, "that I have no way to prove that you were, in fact, with God. I do, however, have a very strong intuition that it's true. And there are some things that point to that conclusion, even if they aren't conclusive."

"Such as?" Sunny asked immediately.

"The very nature of the dream, were it a dream," he began, "is very unusual. I've talked at length with Dr. Heidrich and he agrees that what you initially recounted fits none of the established dream patterns. There is no resolved conflict per se; there is no self-aggrandizement, if you will; it's almost impersonal."

"To imagine that you are a messenger of God sounds pretty personal to me," Sunny noted.

"I might agree if she truly welcomed the role. It appears, however, from everything I've heard, that she does not. If anything, she would like not to believe it."

"That's true," Leah said softly.

"But Leah," Sunny noted impatiently, "didn't the other doctor tell you that you might be, how did you put it, looking for a life purpose or some such thing."

"Yes, he did," Leah acknowledged, looking at Sunny.

Dr. Marcus sighed. "Yes. Again, however, Dr. Heidrich agrees that that would be more plausible if it was a purpose or a role that you welcomed. Your reluctance, he agrees, makes that less likely. It would, he believes, require the presence of schizophrenia, which he is confident you do not have."

Crossing his arms and cocking his head slightly, Dr. Marcus, asked, "Leah, what does your gut tell you? If you set aside whether or not you welcome this role, or whether or not you fear this role, what do you feel in the heart of your soul? Our intuitions are often more objective than our mental analysis."

Leah exhaled deeply. She rubbed her fingers together anxiously on her lap. Finally, she said slowly, "My heart tells me that I was with God, and that he loves me, and he wants me to deliver a message of love to the world."

Sunny gasped. "Leah, please stop," she pleaded. "Do not throw your life away for a delusion. You are not God's messenger!"

Leah looked at Sunny with a piercing look seething with an anger built up over a lifetime of cowering submissiveness. It was so out of character that Sunny actually took a step backward.

"Sunny," Leah said forcefully through clenched teeth, "you and everyone else have told me what to do all of my life. I'm not going to allow you to crush my hope this time. Whether I was dreaming or not, I believe that I was with God and that God loves me. I am not," she spat with emphasis, "going to let you take that away from me. Not this time."

Stunned, Sunny, eyes wide in horror, looked at Dr. Marcus, who sat largely expressionless, but whose face faintly hinted satisfaction at the outburst.

Her shock giving way to embarrassment, Sunny grabbed the bedrail with both hands. "Leah," she finally uttered, "I'm not trying to tell you what to do. I've never knowingly tried to tell you how to live your life. I'm just trying to protect you. You know that you can be an idealist at times."

"Naïve, you mean?" Leah retorted.

"No, no. Innocent, maybe. Oh, I don't know, Leah," Sunny concluded in exasperation. Pausing, she looked again at Dr. Marcus and calmly said, "Maybe now is not the time to discuss this."

Dr. Marcus, still unruffled, almost serene, began to stand. "I must be going anyway. Perhaps we can talk more later," he said placidly.

Turning to face Dr. Marcus, the anger had disappeared from Leah's face, but it had been replaced with an equally uncharacteristic look of resoluteness.

"I'd prefer you stay, Dr. Marcus, if you have the time."

"Yes, of course," he softly replied as he returned to his seated position. "I've got the time."

"Good. Thank you," Leah said, her voice confident and clear.

Looking to Sunny, Leah said, "I'm sorry, Sunny. I know you think I'm crazy. But as much as I've tried to convince myself that I was just dreaming, I can't. As much as the whole idea scares me to death, there's a little voice inside that says it's why I'm here."

Bursting into tears, Sunny lunged forward to embrace her sister. Leah returned the embrace and the two sisters, the younger one sobbing, the older one calm and stoic in appearance, rocked gently back and forth. For the first time in their lives, Sunny surrendered the role of big sister while Leah confidently embraced it.

Finally, Leah put her hands on Sunny's upper arms and gently pushed her backward. Turning to Dr. Marcus, she said, "I'm sorry, doctor. We're acting as if you're not in the room."

"No apology necessary," Dr. Marcus replied reassuringly. "As an only child, I'm quite jealous of the bond between you."

Sunny sheepishly retreated to the bathroom to find a tissue and compose herself.

Finally, Dr. Marcus said to Leah, "If you do wish to move ahead with your mission, Leah, I would like to help, if you'll let me."

"Of course," Leah replied, "but how?"

"Any way I can. Although I am Jewish, I am quite familiar with the New Testament as well as the Old. I might be able to help you through some of the theological issues that are sure to come up. More than anything, I suppose, I'd like to provide encouragement. I think the world is truly on a dangerous path, and if I, in some small way, help you to get it back on track, I know that will bring me great satisfaction; a sense of purpose, if you will."

After contemplating the offer for several moments, Leah raised her arms in front of her and let them drop to the bed, exclaiming with cheery abandon, "Let's do it. What's first?"

"Well, I don't want you doing anything for the next couple of days. You need your rest. I would, however, with your permission, like to introduce you to a very good friend of mine. His name is William Vaughn and he is the managing director of a non-profit organization called Americans for the Advancement of Faith. I am a member, which is how we initially met. It's an inter-denominational group that wishes to promote a faith-sensitive society."

"I've never heard of it," Leah observed matter-of-factly.

"No, I'm not surprised. They operate well below the radar of public attention by design. There are numerous groups that are aligned on the opposite side of the issue. They would like to see a secular society in America, similar to the societies of modern Europe. And they have a very sympathetic ear in the media. A.A.F., and other organizations like it, seldom get favorable news coverage, so they've learned just to stay out of the news."

"What could Mr. Vaughn do to help me?" Leah asked.

"I'm not sure, to be honest. He's very well connected, however, and has a top-notch communications machine already in place. I would think he could help you get your message out. I'm not sure you'll be able to rely on the media to do it for you. Besides, the organization is extremely well funded. Should there be a need for financial assistance, I should think he'd be in a position to provide it."

"Okay, Dr. Marcus. Let's talk to this Mr. Vaughn of yours."

———

After Dr. Marcus left, Sunny emerged from the bathroom and took her seat on the windowsill, staring blankly at the bright summer sun sinking slowing on the horizon.

Leah was the first to break the long silence. "I'm sorry to have snapped at you, Sunny. I guess that had been building for a long time."

Sunny simply nodded in response.

"Now may not be the time to tell you this, Sunny, but I've always been painfully jealous of you. And, as a kid, that jealousy often turned into resentment."

Sunny turned her head to look at Leah, her face remaining void of expression.

"You did everything right. You were pretty; you were athletic; and, most importantly, you didn't let anyone push you around. I, on the other hand, was chunky, inept at anything athletic, and I never stood up to anyone."

"You don't really believe that, do you?" Sunny asked calmly.

Leah thought for a moment before responding. "I came to," she finally replied, nodding her head. "I finally gave in."

Sunny looked quizzically at her sister.

"You weren't aware of this," Leah continued, "but Dad frequently asked me why I couldn't be more like you. He said that if I didn't get a backbone, people were going to walk all over me and I'd have only myself to blame. Eventually, I just surrendered. I didn't even try to stand up for myself. I accepted that I'd never amount to anything."

"Is that why you didn't go to college?"

"He told me it would be a waste of time. He said I should just go out and find a man to take care of me."

Sunny returned her gaze to the sunset. "I didn't know. I'm sorry," she said remorsefully to the window.

"It wasn't your fault," Leah answered. "I eventually realized that it really had nothing to do with you. That's what allowed us to become sisters again."

After both sisters sat quietly in thought for several minutes, Leah asked, "Do you remember Henry Wyatt?"

Sunny shook her head from side to side.

"You would have been only 12 at the time. I wasn't much of a dater, but I had gone on a couple of times with Henry. He was nice enough. Nothing special, which is why, I suppose, he thought to ask me out. At any rate, I was home alone one Friday night. You and Mom were out shopping for my birthday. Dad had gone out to have a beer with his buddies. And Henry called and asked if he could come over. I, of course, was incapable of saying no, so I agreed, even though I knew Mom and Dad would go ballistic if they found him there. I guess I figured that I would somehow miraculously come up with the courage to ask him to leave after a while."

Leah stopped and looked down at her hands before continuing. "Well, Henry had gotten his hands on some beer. He had a snoot-full by the time he got there. I had never seen him when he had been drinking, but it turns out that he wasn't as meek and mild as he seemed. He had a lot of rage bottled up inside and the alcohol let it all come out."

"Did he hurt you?" Sunny asked in horror.

"It never got that far," Leah observed calmly. "First, he wanted sex. I said no. He insisted. We struggled. Before I knew it he had me pinned on the floor. He ripped my panties off and was in the process of unzipping his jeans when Dad walked in."

"What did he do?"

"Dad? He pulled him off and told him to go home and never come back."

"He didn't call the police?" Sunny asked incredulously.

"No. He never even told Mom about it."

"Why?" Sunny asked, desperate to understand.

In a calm, unemotional voice, Leah explained, "Because he thought it was my fault. He said Henry only tried to take advantage of me because he knew I was a pushover and wouldn't resist. He said I got what I deserved."

Tears welling in her eyes, Sunny walked over to Leah's side and put her hand on her arm. "What did you do?"

"The next night," Leah continued, "I found Henry Wyatt and gave him what he wanted."

Sunny began to sob.

"I gave a lot of boys what they wanted after that. I guess I figured that it was my destiny to be the world's doormat."

"That's why we never saw you once you moved out."

"Yeah. Well, thankfully, I eventually met Greg. He didn't ask me for sex. He didn't ask me for anything. And I fell in love with him for it. We were just alike; happy to hide behind closed doors and let the world rush by without noticing us."

"I always wondered if Greg didn't dislike me for some reason," Sunny said ponderously.

Leah laughed. "You made him nervous," she said. "Greg didn't dislike anyone. He never stood in judgment of anybody."

———

Later that evening, Leah was alone in her room when one of the nurses entered. Sunny had left earlier to be with the boys.

"Leah, I'm really sorry to bother you, but there is a woman at the elevator who wishes to speak with you. The guard hasn't let her through, but she's very insistent. I only bring it to your attention because she says that she represents an organization that wants to help you."

After a long hesitation, during which she bit her lip, Leah finally said, "I'll talk to her."

"Okay. I'll send her down."

A minute or two later, a woman peered around the corner and entered Leah's room.

The woman was slightly younger than Leah with a full head of black frizzy hair and heavily freckled skin. She was wearing a black leotard scoop-neck top and a full-length wrap-around skirt fashioned out of an African print. She wore several colored rubber wristbands, but appeared to be wearing no makeup. On her feet she wore a pair of well-worn Birkenstock sandals.

"Mrs. Warner, thank you so much for agreeing to see me," she said as she entered, her hand extended. "My name is Helen Luft."

Shaking her hand, Leah said, "You're welcome."

Fishing deep into the large woven hobo bag slung over her shoulder, the woman produced a business card and offered it to Leah.

"Thank you," replied Leah. "I've always liked the name Helen," she said, looking at the name on the card.

"I heard of your story from a local colleague and was totally fascinated. I'm sure I won't be alone. The Associated Press, I'm told, has picked it up. It will be in every major newspaper in the country tomorrow."

"I didn't know that," Leah replied, as waves of trepidation welled within.

"Yes, it's probably good that they've posted a security guard. I'm sure you're going to have lots of people who would like some of your time."

"I did have a couple of uninvited guests earlier today," Leah noted.

"Yes, well let me get to the point and I will get out of your hair," Helen said in a rapid fire voice that made it clear that she was a very busy woman who expected to accomplish much in a day.

"I represent an organization called A.S.P. - Americans for Social Progress. We're a research organization committed to social development."

"What does that mean, exactly?"

"An end to discrimination of all kinds; economic parity; religious freedom; cultural freedom; and the protection of personal privacy."

"Sounds like an important mission," Leah replied sincerely.

"It is. And when all is said and done, it all comes down to peaceful and hate-free social harmony built on mutual respect. From what I read in the *Dispatch*, you appear to support such an ideal."

"I suppose," Leah replied hesitantly.

"Good. That's why I'm here."

"Okay," Leah replied.

"Do you mind if I sit?" Helen asked pleasantly.

"Please," Leah replied, motioning to the chair against the wall.

Moving it briskly to the side of the bed, Helen sat down quickly and forcefully.

"There's one problem," Helen began, crossing her legs and clasping her hands over her knee.

Leah unconsciously leaned away from Helen, as if she might deliver a physical blow.

"We're concerned that, as well-intended as you may be, framing the concept of social harmony in terms of religion will actually impair social harmony, not promote it."

Leah furrowed her brow. "How so?" she asked.

"Well, there are a lot of religious groups, unfortunately, which use their religion to justify intolerance and prejudice"

"In what way?"

"By demonizing homosexuals, for example."

"I'm not one of those people," Leah responded defensively.

"Good. Then you understand."

"No, I'm afraid I don't."

Helen sighed heavily. "You see," she said, gesturing in the air with her hands, "if you go ahead with your story - and try to spread this message from God – we're afraid it will only serve to embolden the political right, which has already unraveled years of social progress."

"I have no interest in politics, I assure you."

"Yes, but even if you don't, your message will be politicized. It will be abused by those who wish to make God, or their perception of God, the supreme leader of the land."

Leah sat silently in silence, her mind racing to understand.

"What is it you want me to do?" Leah finally asked.

Helen looked intently at Leah, who held her gaze.

"We want you to think about what you're doing before you do more damage than good," Helen finally replied.

"You want me to be quiet?"

Helen sighed deeply and looked down at the floor. After several moments of silence, she looked up and asked, "Leah, why are you doing this? Why do you want to put yourself through all this? Is it money?"

"No," Leah replied indignantly.

"If it is, Leah, money is easy to come by. We would be happy to help you financially."

"You want to buy my silence?" Leah asked in exasperated disbelief.

Helen didn't respond.

"Do you really know what you're getting into, Leah? Do you? Politics is a nasty game. A very nasty game. Sometimes, people even get hurt."

"I don't believe this," Leah replied, shaking her head slowly from side to side.

"Let me tell you how it'll ultimately come down. You can't prove you are God's messenger."

"And you can't disprove it," Leah interrupted.

"Doesn't matter," Helen retorted. "The burden of proof is on you. And you don't have it. That means, in a nutshell, that *you* will be the story. The message of love; the existence of God; all of that will be lost. You, Leah Warner, will be what the battle is all about. Do you really think you're up to that?"

"Up to what?" Leah asked in growing bewilderment.

"Your opponents, Leah, and there will be many, will do everything they can to discredit you; to make you out to be a lying, conniving, opportunist."

"But I'm not," Leah pleaded.

"Everybody's got a past, Leah. They'll dig through every grain of yours. And if they can't find anything, they'll make something up. The end always justifies the means when the stakes are high enough."

"I really don't believe this."

"Remember, Leah, your children will be sitting in the audience as your life story is told. As will your sister and your friends and everyone else you hold dear to your heart."

Leah's face began to turn red, her jaw hardened, and her fists clenched.

"I think it's time for you to go," she finally said in a firm, stern voice.

"Fine," Helen replied tersely. After a long pause, she said, "Leah, you are making a huge mistake. I hope you'll reconsider."

Helen rose brusquely from the chair, threw her handbag over her shoulder and marched to the door in long quick strides. Before leaving, however, she stopped and turned one last time.

"You've been warned, Leah."

CHAPTER 8

A hand went up. Professor Bradshaw pointed.
"Couldn't everyone be wrong?"

"Theoretically, sure. It was long believed by virtually everyone that the sun rotated around the earth. And, we now know, they were all wrong."

Moving to the other side of the floor, Professor Bradshaw said, "There's another potential explanation for universality beyond natural response. It has to do with how public opinion is formed. Anyone care to explain?"

"Public opinion is formed by opinion-makers."

"And who are those opinion-makers?"

"In science, they are the people believed to be the most learned."

"Correct. Universal consent does not require universal conclusion. It could be argued that a relatively small number of people would have to have put forth the notion of a Supreme Being for its acceptance to have become universal.

"Or, of course, we could be wired, as supporters of the argument from universal consent would submit, to know that there is a Supreme Being. The knowledge could be innate."

"Couldn't Darwinism explain it?" a young woman in the front row asked.

"How so?" Professor Bradshaw asked, furrowing his brow.

"As man evolved, the people who believed in God won out in the process of natural selection, perhaps for unrelated reasons."

"Interesting thesis. That would suggest, however, that either there was some Darwinian advantage to believing in God or that the coincidental advantage you refer to required a belief in God, which may, in fact, support the idea that such knowledge is innate. In the end, Darwin explained why some species survived and others didn't, but he really tackled the physical development of beings, not that portion of their mental development that deals with spiritual matters. He did renounce the Bible and Christianity, however. And it is commonly accepted today that he did not recant his theories on his deathbed, as many rumors have suggested over the years. Still, relatively few Darwinists would submit that he categorically disproved the existence of spiritual forces within the universe.

"In fact, this raises an interesting fact that theists often cite in support of their beliefs. It has to do with theism and modern science. Anyone care to guess what that fact is?"

Professor Bradshaw scanned the audience as he stood at the front of the class, chin raised. Finally, a young man raised his hand tentatively.

"Yes?"

"Is it that religion remains popular despite advances in science?"

"Very close. It is that theists and religious philosophers face the same questions today that they have faced from the beginning of time. Not only has science not provided conclusive evidence of alternative explanations, it has uncovered no new questions. That's pretty incredible when you think about it. Despite all of the advances in modern science, scientists have presented theists with no new challenges. None.

"Can anyone tell me who Professor T. H. Huxley was?"

Several hands shot up.

"The young woman in black."

"Known as 'Darwin's bulldog,' he was one of Darwin's first and most forceful supporters."

"Correct. Professor of the Royal College of Surgeons and President of the Royal Society, Huxley wrote a book entitled, *Evidence as to Man's Place in Nature*, published in 1863, which claimed that Darwin's thesis of natural selection could, in fact, be accepted as a matter of fact.

"Huxley, however, also had this to say, according to a passage in the book, *Life and Letters of Charles Darwin*, edited by Darwin's son Francis."

Professor Bradshaw consulted the notes he was holding in his hand, flipping through a couple of pages before finding the quote he was looking for.

"I quote. 'There is a great deal of talk and not a little lamentation about the so-called religious difficulties which physical science has created. In theological science, as a matter of fact, it has created none. Not a solitary problem presents itself to the philosophical Theist at the present day which has not existed from the time that philosophers began to think out the logical grounds and the logical consequences of Theism.' End quote.

"So, did Huxley believe in God, despite his support of Darwinism?" the professor asked.

No hands went up.

"Huxley was an agnostic. In fact, Huxley coined the term agnosticism, from the Greek word agnostos, meaning unknowable. In Huxley's case, however, his agnosticism was not just a function of keeping his options open, as it is for many agnostics, but from his conviction that knowledge is unattainable on many matters covered by religious doctrine. He did not, in other words, despite his support for Darwinian theory, rule out the existence of a Supreme Being.

"Just out of curiosity, does that surprise anyone – that 'Darwin's bulldog' left the theistic door open?"

Most hands were raised.

"I thought it might," Professor Bradshaw noted. "Remember what Socrates said. We don't know nothin' 'bout nothin'. Never let your assumptions lead you down the path of false knowledge.

"And I think that's an excellent point on which to end today. Next time, we'll discuss Thomas Aquinas, now known to Catholics as Saint Thomas. The next four chapters in your text, if you will."

———

The following morning, there was a knock at Leah's door and Dr. Marcus entered with a guest. Sunny was sitting on the far side of Leah's bed and both women were reading magazines.

The man appeared to be in his mid-fifties. He was over six feet in height, wore his stylishly cut grey hair gelled straight back, and was dressed in a double-breasted dark blue suit, white shirt with French cuffs, light blue cuff links, and a light blue silk Hermes tie to match.

"Good morning, Leah, Sunny. This is William Vaughn, the friend I told you about."

"How do you do," the man offered in a deep rich baritone while bending slightly at the waist. He then stepped forward to shake each woman's hand.

Retreating back a step from the bed, Mr. Vaughn unconsciously tugged downward to straighten his neatly pressed suit coat. He stood upright and erect, his chin slightly raised.

"William flew in from Washington this morning and I picked him up at the airport. I've given him most of the details of the story, so he's fairly up to speed on what's happened."

"A fascinating story, I must say," Mr. Vaughn offered enthusiastically.

"Yes indeed," Dr. Marcus agreed. "Unfortunately, I have to run to a staff meeting, but I thought the three of you could spend some time together just to get acquainted. As I said, I'm not sure how A.A.F. can help you, Leah, but I think it's a good contact to have and I'm sure you will find William to be a most engaging conversationalist."

"I've just met these fine ladies and I'm sure I'm blushing already," Mr. Vaughn observed, smiling broadly.

Dr. Marcus patted him on the shoulder amiably and turned to leave.

"Please be seated, Mr. Vaughn," Leah offered, gesturing toward the chair next to the bed.

"Yes, thank you," he replied, deftly unbuttoning his suit coat and carefully lowering himself onto the chair.

"Dr. Marcus told us a few things about you, Mr. Vaughn," Sunny began immediately, "but perhaps you could tell us in your own words."

"Yes, of course," Mr. Vaughn replied before clearing his throat.

"Simply put," he began, "A.A.F. is an organization devoted to the promotion of faith. We're a non-profit organization, registered with the

Internal Revenue Service under Section 501(c)(3) of the Internal Revenue Code."

"So you're a religious organization?" Sunny asked.

"Yes, but we are not a church and we do not formally align with any single religion, although we do support only the monotheistic religions – Christianity, Judaism, Islam, etc."

"And where does your money come from?" Sunny continued.

"Our members, mostly. We do get grants, as well, from private trusts and foundations."

"And what kind of people belong to your organization?" Sunny pressed.

"I'm afraid we don't disclose our membership list, not even to the members. Let's just say it's a very diverse group. Some names you'd surely recognize. Others you wouldn't."

"But they're all conservatives, I assume," Sunny went on.

Mr. Vaughn chortled. "Certainly not." He paused to raise his hand, forefinger extended, to his lips. "You must understand a couple of things about Washington and the people who have a direct interest in what goes on there. For starters, no one is who he or she appears to be. Their public identity is only the identity they've chosen to acquire power. Who they really are, however, is another story. There is often little similarity between the two personas. And, secondly, power is acquired through conflict. Without conflict, the voters have no reason to vote for either side. There must be a political enemy, so a good politician will create conflict even where none really exists. As a result, most politicians are fictitious characters in the end. They only appear to hold vastly different ideals. In reality, they are all remarkably the same. They all lust for power."

Speaking for the first time, Leah asked, "Are there politicians that belong to your organization?"

Mr. Vaughn grimaced thoughtfully before answering. "Politicians, you must understand, are mere figureheads. They are the tip of the iceberg that you can see above the water. Virtually all of the icebergs in Washington are a part of our little coalition at some level, just as they are all a part of our competing coalitions. As a practical matter, however, only those politicians who have chosen religion as a theme on which to further their power are themselves members. And some of them, I assure you, are a lot less religious than some of those politicians who have chosen to acquire power by railing against religion. It's all very topsy turvy, which is what makes it so much fun," he concluded, again smiling broadly.

"Doesn't that violate the separation of church and state?" Sunny asked suspiciously.

Again, Mr. Vaughn chortled in response to the question.

"The principle you cite is one of the least understood principles of our democracy. School children are taught that the Founding Fathers wished to secularize the political arena. In fact, that's not the case at all. The doctrine of the separation of church and state actually has little to do with religion per se. It has to do with power."

"How so?" Sunny asked, furrowing her brow.

"You see," Mr. Vaughn continued, "the Founding Fathers, more than anything else, wanted to limit the size and reach of government, particularly the federal government. They attempted to accomplish their objective, in part, through the wording of the Constitution. Through the work of generations of politicians on both sides of the aisle, however, their efforts to limit the reach of government have been greatly compromised over time. There is, at the current time, virtually no limit on the potential size or reach of our federal government.

"The Founding Fathers, I believe, recognized the potential for such an eventuality. This is why they went to such great lengths to promote the idea of a faith-based society in America, which, at the time, of course, meant a Christian society. Religion, you see, puts a natural constraint on the power of government. There's a limit to how much power a person of faith will concede to the government because his faith outweighs his sense of civic obligation. To the person of faith, God is the source of ultimate authority, not the government.

"Have you ever noticed that most of the totalitarian and despotic governments of modern times have been averse to religion?" Mr. Vaughn continued enthusiastically. "That is not a coincidence. A religious society will never tolerate an all-powerful government. Anyone who wants to install an all-powerful government, therefore, such as the Leninists and others, must first marginalize religion."

"I'm afraid I don't understand, Mr. Vaughn," Leah offered.

"Yes. Well, what I just said would seem to argue that those who want to limit the power of government would want to integrate, not separate, church and state. The problem is that when religion becomes state-sponsored, as it was in Afghanistan and still is in Iran, it becomes a political institution, its leaders become politicians, and it loses its tempering influence on the consolidation of power. Church leaders inevitably succumb to the political temptation to acquire more and more power. The histories of Europe and the Middle East provide numerous examples.

"What the Founding Fathers did not want, therefore, was state-sponsored religion. And that, pure and simple, is the reason for the separation of church and state doctrine."

Leah and Sunny exchanged looks of confusion.

Sensing their puzzlement, Mr. Vaughn added, "You see, A.A.F. does not wish to promote state-sponsored religion. We only wish to promote a faith-based society."

"So you agree with keeping religion out of politics," Sunny offered.

"Technically, yes. Conceptually, no." Mr. Vaughn paused while he reached up to smooth his hair. "To understand what we want, you have to understand what our opponents want."

"And who are they?" Sunny interrupted.

"Broadly speaking, the secularists. You see, the problem arises in that most secularists are not who they say they are. They claim not to be anti-religion. In fact, they cleverly frame their debate in terms of religious tolerance, arguing that religion is a personal matter that should be left to the individual."

"Frankly, Mr. Vaughn, that is a position I generally support," Leah noted.

"As do I, in principle. Remember, however, that nothing is as it seems in Washington. That is what the secularists say; that is not what they mean."

"How do you know that?" Sunny challenged.

Unfazed, Mr. Vaughn calmly replied, "Why would anyone who truly believed that faith is a private matter, but otherwise fine and dandy, go to such trouble and expense to remove the phrase 'Under God' from the Pledge of Allegiance; or to ban school children from singing Christmas carols in a school recital; or to have the Ten Commandments removed from courthouse walls? If your real agenda is simply to promote the right not to believe, these initiatives all seem like an awful lot of fuss about nothing."

"So, what is their real purpose?" Sunny asked.

"Their real agenda has little to do with religion per se," replied Mr. Vaughn, speaking in a monotonous tone that suggested he had given these answers a million times before. "Their real agenda is power; power which they can then use to pursue their government-centric social agenda. In short, they want to empower themselves through expansive government and they realize that in order to do that they have to drive religion off the American social stage."

"I'm afraid I find it hard to believe that Dr. Marcus would be so politically minded," Leah observed.

"Dr. Marcus is perhaps our least political member," Mr. Vaughn agreed, smiling broadly. "He, like many of our members, is interested in the promotion of faith on its own merits. They have little interest in the political implications. Nonetheless, there is an alignment of interests between those who simply wish to promote faith and those who wish to promote faith for political purposes."

"And why would your organization want to help me?" Leah asked. "That, of course, assumes that you do, which may or may not be the case."

"Your story promotes faith," Mr. Vaughn answered matter-of-factly. "And it's church-neutral." A pause. "Have you contacted any churches yet, Mrs. Warner?"

"No."

"If I may be so bold, I suspect that you will find the institutions of religion somewhat reluctant to support your cause."

"Why?" demanded Sunny.

"A church or a synagogue or a mosque, at the end of the day, is an institution. And institutions have interests of their own. Self-preservation is key among them. And maintaining relevance is not far behind.

"In this case," he continued, "God did not appear to a church leader. God appeared to an average citizen who, by her own admission, was not a religious person beforehand. In this case, therefore, the church, as a metaphor for all religious institutions, was, if you will, a by-stander. In short, the church was marginalized. I seriously doubt that is a result that the church will want to promote."

The room fell silent while the two women exchanged looks, each recalling the less than supportive comments made by Pastor Rataj. Mr. Vaughn, for his part, crossed his legs and leaned back in his chair, appearing as relaxed and calm as if they had just been discussing the beautiful weather.

Finally, Sunny asked, "And what kind of help are you willing to provide, should Leah decide to accept it?"

"Financial support; security, if it becomes necessary; communication tools; infrastructure, if you will."

"Why would she need security?" Sunny interrupted.

"I'm sure you realize, Mrs. Warner, that if you are successful in getting your message out, you are sure to become a most controversial figure. Your story will bring emotions among the extremists on both sides of the religion question to a frothing boil."

"Do you really think that someone will actually want to hurt me simply because I deliver a message of love from God?" Leah asked incredulously.

"Yes. I'm afraid so," answered Mr. Vaughn. "There are a lot of very disturbed and desperate people in the world. You will motivate all of them to come out into the open. Having said that, however, I don't believe you should be fearful of those people. Disturbed people typically have a hard time getting organized enough to spread real terror."

"So why would I need security?" Leah continued.

"You have security now," Mr. Vaughn pointed out. "There is a rather sizeable security guard stopping anyone who comes off the elevator. Security isn't just about protection. In most cases it's more about managing access for practical, rather than protective, reasons."

There was another prolonged silence.

Finally, Leah offered, to no one in particular, "I have no interest in getting involved in politics. I never have."

"Mrs. Warner, please do not take offense at this, but I think it is naïve to think that you and your story will not become politicized, whether we are involved or not. In the world of politics, everything is political. Everything is partisan. We can no more take the politics out of any issue today than we can take the water out of rain. Everyone has a perspective. And perspective, at the end of the day, is the basis of political ideology. And political ideology, as it were, is the weapon with which politicians joust for power. And power, of course, is what politics is all about. It's the Siren's Song that lures politicians into the political arena."

"That's a rather cynical assessment," Sunny noted.

"A realistic assessment," Mr. Vaughn retorted.

After another long pause, Leah asked, "Mr. Vaughn, are you familiar with a woman named Helen Luft?"

"Helen Luft," he replied with emphasis. "A senior official with A.S.P. – Americans for Social Progress. She's already paid a call, has she?"

"Yes, last night."

"And she wanted to help, did she?"

"No, not really. She wanted to buy my silence."

Mr. Vaughn laughed in a mockingly abandoned way. "They so underestimate people who aren't one of them," he said wryly. "Helen Hunt is a secularist. And, by the way, a big-time political operative, although she'll never admit it. She likes to portray herself as an innocent researcher dedicated to helping the poor and oppressed."

"You don't sound like a fan," Sunny noted.

"Oh, I am. Helen is a brilliant lady; very shrewd; and very, very driven. I'd love to have her at A.A.F."

"I don't think she'd be very supportive of promoting faith," Leah observed.

"Oh, I don't know," Mr. Vaughn replied slowly. "She's a Washington player. Remember, nothing is as it seems. At the end of the day, Helen enjoys power. If she thought she could get more of it by switching sides, I think she'd flip in a heartbeat."

"Does that go for you too, Mr. Vaughn?" Sunny challenged.

Mr. Vaughn again laughed with abandon. "Very good. I like your spunk. And your skepticism will serve you well in this endeavor."

———

"You're listening to WKND, Detroit's hottest talk radio. I'm Dennis Ronson, and for the next two hours we're going to be discussing the most controversial news items of the day. We don't shy away from controversy here at WKND; we take it by the horns and we wrestle it to the ground. Our mission, and we do accept it, is to give you simple, objective explanations of both sides of the issues so that you can decide for yourself where you stand.

"Our topic today is Leah Warner, who has sparked some heated controversy over her claim to be a messenger of God. Joining us in studio to provide his interesting perspective on the topic is Professor Steven Bradshaw, Distinguished Professor of Philosophy at Great Lakes University, and author of the book, *The Myth of Truth*. Professor, great to have you with us."

"Thanks for having me."

Dennis Ronson was a middle-aged man of immense physical proportions. Weighing close to 350 pounds, he often quipped that he was the largest thing in Detroit radio. Born in West Texas, he was an avid hunter and competitive skeet shooter who had won the Michigan state championship on three occasions.

"Before we start, Professor, I just want to give our listeners the facts of this case. There aren't many. Basically, we have a 38-year-old widow and mother of two; a stay-at-home mom. She has a head on collision with a drunk driver and suffers all kinds of serious injuries, including several broken bones, lots of cuts and bruises, and severe head trauma. She's in a coma – what they call a Level I coma, which is the most serious kind. In fact, she eventually stops breathing as a result of her head injuries and has to be put on a mechanical ventilator to help her to breathe."

"That's my understanding," Professor Bradshaw agreed, sitting at the guest microphone on the other side of the broadcast booth.

"A couple of weeks later, however," Dennis continues, "some kind of alarm goes off indicating that the patient has just gone into cardiac arrest; the nurses rush in; and there's Leah Warner sitting on the side of the bed praying. And if that wasn't miraculous enough, all of her cuts and bruises have healed, and, x-rays would later show, her broken bones are healed to a degree that is inexplicable."

"Again, that is my understanding," concurred Professor Bradshaw.

"Now here's the kicker. Mrs. Warner says that she has talked to God and that God has asked her to deliver a message to the people of the world. The message is that God loves each and every one of us and wants us to learn to love each other just as much."

"Yes, but God, according to Mrs. Warner, wants us to love in a very specific way. God wants us to serve each other. That, of course, would require that we abandon our current cultural focus on achievement and acquisition, and to embrace humility and selflessness instead," elaborated Professor Bradshaw.

"Sounds harmless enough," Dennis responded. "So where's the rub?"

"Well, that depends on who you are," Professor Bradshaw began. "For those involved with organized religion, the rub appears to come from the fact that such an event does not align with accepted religious doctrine and, to a lesser degree, perhaps, the possibility that such an event could challenge existing religious hierarchies and affiliations."

"If God will talk directly to a homemaker from Michigan, in other words, why do we need churches? Is that what you're saying?"

"I wouldn't put it quite that way, but essentially, yes," replied Professor Bradshaw.

"Who else is rubbed the wrong way by this?"

"Well, certainly those who wish to promote a secular society have no interest in a God who sends messengers and tells people how to behave," Professor Bradshaw noted.

"I guess they'd have a hard time convincing people to take 'under God' out of the Pledge of Allegiance if, in fact, Mrs. Warner's story is true," snickered Dennis. "Anybody else getting bent out of shape over this one?"

"I don't know about bent out of shape, but it appears that this case has just about everybody thinking, and more than a few just a little uneasy. There are, of course, those, and it appears to be a growing number, who believe Mrs. Warner's story. Those people, not all of whom were religious beforehand, are generally euphoric over the prospect of a loving God. These individuals, however, are now faced with a call to action, it seems to me. How can you believe her story and not feel some sense of obligation to help re-shape our cultural and political institutions."

"And that means money and power, so things could get ugly," Dennis interjected.

"Exactly. A lot of people would say, 'I don't care what you believe as long as you keep it off my lawn.' Sparks typically fly, however, when one group of people tries to tell another how they should live."

"I went to the Tigers game at Comerica Park last night," Dennis offered, "and everybody was talking about it. In many ways, the game seemed to be a sideshow."

"Well, it obviously raises a lot of pretty significant issues."

"And one of those, of course, is 'What does it take to prove God's existence?' Is one medical miracle enough? Or was it even a miracle? We'll address those questions and more. Now, however, we need to take a short commercial break. Loving God or not, we still gotta pay the bills. We'll be right back, so stay with us."

During the break, Dennis asked the engineer to lower the air temperature in the broadcast booth. "You got it set for a skinny guy," he said jokingly.

After rummaging through a few papers, Dennis looked over at Professor Bradshaw and asked, "You like cars, professor?"

"I do indeed. Drive a '68 charger."

"Really. That's a classic. What engine you got in it?"

"426 Hemi"

"They didn't make many of those that year, did they?"

"No, they're pretty rare," Professor Bradshaw proudly replied.

"Sweet," Dennis said enthusiastically.

"Ten seconds," said a voice over the headphones.

"We're back. I'm Dennis Ronson and I'm joined by Professor Steven Bradshaw, Distinguished Professor of Philosophy at Great Lakes University, and we're discussing the case of Leah Warner, the Michigan woman who claims to be a messenger of God. So, Professor, we want to talk a little bit about proof. What does it take to prove the existence of God and does this case meet the standard. As the author of a book on the subject of truth, you've got some thoughts, I'm sure. Please share them with us."

"Yes, thank you. Well, as the title of my book suggests, contrary to popular perception, there really is no such thing as irrefutable truth. There is only our perception of truth, and that is invariably influenced by our past experiences and the core belief system that we have come to accept over time."

"But aren't there scientific facts to which there are simply no exceptions. Water can't flow up hill, for example. The speed of sound is always whatever it is. Things like that."

"The way I use the terms, facts and truths are two different things. A fact is a piece of data, an observable and measurable reality. Yes, sound does travel at a constant speed. A truth, however, requires an extrapolation of that fact into a larger observation or belief. In the case of sound, for example, scientists have long been able to measure the speed of sound. Until Chuck Yeager broke the sound barrier, however, it was a matter of hot debate as to what would happen if an airplane exceeded the speed of sound. While there were theories, no one really knew until it was actually observed.

"Science," Dr. Bradshaw continued, "is not a collection of established truths. Science is no more nor less than a methodology for evaluation;

an attempt to explain reality. It is a way to approach the development of knowledge. It is not a body of knowledge itself."

"But what about," asked Dennis, "when we read about some big new scientific discovery? Isn't there usually some broad conclusion involved, like chocolate is bad for you, or whatever?"

"Yes, and those conclusions frequently turn out to be wrong in the long run. A very large percentage of scientific study is ultimately proven to be erroneous, not because the facts are wrong necessarily, although that does happen, but because the conclusions drawn from those facts are wrong."

"So what about Leah Warner?"

"In the case of Leah Warner," Professor Bradshaw continued, "her medical recovery appears to be an observed fact. I haven't heard of anyone who disputes the fact that she healed with inexplicable swiftness. So that, I believe, is a fact. Does that, however, prove the existence of God or the veracity of her claim to be a messenger of God? Your answer to that will depend on what you want to believe, or, perhaps more accurately, what you are willing to believe. If you are a deeply religious person, for example, you will be inclined to accept the story at face value. If you are an avowed atheist, on the other hand, or if the veracity of Mrs. Warner's story would somehow turn your life on its ear, you will probably need more 'proof.'"

"You'll just write it off as a medical miracle, but nothing more."

"Yes."

"Okay. With that explanation, and I thank you for it, Professor Bradshaw, I think it's time to hear what some of you have to say on this very interesting subject. If you have a question for the professor, or you just want to tell us what you think, please call us at 1-800-599-3517. Before we take the first call, however, it's time for another quick commercial break. Don't go away. We'll be right back."

Revisiting their conversation from the prior commercial break, Dennis told Professor Bradshaw, "I drive a Hummer. It's the only vehicle I've ever owned that doesn't tilt when I get in it," he laughed.

"The original?" inquired Professor Bradshaw.

"Yep, the H1. Only gets about ten miles to the gallon – it's a beast."

"Do you go off-road with it?"

"Don't like to get it dirty," Dennis chortled. "I must admit, I wouldn't expect a professor of philosophy to drive a '68 Charger."

"A lot of people think that's why I do," the professor responded, smiling mischievously.

"Oh, there's one of our sales jockeys with a potential client. Must be giving him the tour. Smile, Professor," Dennis said jokingly. "Oh yeah," he continued mockingly, while waving enthusiastically, "Let's go see the fat guy in the glass booth."

"I heard that," a voice came over the headphones.

"They didn't," Dennis noted as he continued to wave.

"Ten seconds," came the voice again.

"And we are back. For those of you just joining us, I'm Dennis Ronson, your host, and I'm joined in studio by Professor Steven Bradshaw, Distinguished Professor of Philosophy at Great Lakes University and author of the book, *The Myth of Truth*, and we're discussing the case of Leah Warner, the Michigan woman who claims to be a messenger of God. So, let's take our first call. It's from Bob in Havana.

"Hi, Bob. I assume you're not calling from Havana, Cuba, Bob."

"No, Havana, Michigan, up here in the great UP."

"You're a Yooper."

"That's right."

"Before you give us your thoughts on the Leah Warner case, Bob, why do they call it Havana? Is it named after the capitol of Cuba?"

"I have no idea."

"How long you lived there, Bob?"

"All my life."

"Okay, Bob. Not big on trivia, I guess. So what do you think about Leah Warner?"

"Well, I really don't care if she's telling the truth or not. I think people are making way too much of this whole thing. I'm gonna live my life the way I want to live it and that's that."

"An interesting perspective," Dennis replied. "Bob, do you believe in God?"

"I believe in gettin' up in the mornin' and going to work. And I believe in having a cold beer when I get home at night. Beyond that, I don't waste my time worrying about what to believe or not."

"Well, thanks for calling, Bob. Professor Bradshaw, any thoughts?"

"Well, I'd say that was a caller who had established a belief system and wasn't about to let anything interfere with it. I'd say his standard for accepting a new truth is about as high as it can get."

"No question about that," Dennis agreed. "Let's go to Rhonda on the west side of the state, in Grand Rapids. Hi, Rhonda."

"Yes, hi Dennis. Hello Professor Bradshaw. Well, I, for one, am very disappointed in the Christian churches. I think the churches should be supporting her. Most of the religious leaders I've seen interviewed, however, don't seem to be doing that."

"Do you believe she's telling the truth, Rhonda?" Dennis asked.

"Oh yes, I do indeed. Let's face it, our culture is filled with filth. It shouldn't be any surprise to anyone that God is fed up and wants us to change our ways."

"So you think that we should all listen to Mrs. Warner," observed Dennis.

"Yes. I pray daily that we do."

"Okay. Well, thank you Rhonda. Let's go to Ann Arbor and Ryan. Hi Ryan."

"Hi. I have to disagree with Dr. Bradshaw's characterization of science. I'm going to be a senior this fall, majoring in biology, and I know for a fact that there are certain scientific truths that are irrefutable. Evolution is one of them. And since evolution is a scientific fact, the Bible is essentially a hoax."

"Professor Bradshaw?"

"Well, Ryan, I would agree that evolution is established science. Having said that, however, I wouldn't say it's irrefutable. There are some pretty highly respected scientists who question the basic theory and many evolutionary biologists who support the basic theory of evolution but question some of the detailed conclusions drawn from it. At the end of the day, the basic process of evolution has never actually been observed in the sense that we observed Chuck Yeager breaking the sound barrier, so, while I personally support the basic theory, it is not, by any stretch, an irrefutable truth.

"I think, Dennis, if I may," continued Dr. Bradshaw, "that this call really illustrates the reason for such diverse reaction to Mrs. Warner's claims. Wherever you come down in the argument of creationism versus evolution versus intelligent design, it is tough to argue that scientists and educators don't have a vested interest in rejecting creationism in the same way that religious leaders have a vested interested in rejecting evolution. After all, if the Bible has all the answers, what do we need scientists for? So it is no surprise to me that when presented with inconclusive or incomplete facts regarding the origin of life, scientists, with some exceptions, as I noted earlier, are inclined to read non-creationist explanations into them. That's not to say that evolution is wrong. As I said, I am a believer. It is to say, however, that we should bring a healthy skepticism to a debate with any individual who has something to gain – or in this case lose – from the ultimate truth. At the end of the day, that was the message of Socrates. Unfortunately, I believe that we, as a society, and our institutions of higher learning, in particular, have strayed from the Socratic Method."

"How so?" Dennis asked inquisitively.

"We don't challenge our assumptions. And we don't, as a rule, have much tolerance for those who do. We immediately take sides on every issue without subjecting that issue to objectively skeptical investigation. As academicians, we often make the mistake of telling students what to think rather than giving them the tools to think for themselves."

"It's my way or the highway."

"Intellectually speaking, yes. And it's not limited to the academic community. Most of us are not very accepting of people who disagree with us."

"Good point. But back to this issue of personal incentive and how that influences our perception of things. Can you explain that a little further?"

"Sure. It's a problem that I myself face on a daily basis," explained Dr. Bradshaw. "As a professor of philosophy, I have an incentive to appear learned. It allows me to keep my job, justify my pay, and reinforce my self-esteem. Because of those incentives, however, I have to be very careful not to draw complex philosophical conclusions where a very simple conclusion is warranted just because complex conclusions are more inclined to be seen as learned.

"In Mrs. Warner's case," Dr. Bradshaw went on, "there are a whole lot of people, as I discussed at the beginning of the show, who have incentives not to believe her. In fact, the one thing, in my mind, that tends to argue for her veracity is the fact that I can come up with no personal incentive powerful enough to warrant her making her claim in the face of the criticism and pressure she has come under."

"Another good point. Let's take another call. Angie from Chesterfield."

"Yeah, hi. I think this is all about money. I think she made the whole thing up just so she could write a book or something."

"Well, I suspect you're not alone in thinking that," Dennis responded, with a note cynicism. "Unfortunately, a lot of people seem to be doing just that these days."

"The only problem with that theory, however," interjected Dr. Bradshaw, "is that she's not going to get anyone to pay her a lot of money for her book unless her story is widely accepted. She's making progress, but I'd say she still has a ways to go before any publisher is going to write her a big fat advance."

"Well, Professor Bradshaw, we certainly are getting a flavor for the diversity of opinion about this case."

"We are a divided country," Professor Bradshaw noted.

"That's for sure. Any other thoughts on why that is?"

"Personally, I think some of it has to do with deteriorating standards of communication, particularly the propensity for hyperbole and the excessive use of word association."

"You lost me, doc. Explain."

"We've become very undisciplined in how we write and talk. As an example, how often do you hear the phrase *very unique* today? Technically, the phrase is redundant. Unique means one of a kind. Something can't be very one of a kind. Yet it's used all of the time because the word unique just doesn't rise to the level of hyperbole common to our modern communication."

"And what is your point about word association?"

"Well," Dr. Bradshaw explained, "by that I mean that anyone who wants to influence opinion, which appears to be everyone these days, including the media, attempts to do so through word association. There's no attempt at objectivity. Instead of communicating the known facts, we throw out words that are associated with a certain perspective or worldview. In doing so, we both expand the topic and change the subject. The objective is not to communicate, but to influence."

"Interesting. Well, we're running out of time. So what d'ya think, doc? Is Leah Warner ever going to get her message through?"

"If support were to grow, it could grow quickly, but I think she'll have a challenge getting the ball rolling."

"I'm sorry to interrupt, doctor, but our producer, Jeannie, has just informed me that we have a very special guest on the line and that we're going to take the unprecedented move of extending the show in order to take her call. Hello caller."

"Yes, hello."

"And you are?"

"My name is Gail Harmon. I was the night shift nursing supervisor in the Critical Care Unit at Saint Mary's Hospital where Leah Warner was treated."

"So, did you get to meet Mrs. Warner?"

"I was the first one to find her sitting up in bed praying."

"Oh, wow. Can you describe what happened? I'm sure our listeners would love to hear."

"Well, it was 5 o'clock in the morning. I was just returning from a break and as I approached the central nurses' station in the CCU, an alarm went off, indicating that a patient was in cardiac arrest. That patient was

Mrs. Warner. The other nurse and I immediately ran to her room and when we opened the door, Mrs. Warner was sitting on the side of the bed praying."

"So what had caused the alarm to go off?" asked Mr. Ronson.

"No one knows for sure."

"But you were obviously surprised to see her sitting there."

"More than surprised, yes. I can't even think of a word to describe it. She had also removed the ventilator tube that she had required to assist her in breathing."

"So, what happened after you got over the initial shock?"

"I haven't gotten over it yet. But we got her to lie down again and re-attached the sensors. As we did so, however, we realized that all of her bruises and lacerations were gone. Her skin was as smooth and soft as a young girl's. In fact, she was radiant, like a young girl who had just fallen in love for the first time."

"And what did the monitor indicate once you had re-attached the sensors?" asked Dr. Bradshaw.

"Everything was perfectly normal."

"Now, when you say that her cuts and bruises had gone away, can you put that into some kind of perspective for us? How noticeable had they been?" Dennis probed.

"Well, if you've ever seen anyone in a serious automobile accident, particularly a head-on collision, it can be a pretty gut-wrenching sight. Mrs. Warner was as bruised and cut up as anyone I have ever seen. I've been a nurse for 30 years and even I had a hard time seeing her and not getting a knot in the pit of my stomach. I dare say that most people would have looked away if they had seen her."

"And when had you seen her last?"

"Just a few hours before, at the beginning of the shift, when I made my rounds."

"And she was, at that point, still pretty banged up?"

"She was months away from healing."

"And did she talk? What were the first words she said?"

"She said, 'I'm all right.'"

"And what then?"

"I asked her a bunch of questions about her pain and such. And she said she didn't have any. Even her broken bones weren't bothering her."

"And they proved to be healed, is that right?"

"Not completely. But they had healed to an extent that normally would have taken months."

"And did she say anything about God while you were there?"

"Yes. But before I go into that, I asked her if she knew where she was and she answered correctly without the slightest hesitation. Since she had been in a coma since arriving, and since she didn't live nearby, that struck both me and the other nurse as rather incredible."

"I agree. Please go on."

"Well, when she first mentioned God, she was basically expressing her amazement that God had chosen her of all people."

"So she talked about God almost immediately. Is that correct?"

"Yes. She was clearly in awe of what had happened to her."

"No doubt. And how did you take what she had to say about being God's messenger. Did she appear delirious, or groggy, or dis-oriented perhaps?" Dennis asked.

"Not at all. She was very calm, very alert. She spoke with great clarity."

"And did you believe her?"

"At first, I tried not to think about it. I just tended to my duties. When I went home, however, I couldn't stop thinking about it. And for the first few days I tried hard to convince myself that there was some alternative explanation. I guess I was a little bit afraid."

"And did you change your mind?"

"Change, no. But I finally accepted what I had known in my heart was true all along; that she was telling the truth."

"Well, Gail, I have to admit that you're pretty convincing," Dennis noted. "Professor, any observations?"

"I think that noise we hear in the background may be a ball starting to roll," Professor Bradshaw quipped.

CHAPTER 9

"Saint Thomas Aquinas," began Professor Bradshaw, as he stepped out from behind the podium of the Davis lecture hall, "was a 13th Century philosopher and theologian. The Roman Catholic Church, which adopted the Thomistic school of philosophy as its own, considers him to be the greatest theologian of all time. Hence the saint. A philosopher in the Scholastic tradition, Aquinas offered five ways, as he called them, to prove the existence of God. Can anyone give me the first?"

Several hands went up.

It was a clear fall day, so bright shafts of light streamed through the upper windows of the hall. The position of the sun at the moment was such that the shafts were just above the heads of the students, so while the students themselves weren't illuminated, their raised hands were, creating the illusion of hands floating in space.

"Yes, the young man with the obscene tee shirt."

"The argument from motion," he replied, looking down at his tee shirt, which was solid blue, to determine what had sparked the professor's comment.

"Correct. And what is that argument?"

A young woman raised her hand, but didn't wait to be called upon to answer. "The world is in motion and for everything that is moving there must be a mover."

"Also correct. Aquinas argued that motion is the actualization of potential. My hand," Professor Bradshaw explained, holding his hand aloft to demonstrate, "has the potential to move. And now it is moving," he concluded, making a sweeping motion toward the class.

"The state of potential and the state of actuality are two very different states. They cannot co-exist," he continued. "If something merely has potential, it isn't yet. But if it is, it no longer has potential. It already is. What conclusion does a Thomist draw from that?

"Yes."

"Something in a state of potential cannot move itself."

"Correct. Only something already in a state of actuality can move something in a state of potential. And since the universe is moving, there must have been something already in a state of actuality when the universe began. That something, of course, according to Aquinas, would have to be God. What's the second way?"

"Efficient cause," someone in the back shouted.

"Yes. Behind every effect is a cause. And behind every cause is a prior cause, which means that there must have been a first cause. That first cause must have been God."

A hand went up.

"Yes."

"Why can't the process be infinite?"

"If it were, there would be no ultimate effect, so there would be no cause and effect," Professor Bradshaw answered. "Which is why Aquinas considered the universe to be finite." A pause. "Third way?"

"Everything that can be can also not be," a young Indian woman offered.

"Yes. If something cannot be, then at some point it must not have been. So what?"

No hands went up.

"Being and not being," Professor Bradshaw explained, "are mutually exclusive. Nothing can exist and not exist at the same time. Nothing that does not exist, therefore, can cause itself to exist. Something that already existed must have caused it to come into existence from non-existence. Because everything in nature cannot exist, moreover, there must have been a time when nothing existed. And if nothing existed, who, but God, could cause it to exist?"

————

As Leah's story spread, it came to dominate conversations and headlines everywhere. The reaction, however, was decidedly mixed. The emotions stirred ran the gamut from hope to despair, rapture to outrage.

By the fourth day following her re-awakening, the hospital was besieged with people trying to get through to Leah. From reporters seeking stories to the sick and infirm seeking cures, people came to Saint Mary's en masse, quickly overwhelming the hospital security staff and disrupting hospital operations.

The Oakland County Sheriff's Department was brought in to help maintain order and security. The maze of checkpoints and access barriers that deputies erected, however, created great inconvenience for employees and legitimate visitors, fouling moods and fanning tempers among the hospital staff.

The hospital administration felt understandably conflicted in its reaction. While welcoming the notoriety and publicity surrounding such a high-profile patient, the cost of heightened security and the impairment of routine operations were of rising concern.

Whitney Sharpe was particularly anxious that one of the visitors seeking access to Leah might get hurt on hospital property or that the disruption of normal services might lead to claims of malpractice. He begged both the hospital's CEO and Chief of Staff to pressure Dr. Marcus to release Leah as soon as possible. Both prudently declined, however, knowing that the doctor would be unresponsive to any such coercion.

Leah's home was equally overrun with people waiting for her release and return. Both of her neighbors had to erect temporary fences in order to keep the crowd from trampling their own well-groomed lawns. And the incessant barking of dogs now shattered the normal tranquility of the neighborhood.

"Do you know what's going on outside?" Sunny asked as she arrived on the fifth morning.

"No, what?"

"It's a zoo. There are people and police everywhere. Even the television stations are all here now. Took me half an hour to get here from my car."

"Why?"

"You're not serious," Sunny replied, mocking incredulity. "They're here to see the lady with the message from God."

"Really?"

"I guess so. They ain't here for the food."

Leah furrowed her brow as she considered the news.

"To be honest, a lot of people didn't seem very happy about the whole thing," Sunny continued. "There's a fair amount of angry shouting going on."

"Between who?" Leah asked with a note of concern.

"Hard to say. But they've got signs and everything."

"How could anyone be angry over the news that God loves us?"

"It rocks their world," Sunny shrugged. "It's the same scene at your house. I stopped by there last night to get a book that Ryan needed for school. When I saw the mob, though, I just kept driving."

"What about your house?"

"Not a problem yet. I guess nobody's figured out where I live yet, probably because I have a different last name."

After a long pause, during which Leah stared contemplatively off into space, Leah asked, in a vulnerable tone, "What do I do?"

"I don't know, Leah. I really don't know. I said I'd stand by you, and I will. I wonder if either one of us knows what we're getting into, though."

At that moment, there was a short knock at the door and Dr. Marcus entered.

After greetings were exchanged, he said, "Looks like you've become quite a celebrity. The hospital's almost under lockdown."

"That's what I hear," Leah replied. "Makes me feel very guilty, to be honest."

"It's not your fault," Dr. Marcus replied kindly. A pause. "So, how are we feeling today? Any change?"

"Nope. Feel fit as a fiddle, other than a little anxiety about everything that's happening."

"That's understandable. Any trouble breathing? Blurred vision? Headaches?"

"No."

"Splendid. So, have you thought any more about William Vaughn's offer to help? I talked to him again last night and he seems quite keen to get involved. Said he thought your need for security was inevitable and, on that front, it would appear he's correct."

"He's a little slick for my tastes," Sunny offered immediately.

Dr. Marcus laughed. "Some would say he's charmingly cosmopolitan, but I can accept slick. He lives in a very slick world. He can also be rather cynical, I'm afraid. That sometimes makes him seem more conniving than I think he really is. Despite appearances, however, he is a very religious man who is committed to making the world a better place."

"What's his religious affiliation?" Leah asked.

"Evangelical Christian. Born and raised a Baptist, I believe. His parents were missionaries."

"He does make it sound like his organization is more political than religious," Leah observed. "I have to admit that bothers me a little."

"Understood," Dr. Marcus replied, nodding his head. "I've wrestled with that issue myself, to be honest. William, of course, argues that there is a political side to every issue, including faith, and I suppose he's convinced even me of that to a point. I will say, however, that the organization as a whole is not as politically oriented as he is. To some extent that's his job. And there's no doubt he relishes the role. I would point out, however, that there is a board of directors that really sets the agenda and is nowhere near as pre-occupied with the political aspect of things. I've met several of the members and I can assure you that the people I worked with were of the highest integrity."

"Well, judging from the crowds outside this morning," Sunny noted, "we may not have much choice but to accept his offer to provide security at least."

"Yes," Dr. Marcus agreed. "I must admit that I was shocked and dismayed by the apparent amount of animosity in the air. Even the police seem very much on edge."

"Can we trust him?" Sunny asked suspiciously.

"Well, if my opinion counts for anything," Dr. Marcus replied, "I believe you can. I do not hesitate to vouch for his honesty and integrity."

"Okay," Leah concluded, sighing deeply. "I guess I don't have much choice. I trust your judgment, Dr. Marcus. I'll call Mr. Vaughn today."

"When is Leah going to be ready to go home?" Sunny inquired.

"Well, I'd say as early as tomorrow, but I can always come up with a reason to keep you another day or two if William needs the time. I would like to schedule one more CT scan for tomorrow morning, just to be sure."

"Okay," Leah concluded.

"For what it's worth, Leah, I seem to recall you saying that when you were with God he sensed your fear about being successful in your mission and was reassuring."

"Yes," that's right, Leah replied, her voice rising with renewed optimism.

"You have every reason to be anxious," Dr. Marcus continued. "It doesn't strike me, however, that God is going to send a messenger and then abandon her. I have to believe God is going to be looking out for you."

Leah nodded, reassured by the observation.

———

Later that morning, Leah called William Vaughn at the number on his business card. When she told the woman who answered who she was, her call was put through immediately.

"Mrs. Warner," he said cheerily upon answering. "How pleasant to hear from you."

"Mr. Vaughn, I've decided to take you up on your offer to help. Actually, I'm not sure I have a choice."

He laughed light-heartedly. "That's wonderful. I've been watching the newscasts coming out of Michigan. It looks like a full-blown media feeding frenzy there, both at the hospital and at your home."

"That's what I understand."

"Well, I've already looked into security companies and have one tentatively lined up. They're top shelf. All ex-military. They can be in place in less than 24 hours."

"That's good, because Dr. Marcus said that I could be released as early as tomorrow."

"Then I will get right on it. They did suggest that we rent a furnished home that's easier to secure than your own. If you're willing, I think it's a good idea. From what I've seen on the television, it looks as if it would be hard to keep the mob at bay at your current home."

"I'm not sure I can afford that," Leah replied uneasily.

"Oh, don't worry about that. We'll pick up all your living expenses in addition to the cost of the security firm."

"But how will I get the message out if I'm in hiding?"

"You wouldn't be in hiding per se. Don't worry, we'll get your message out. We just need to manage access and this would make it significantly easier. My assistant has already tracked down a perfect furnished home not too far from your own. I think you'll be very comfortable there. We can execute the lease this afternoon, if you agree."

"You're very efficient, Mr. Vaughn."

There was no response.

"Mr. Vaughn," Leah said quietly.

"Yes?"

"What about Helen Luft?"

"Well, I'm afraid we can count on her following through on her threats."

"About trying to discredit me?"

"Yes, I'm afraid so."

The phone line was silent.

Mr. Vaughn spoke first, saying, "I took the liberty of calling an acquaintance I've worked with before, a private investigator. I asked him to discreetly look into what Ms. Luft and her crew might dig up from your past."

Leah gasped.

———

The following afternoon, the front doors of Saint Mary's hospital parted, revealing Leah Warner in a wheelchair being pushed by Dr. Marcus himself. Sunny had the boys and would be waiting at their new home.

The dozens of reporters, cameramen, and photographers waiting for Leah's appearance immediately cascaded in on the barricades that had been set up by the police to allow Leah to leave the hospital safely.

It was a beautiful summer day in southeast Michigan. Fluffy cumulus clouds floated lazily through the blue sky on a soft breeze. The temperature was a pleasant 79 degrees and the humidity was unusually low.

At the end of the cordoned off walkway waited a shiny black Suburban with tinted windows. Two men in dark suits stood next to the open rear passenger door. Both wore dark sunglasses and both had ear pieces connected to chords that ran underneath their jacket collars. Closely shorn, young, large, and obviously fit, both stood stiffly upright, arms hanging in front of them, one hand holding the wrist of the other. Another man could be seen through the open door behind the wheel of the vehicle.

In addition to the media representatives, there were approximately three hundred people in the crowd, including a group of nuns. The old man with the walker was there. So, too, were several families. More than a few of the youngest children sat atop their father's shoulders to get a better view.

Some members of the crowd cheered, while some openly wept. A few stroked Rosary beads, while others held their hands aloft in praise. Many just watched, curious to see the woman who claimed to have been with God.

There were those, however, who, for a variety of reasons, were there to voice their disapproval of Leah and her message. Some were atheists who simply refused to believe. Others were fearful of religion in the public square and the potential for it to encroach on the political process. Still others were simply there because the television cameras were. They were protesting against a myriad of unrelated causes, from offshore drilling to the use of hormones in dairy cows.

One group of approximately thirty protesters carried signs that read, *Citizens for a Secular America*. One man with a long gray beard and pony-tail carried a sign that read, *Atheists Unite!* Yet another protester was dressed up in a crimson red devil costume. He was performing a ritualistic dance with greatly exaggerated arm and leg movements.

Two sheriff's deputies on motorcycles were parked in front of the highly polished Suburban, apparently intending to escort the vehicle through the sea of people and vehicles.

Leah was smiling, although she made no attempt to reach out to touch the many outstretched hands. She also ignored the dozens of questions shouted out by reporters. She merely looked around in disbelief, struggling to accept that she could be the center of such attention.

About halfway down the walkway, Leah turned her head around and asked Dr. Marcus to stop. She apparently wanted to address the crowd. It took several minutes for the crowd to quiet down, but a sheriff's deputy standing off to the side approached her with a bull horn he had been using for crowd control and handed her the attached microphone.

"Good afternoon," she began, after the officer pointed to the button on the side of the mouthpiece. She paused, surveying the crowd in silence. "I'm afraid I don't know where to begin," she finally continued. "As most of you have obviously heard, I was in a terrible automobile accident several weeks ago and was brought here to Saint Mary's in a coma. Several days ago, however, I awoke and all of my injuries were largely healed." A further pause. "I'd like to thank the staff here at the hospital for their outstanding care. They've all made me feel very much at home.

"While I was in the coma," Leah continued hesitantly, "God was with me." The crowd immediately erupted in a loud cacophony of cheers and jeers. One young man in a tee shirt that read, "Jesus Rocks," got into a fracas with one of the more impassioned detractors, an older man in wire rim glasses with a full head of thick, bushy hair. A sheriff's deputy immediately stepped in and separated them.

After waiting for the ruckus to die down, Leah continued. "God asked me to deliver a message to the world. God asked me to tell each of you that you are truly and deeply loved. And God asks us to love each other through selflessness and humility. We are too occupied with acquisition and achievement."

The crowd erupted again, with even more emotion. Someone in the back hurled an open can of soda toward Leah. The can landed next to her, but its contents spewed across Leah's face and upper body. Leah shrieked and a look of fear washed over her face.

The sheriff's deputy lunged forward and took the megaphone from Leah, pleading with her to get to the car as quickly as possible. Dr. Marcus immediately rolled her forward, a look of anxious foreboding on his face.

The two security guards leapt from their posts and sheltered Leah between them. When they reached the Suburban, they virtually whisked her out of the chair and into the back of the Suburban. One of the security guards immediately closed the door and moved to climb into the front passenger seat, scanning the crowd behind his dark glasses as he did so. The other man moved quickly around the rear of the vehicle and climbed into the rear seat on the far side.

The motorcycles moved forward with a lurch, their lights ablaze and sirens blaring. Soon the procession was moving quickly down the hospital driveway. Leah looked back to see Dr. Marcus still standing behind the chair. She hadn't even had a chance to say goodbye.

Leah and the three men rode silently through the streets of Waterford, eventually turning onto the entrance ramp for westbound Route 78, at which point the motorcycles escorting them silenced their sirens, doused their flashing lights, and peeled off to the side of the rode. The driver of the Suburban, who wore a headset and was in radio communication with the officers, thanked them for their help and wished them a pleasant day.

Speeding down the interstate, Leah calmed down enough to realize that she was trembling. She clutched her arms in front of her chest, dropped her shoulders, and leaned forward in a vain attempt to fight a deep chill.

The security guard next to her offered a white linen handkerchief.

"It's clean," he noted, smiling kindly. "You still have some soda on your face."

Leah accepted the offer and wiped her face and dress, slowly regaining her composure. After a few minutes, she was calm enough to talk and sought to release the tension that engulfed her.

"How long will it take to get there?" she asked meekly.

"About forty-five minutes," responded the man in the front passenger seat, looking over his shoulder.

"Are my sons there?"

"Yes m'am," the same man replied. "They're already there with your sister."

"Are they all right?"

"Yes, m'am."

After riding in silence for another fifteen minutes, Leah asked, "How is this going to work, exactly. I've never had the need for security before. Will I be free to go to the grocery and what not?"

"We're just here to protect you, m'am. You're free to leave whenever you wish, but we'll accompany you, of course. As far as food and the like, we'll do the shopping for you."

"Will you be staying at the house too?"

"The contract calls for 24/7 security. There will be a minimum of three members of the detail on the premises at all times. There's a guest house on the property that we will use as our command post and where off-duty personnel can eat and sleep."

They again rode silently for several minutes.

"So, do you guys have names?" Leah finally asked.

"I'm Jim Roberts," responded the man in the front passenger seat, the only one to have spoken so far. "I'm the team leader. Next to you is Jack Hillman and behind the wheel is Jose Garcia."

"And you guys work for A.A.F.?"

"No, m'am," Jim Roberts responded. "We work for Pinnacle Security. Our company has been hired by A.A.F. We're all ex-military – Special Ops, Navy Seals, and such. The three of us have spent the last two years in Iraq or Afghanistan."

"Well, God loves you," Leah said anxiously, smiling as if she had just cracked a wonderfully funny joke.

"Yes, m'am," replied Jim, maintaining his all-business demeanor. Jose did smile, however, she could see in the rearview mirror, exposing what Leah knew instinctively was genuine kindness.

Leaving the highway, they entered the town of Oakville, a wealthy bedroom community thirty miles northwest of Detroit. They proceeded through the quaint downtown, home to a variety of swank restaurants, upscale boutiques, and art galleries.

On the southern end of town, they turned right onto a street lined with stately, older homes that sat on large, beautifully landscaped lots.

At the end of the street, they drove through an ornate brick gateway. A brass plaque read, "Forest Glen."

Passing through the entrance, the homes were much newer and even statelier than the ones just passed. Large and grand, almost pretentious, each home was obviously worth millions of dollars. Not exactly humble, Leah thought to herself. .

"Who owns the house?" Leah asked.

"Auto exec," replied Jim. "Been assigned to run their European division for a few years."

"It's going to seem a little hypocritical," Leah said to no one in particular, "me living out here and telling people that God wants them not to focus so much on acquiring things."

"It's for security, m'am," Jim answered. "There was no way we could secure your current home."

"That wasn't really a consideration when Greg and I purchased it," Leah noted. "And please, if we're going to be together for awhile, I'd prefer that everyone call me Leah."

"Yes, m'am," replied Jim. Jose, Leah noted, was again smiling. She smiled in response.

Toward the back of Forest Glen, the vehicle pulled up to a large black wrought iron gate sitting between two ornate pillars in the middle of a brick wall that apparently encircled the entire property. Jose pressed a button on a small box that was sitting on the dashboard and the gate slowly opened. When it had opened sufficiently to drive through, the Suburban moved ahead, stopping on the other side to wait for the gate to close before proceeding to the house.

The large brick house sat several hundred yards beyond the front gate. The driveway was made entirely of brick pavers and was lined with ornamental trees that were still in blossom. For aesthetic rather than topographical reasons, it wound its way to the front entrance in a series of gentle curves.

The house was a brick manse in the French Provincial style of architecture. Modeled after a stately French country chateau, the house had a steep hipped roof and was built with both balcony and porch balustrades. The second story was outfitted with symmetrically positioned double French windows with shutters, each with a curved top that extended through the cornice, adding to the sense of the home's extraordinary height.

As they drove up the driveway to the front porch, Sunny, Tyler, and Ryan emerged from the house and came down the stone steps. Leah virtually jumped out of the vehicle to embrace her sons.

After a long embrace, Leah reached out, putting her index finger under Tyler's chin to raise his face so that she could see it more clearly. "What happened to your eye?"

"Fight at school," Ryan answered for him.

"Over me?"

"Yeah," Tyler answered quietly.

"You should see the other guy," Ryan said enthusiastically. "Tyler shel-lacked him."

Tyler just looked at his brother and grimaced.

"Did you start it?" Leah asked Tyler.

"No."

"What happened?"

After pausing, Tyler explained. "Johnnie Holcum said you were crazy and should be locked up in the nut house. All the kids were laughing."

"So you did hit him first," Leah observed calmly.

"Yeah. He wouldn't shut up."

"You know that's no excuse," Leah said, lowering her chin in a non-threatening fashion.

"I know," Tyler agreed.

"Okay. Well let's all get inside so I can get a look at our temporary home."

"You're not going to believe it," Sunny offered, falling in behind Leah and the boys as the re-united family went up the steps and entered the house.

"I don't already," Leah replied.

CHAPTER 10

Professor Bradshaw walked back to the podium and took a sip from the glass of water he had placed there.

"Fourth way?" he asked after putting the glass down.

"Yes."

"Relativity requires an absolute."

"Good. Explain."

"If there is good, better, and best, there must be a best against which all things are judged."

"Excellent. And why can't man be that ultimate standard?"

"Because all men are capable of good and bad."

"Well done. Yes, only God is perfect." A pause. "And the fifth way?"

"Everything has a purpose," a young man in the front answered.

"Yes. There is very little random activity in the world. Animals, for example, seem to act in an innate way in order to live and survive. A lion doesn't wake each morning and spend his day unlike any other day. He does things, like hunting for food, in pretty much the same way each time. And in each case, that way is typically acknowledged to be the most efficient way with the highest probability of success. It's not, in other words, random." A pause. "So where does that knowledge come from?"

"Experience?" offered a young Asian woman.

"Some of it, perhaps. To argue that all action is a result of previous action, however, is to argue against the existence of instinct. That, I submit, is a tough argument. It's certainly not one that Aquinas would have accepted." A pause. "Aquinas, of course, believed that the only explanation for instinct is God.

"Interestingly," Professor Bradshaw continued, lowering his head and bringing his index finger to his lips, "Aquinas was a huge fan of Aristotle and borrowed heavily from his work. The path from Aristotle's philosophical doctrine to Aquinas' theological doctrine, however, is not, on the surface, an obviously logical one. How did Aquinas reconcile the extrapolation of the former into the latter?"

Only one hand went up.

"Yes."

"He asserted that certain words and phrases had dual meanings."

"Correct. He actually believed that philosophy was a subset of theology. All theologians are philosophers, he maintained, but not all philosophers are theologians. Hence the potential for dual meaning. And while these dual meanings are difficult to accept at face value, modern scholars of Aristotle generally accept that Aquinas' Christian interpretations are at least plausible."

A hand went up in the back.

"Yes."

"Hasn't the modern Roman Catholic Church repudiated some of Aquinas' beliefs?"

"Yes. Aquinas supported slavery, for example, and actually argued that slave owners have the right to beat their slaves. That, of course, would be a problematic position for the Church to take today."

There was some laughter in the hall.

"Aquinas also believed that women were mentally inferior to men, a view not currently shared by most, but probably not extinct."

Several young men laughed, causing the women around them to cast stern looks in their direction.

"Aquinas actually stopped writing late in his career. In fact, his most famous work, the Summa Theologica, was never finished. Can anyone tell me why?"

Several hands went up.

"Yes, way in the back."

"He had a mystical vision," the young woman called out.

"Yes, while celebrating mass." Consulting the notes he held in his hand, the professor continued. "Afterward he said, 'All that I have written seems to me like so much straw compared to what I have seen and what has been revealed to me.' This represents another argument for the existence of God. Can anyone tell me what it is?"

"The argument from revelation?" a young man called out.

"Yes. The argument from revelation, however, differs from all of the other arguments we have discussed because it is a theological argument rather than a philosophical one. Nonetheless, we will wrap up our series next time with a discussion of this argument in the interest of completing the picture that we have drawn to date. In doing so, we will leave our long-dead philosophers behind and jump ahead to the current day and look at the most talked about and hotly debated revelation of our time – the revelation to Leah Warner."

————

As Leah was leaving the hospital, Helen Luft was sitting down for the weekly meeting of A.S.P.'s senior staff. The group of approximately fifteen staffers was, with a few exceptions, young, stylishly groomed, and casually dressed. Nearly all held PDAs and several were busy sending last minute e-mails as the last participants arrived.

The meeting was held at A.S.P's national headquarters housed in an old Georgetown brownstone. The conference room was tastefully furnished and comfortable, but modest in size, requiring some of the less senior staff to sit against the wall. Howard Dreyfus, the managing director of A.S.P., and Helen's boss, was sitting at the head of the polished wooden table.

"So, Helen," Howard began, "why don't you tell us about your visit with Mrs. Warner."

"Not much to tell. She wouldn't go along," Helen said with a hint of disgust.

"Not even for money, huh?" Howard asked.

"No. She's a pious bitch," Helen answered snidely.

"Is she convincing?" asked a young man dressed entirely in black seated at the table to Howard's immediate right.

"Not to me," Helen replied.

"That wasn't the question."

Giving the questioner a sharp look of rebuke, Helen replied, "Will she be convincing to some overweight housewife in Iowa who thinks New York is the capitol of Europe? I don't have a clue."

The questioner relented, looking down at his notes.

"And we think she's getting support from A.A.F., is that right?" Howard queried.

"It's confirmed," answered a young woman seated against the wall across from Helen.

"Surprise, surprise," Howard replied in feigned shock. "I would never have guessed," he continued, prompting snickers around the table.

"Bunch of Fascists," Helen sneered.

"They're good," her boss retorted. "Never underestimate your enemy, Helen. Besides, at the end of the day, they're one of us. Let's face it, we're both just power-brokers who use each other for our own gain. And I have no doubt that we share many of the same supporters. Don't think for a minute that the people who are willing to buy the power we broker really give a rat's you-know-what about ideology."

There was more laughter around the table.

"That's the beauty of politics," Howard went on. "So long as there is so much power at stake, there will always be plenty of money to go around."

"She'll come off as their pawn. Her association will discredit her," Helen observed.

"Maybe," Howard replied, nodding his head pensively. "The people who will be most offended by that, however, are the ones who aren't going to buy her story anyway. Vaughn is not an amateur. Whatever you think of him personally, he knows what he's doing."

"She's got a past," Helen interjected nonchalantly.

"What kind of past?"

"Arrested for shoplifting at 15; moved out of the house at 18. Was a bit of a slut, it appears. And she was arrested for possession of marijuana at 19. Not exactly the kind of background the religious rubes take a shining to."

"Who have you given it to?" Howard asked, his hands tented in front of him.

"Nobody yet. I think we should let her make her first move before we pounce. We don't want people getting sympathetic for her before the battle starts."

"Agreed. But when the battle is engaged, who can we put in front of the cameras? It's doubtful that we'll get any politicians to carry our water at this point," Howard observed.

"University professor by the name of Franklin. He's a known atheist; written a couple of books. He isn't politically active, so he can't be easily politicized. He does, however, share our values."

"And our theme?" a young man sitting behind Helen asked.

Without turning around she said, "Religious freedom. Warner doesn't have the right to push her religion on the rest of us."

"And our tactical strategy?" Howard asked.

"It was all a dream," Helen replied curtly.

"And if that doesn't work?" Howard continued.

Looking directly at Howard, Helen replied, "Then we plant the rumor that she has a history of mental illness."

Howard smiled devilishly and said, "I hope I'm never on the wrong side of your claws, Helen, my dear."

Helen immediately flashed an obscene gesture at Howard.

"Well," Howard said to the group, "I wouldn't get too worked up over Leah Warner. She's not going to change anything."

"How can you be so sure?" the man who had questioned Helen earlier queried skeptically.

"Do you really think that people are capable of living selflessly?" Howard asked him. "Self-interest makes the world go 'round."

"What if it's in their self-interest to believe?" the man continued.

"Let 'em," Helen said scornfully. "It doesn't really matter what the masses believe or want. What matters is that the people with the power to actually change things have no desire to. One little housewife from Michigan isn't going to move the status quo."

"Cynical, but true," Howard concluded. "Whether she's telling the truth or not won't really matter in the end."

———

Having given Leah a few days to acclimate to her new surroundings, William Vaughn and an entourage of publicists, advertising experts, and marketing specialists flew to Michigan to meet with Leah and draw up a plan to share her story with the world.

They met in the spacious living room of Leah's new home. The room was situated in the middle of the first floor. There was a large wooden table that ran from front to back in the very middle of the room, on which were placed a large urn of artificial flowers and several antique vases.

The furniture was arranged to create distinct sitting areas on either side of the center table. Like the house itself, the room was perfectly symmetrical, with identical furniture in each sitting area. The group assembled in the left sitting area, although several chairs from the right side were also moved into place to accommodate the large number of people.

Sunny sat next to Leah on a lush love seat. Dr. Marcus was also there and sat on the other side of the circle next to William Vaughn.

"And how are you adjusting, Mrs. Warner?" Mr. Vaughn asked pleasantly, as the dozen or more meeting participants found seats and settled in.

"Other than feeling a bit like a hypocrite and a prisoner, I'm doing fine. It took me a few days to get used to the surroundings, but we're doing all right. The boys love the big screen tv."

"Good," Mr. Vaughn said, smiling. "Well, the media coverage has been quite extensive. The footage of your departure from the hospital was shown repeatedly by the cable networks. Frankly, I doubted that the media would embrace this story. It doesn't fit their agenda."

"At the end of the day," one of the others noted, "the media's out to make money. If the story's big enough, they'll follow it."

Several people snickered in response.

"Yes," Mr. Vaughn continued. "True enough. I think that does change the flavor of our challenge, however. Instead of focusing on getting the word out, it seems appropriate to focus now on converting the doubters."

"Agreed," said another participant.

"We'll still need to do more media interviews, however," Leslie Paul, the independent publicist who had been hired by A.A.F. interjected.

"Absolutely. People need to see her tell her story, rather than just read about it," added Mr. Vaughn. "Anything lined up yet?"

"We're working on it," Leslie assured him.

"John, why don't you walk us through the preliminary media plan," suggested Mr. Vaughn.

As the media plan was unveiled, it was apparent that A.A.F. was planning to spend tens of millions of dollars to help Leah gain credibility and support. The major media markets would be saturated with television and radio spots for two weeks. The print campaign would concentrate on popular women's magazines on the assumption that women would be more receptive to the message than men. The latter, John offered, are more apt to ignore print ads anyway.

After the presentation was complete, Leah asked, "Where is all this money coming from?"

"Our membership," replied Mr. Vaughn, smiling contently. "To be perfectly honest, the money is pouring in. Our members are quite enthusiastic about our involvement."

"What about endorsements?" Leslie asked.

A young woman leaned forward in the large leather chair in which she was seated and replied, "We've got a few politicians lined up already, but most of them are waiting on the sidelines until they see how much support she gets."

"I can tell you that some of the secularists are sweating bullets," a middle-aged man in a suit offered. "They're political base is putting up a lot of fuss.

They know that if the story gains momentum they'll be between a rock and a hard place."

"Perfect place for a politician," a young man chortled.

"What about religious leaders?" Leslie asked.

"None so far," the young woman replied. "Some have actually gone on record against her story."

"What about Donny Hammond?" Mr. Vaughn asked. "He's immensely popular. His church service is carried by television stations around the country. If you can't get him to help us, let me know. He's a good friend."

"Will do," the young woman replied.

"What about a book?" yet another participant asked.

"I don't think I could write a book," Leah offered. "I didn't go to college."

"We'll hire someone to write it," the man replied.

"Somebody with credibility," Leslie added.

The room was silent for several moments as everyone thought of possible names.

"How about the newspaper reporter that wrote the original story in the *Detroit Dispatch*?" Sunny suggested, looking at Leah, who was sitting to her left. "He seemed pretty nice and said that he wanted to see you succeed."

"That's a good idea," Leah agreed, winking playfully at Sunny. "I don't know if he'd do it, but I think I could work with him."

"Let's get in touch with him," Mr. Vaughn said to Leslie.

"Will do. We're also, so that everyone knows, putting together e-mail and letter campaigns using rented lists. We've got twenty or so lists that we're getting ready to test. I've got the recommended copy here," Leslie said, holding up a sheaf of papers for Leah to see. "You, of course, will have to approve it."

"Dr. Marcus," Mr. Vaughn stated, "sitting to my right, for those of you who haven't had the chance to meet him, was Mrs. Warner's attending physician and has agreed to support our efforts." Soft applause erupted around the room, accentuating the sense of excitement that hung in the air.

"Dr. Marcus is a nationally recognized neurologist, a devout Jew, and a member of A.A.F. We've been good friends for many years."

Raising his hand slightly, Dr. Marcus leaned forward in his chair and offered, "I have also been approached recently by Gail Warner. She's the nursing supervisor who first discovered Leah after her awakening and is very interested in supporting Leah's effort."

"Splendid," Mr. Vaughn said jubilantly. "That is great news. She is sure to add credibility to the effort. Leslie, why don't you contact her as soon as you can."

"As soon as we break up," Leslie replied enthusiastically.

The meeting lasted a total of two hours, at which time the assembled group began to noisily disperse.

Leaning forward in his chair, Mr. Vaughn, asked, "Leah, could you spare a few more minutes? There's something I'd like to discuss with you privately."

Several of the departing participants overheard the question and looked knowingly at each other. Leah, caught by surprise, looked to Sunny, and then Dr. Marcus. "Sure," she finally replied. "But, if you don't mind, I'd like Sunny and Dr. Marcus to stay."

"As you wish," Mr. Vaughn agreed.

When the final stragglers had left and closed the door to the front entranceway behind them, Mr. Vaughn leaned forward in his chair, resting his elbows on his knees. "Leah," he began, "I've heard back from the friend I told you about; the one I asked to see what your opponents might use to discredit you."

"Yes," Leah replied, her chest tightening.

Mr. Vaughn bit his lower lip and said, "Well, it turns out that he did find a few things that they're likely to use."

"Such as?" Sunny demanded.

Continuing to look directly at Leah, Mr. Vaughn continued. "It seems that you were arrested for shoplifting at the age of 15."

"That's not true," Sunny protested.

"I'm afraid it is," Leah admitted. "A girl I thought was a friend convinced me to stick a bracelet she wanted into my pants. I didn't say no," she lamented.

"Yes, well," replied Mr. Vaughn. "It appears that you were also arrested for possession of marijuana at 19."

Sunny's mouth was agape.

"That's true too," Leah conceded. "Unfortunately. I was driving back to my apartment after a party with a guy I was dating and we got pulled over. He pulled out a bag of marijuana and told me to put it in the front of my bra. He said the cop wouldn't be able to look there." A pause. "He was right, as it turned out. The cop, however, dragged us down to the police station, where a female officer did take a look."

Mr. Vaughn exhaled audibly. "And were you, Leah, sexually active at that time?"

"Was I a slut? Is that what you mean?" Leah challenged.

Mr. Vaughn didn't respond.

Finally, Leah said, "I was stupid, Mr. Vaughn. I was a young girl with very low self-esteem who hated her father and wanted to disgrace him."

A heavy disquiet hung in the air. Finally, Dr. Marcus said softly, "We've all got a past, William."

"Yes, of course," Mr. Vaughn responded quickly. "Not all of us are claiming to be messengers of God, however."

"Does that mean you no longer want to help me? Why didn't you say so before the meeting? You would have saved us all a lot of time."

"I didn't say that, did I? I'm sorry to bring up what are undoubtedly uncomfortable memories. Ms. Luft and her friends, however, are sure to discover these same facts. And they are sure to use them, as she threatened. It would do little good to pretend they didn't exist."

"It's not too late to back out," Sunny said to Leah in a non-threatening tone.

Leah continued to look directly at Mr. Vaughn. "I'm not backing out," she said. "I know what I've done. And it's all the more reason I have to do this now. There was a time when I cared too much about what people thought. I'm trying to move on."

"Are you sure they will discover these things, William?" Dr. Marcus asked hopefully.

Mr. Vaughn smiled and said, "Yes, David, I'm sure. Digging up dirt on people is a big business in Washington. They'll be lined up to sell our enemies the information."

"What about the boys?" Sunny asked Leah hesitantly.

Leah turned to look at Sunny, a wave of concern washing over her face. Finally, she said, "I can't run from my past forever. At least I can show them that I'm trying to make up for my past mistakes. Hopefully, some day they will forgive me."

———

In front of a live studio audience, late night television comedian, Frankie Houston, walked onto the stage to thunderous applause to begin his opening monologue.

"Thank you. Thank you," he said, waving to the crowd.

When the applause subsided, he began. "Wow! Such enthusiasm. I have to admit, I've been a little worried that the comedy gig was over for me. I mean, how can I compete for people's attention with a lady who talks to God?"

Laughter from the audience.

"And let's face it, unlike the Monica Lewinsky story, this story isn't exactly fertile ground for comedy. 'People of the world, God loves you,'" he says in a deep, omnipresent voice, mimicking the voice of God.

More laughter.

"There just aren't many laughs in that kind of love. Now marriage, that's another story. There's a gag a minute in most marriages. But we're talking the love of the creator of the universe here. That just doesn't tickle the ole funny bone, if ya' know what I mean.

"Now, I mean no disrespect toward Mrs. Warner, the Michigan lady that claims she was drafted to be God's messenger. And I am genuinely thrilled that she has recovered from her injuries. I really am. But." In the background plays the theme music from *The Twilight Zone*, and the host says, in a voice impersonating Rod Serling, "Imagine. You arrive home from a hard day at the office and your wife says, 'The damndest thing happened today.' 'Oh yeah, what? Does it involve the car?' 'No. I was with God and he asked me to deliver a message of love to the world.' 'Really?' A pause. "What's for dinner?'"

Uproarious laughter.

"And what is this stuff about humility and selflessness? That kind of thing might play in Michigan, but here in New York that crap just doesn't sell. Can you imagine some guy walking his dog in Central Park and saying to a homeless guy, 'Hey buddy. Here, take the keys to my penthouse. My turn to live in the box for a while.'"

More laughter and applause.

"And traffic, of course, would be at a standstill. Can you imagine if the cabbies all drove politely? 'After you.' 'No, after you.' 'Oh, I insist.' Manhattan would be gridlocked."

"Actually, she seems like a very nice lady. A little too wholesome for me, but nice nonetheless. Did you see her leaving the hospital? And how about the guy in the devil costume? Who said all the kooks are on the coasts?"

More laughter.

"No, seriously. I read in the paper the other day that she said that there's no reason for anyone to be angry with her." A pause. "This is America, for Christ's sake. We have a right to angry. We're just not happy unless we're angry."

Intense applause and laughter.

———

Leslie, who had rented a temporary office near Leah's new home and was living in a residence hotel, contacted Gail Harmon and made arrangements for Gail, Leslie, and Leah to meet that evening, after Vaughn and his entourage had boarded their private jet and returned to Washington.

Gail was in her middle 50s. Standing 5' 5" tall, she was what is frequently referred to as big-boned; large, but not fat. And while she went to the hairdresser weekly, she didn't bother to hide the increasingly grey color of her hair.

Leslie, by contrast, was in her early 30s, thin, and quite beautiful, a fact that even the heavy, utilitarian glasses she wore did little to mask. She wore her jet-black hair in the kind of stylish short cut common to many professional women who want to be fashionable but not burdened by the care of their hair.

They met that evening around Leah's kitchen table. For the first hour or so, they introduced themselves to each other by sharing their life stories.

Leslie, it turned out, was the daughter of a former United States Senator from Tennessee, Senator Winton Paul. She considered Washington, as a result, to have been her real childhood home.

"Did you go to school in Washington or Tennessee?" Gail asked.

"Washington," Leslie answered. "Sidwell Friends. It's where Chelsea Clinton went. It's a Quaker school, actually. I got a good education there, but it was a pretty sheltered existence."

"Did you go to college?" Leah inquired.

"Vanderbilt. In Nashville."

"So, are you a country music fan?" Gail asked jokingly.

"No," Leslie smiled. "I'm a Yo Yo Ma fan. Nashville was, for a long time, one of the great undiscovered cities. People have always thought of it as being all about country music, but it's actually very cosmopolitan. You actually have to go looking for the country music."

"Any family?" Leah asked genuinely.

"Well, my parents retired and moved back to Tennessee. I had a younger brother, but he was killed in the Gulf War — the first one."

"I'm sorry," Leah offered with sincerity.

"Yeah. He was a good kid. But he was doing what he wanted to be doing." A pause. "He was very idealistic about duty and honor and that kind of thing."

"Didn't want to follow in his father's footsteps, huh?" Gail inquired.

"No. Most politicians' kids don't. I love my father, but I know that he loved being a senator more than he loved being my daddy. You have to be consumed by it, because it will sure as hell consume you."

"I see a beautiful wedding ring. Do you have any kids?" Gail asked innocently.

Leslie laughed, extending the fingers of her left hand to look at her ring. "Actually, I'm not married. I wear this just to keep the scoundrels at bay." A pause. "Almost got married once. To a political aide. Finally decided I didn't want to live my mother's life, though. So now I just have a cat."

After a pause, during which Leslie appeared to be contemplating her near-marriage, Leah asked, "What about you, Gail? Tell us about yourself."

"Not too much to tell. My father was an autoworker in Pontiac. My mother was a sales clerk at Hudson's; or what used to be Hudson's. Now it's Marshall Field's or Macy's or whatever. Graduated from the public high school where I lived and went to Eastern Michigan University to get a degree in nursing. Unfortunately, I got pregnant during my last year. As big of a mistake as that was, however, my bigger mistake was marrying the father. I should've known better than to marry a man named Cecil," she chortled.

"Cecil? What kind of name is that?" Leslie asked without judgment.

"Family name. Some long lost relative of his on his mother's side. At any rate, we struggled through for several years before he found somebody younger who thought the name Cecil had a lot of class. He left me with two kids and rode off into the sunset. I hired a private investigator to track him down so that I could get some child support out of him, but he never found him."

"What'd he do for a living?" asked Leah.

"A mason. A mason named Cecil. Go figure." Pause. "Never owned a credit card. Paid for everything in cash. Investigator said that's why he didn't leave any trail. Didn't even have a credit history."

"At least you had some marketable skills," Leah observed.

"Yeah, I starting working as soon as I had my degree, so I could support myself and my two kids. It wasn't easy, but we got by. They're both grown up now. My daughter has a family of her own."

"It seems like nursing would be a very rewarding job," Leah observed.

"I enjoyed some of it," Gail agreed. "I made some good friends among the other nurses. Some of it wasn't so nice, though. The doctors can be pretty condescending. And a lot of the patients are totally unappreciative of what you do for them. They treat you like a servant. You get to see who a person really is when they're sick. Unfortunately, there are a lot of angry people out there."

"Did you always work in the CCU?" asked Leslie.

"No. I worked in maternity for a long time. I loved the babies," she said, smiling in response to some pleasant memory. "The mothers kept getting younger and younger, though. Some of them weren't old enough to drive a car. They had no idea what they were getting into. Only concern they had was how quickly they would lose their pregnancy weight."

"We're a self-absorbed society," Leslie noted.

"That we are," Leah concurred.

After they each told their story, the conversation turned to Gail's role in helping Leah get her message out. Both Leslie and Leah agreed that Gail would lend tremendous credibility to Leah's story and should, therefore, join Leah in most of her public appearances. Gail also offered to help answer e-mails and letters from supporters and agreed, at Leslie's request, to coordinate Leah's schedule with everyone involved.

Finally, nodding at the clock over the kitchen sink, Leah said, "It's getting late. I'd better get the boys to bed. They're watching movies with Sunny."

"Yeah, it's been a long day," Leslie noted. "And tomorrow will be another one."

"And I've got to get ready for work," Gail observed as she stood.

"Any second thoughts?" Leah asked Gail before getting up.

"No. Why do you ask?"

"Wouldn't be normal if you didn't. I know I've had 'em. And third thoughts. And fourth thoughts. And fifth thoughts."

"You're going to do great," Leslie said encouragingly.

"Thanks. I just don't know what I'm doing. I wish God had given me a little instruction manual or something. I might have even read it for once."

"I guess he figures you'll know what to do," Gail responded.

"Well, he did say he'd help me. And he has sent me you two." The three women exchanged tired, but warm smiles.

———

A few days after the planning meeting, a video crew showed up with Leslie to film a series of ads that would be aired on television stations across the country. Leah had read and approved the script with only minor modifications. The A.A.F., it seemed, was true to its claim not to have any agenda other than helping Leah get her message out.

The videographer asked if Leah would consider having her hair restyled for a more contemporary look, but she adamantly declined. She did agree to be made up by the professional makeup artist that was part of the crew, however, and to allow Leslie to choose her wardrobe.

In the meantime, Leslie had contacted Brad Frank, and after discussing the matter with Harry Snyder, who in turn reviewed it with Marvin Granger, Brad agreed to write the story of Leah Warner and her mission from God.

One day, as a result, Brad called to ask if he could come over in the evening in order to start gathering background information. When he arrived, Sunny and the boys were again watching a movie in the den. Leah and Brad went to work at the kitchen table.

"So, you must have been a little surprised to get Leslie's call?"

"I was. She said it was your idea. Is that true?"

"Sunny's, actually. But I thought it was a good choice," she replied, smiling. "Would you like some coffee?"

"No thanks. I don't sleep well as it is."

"You're under a lot of stress, I'm sure," Leah noted.

"Yeah, the deadlines can be brutal. I love to write, though, and I'd like to think I'm a decent writer, so I generally don't get that worked up over them."

"It must be exciting."

"Hmph," Brad snorted softly. "It used to be. There's no one more confident of his ability to change the world than a cub reporter. Eventually, however, you discover that most of the people you're going to be reporting on think of you as their little pawn. Reporting, it's sad to say, is more about manipulation than reporting."

"How so?" Leah asked, cocking her head slightly.

"Have you watched any news conferences lately? Whoever's holding the news conference has no interest in answering the kinds of questions that would make for good reporting. They have a message to get out and the press is the messenger. They want the story told as they want to tell it, however, so they come in with a few points that they want the media to pick up on and whatever questions are asked, those are the answers they give. They generally have no relevance whatsoever to the questions actually raised. Politicians are the worst, but there are no innocent players in the news game. Everybody has a perspective and an agenda. Publishers have an agenda; editors have an agenda; even reporters have an agenda. It's not uncommon for a story to be largely written, in the reporter's head anyway, before there's been any real investigating. In that case, we become the manipulators. We manipulate the facts and the people involved to get the story we want."

"So, do you think that I'm going to try and manipulate you?" Leah asked. "Trust me, I'm not that clever."

Brad looked at her, hesitating before he answered. "I know what I'm getting into. A.A.F. is paying me a lot of money to write a compelling story. It is what it is. I don't have a problem with that."

"Does it matter if you believe me or not?"

Brad thought for a moment. "Not really. I know what A.A.F. is looking for and I plan to give it to them. Having said that, however, I'd like to come away from this project believing. As I told you, I think the world needs a message of love. I think we need some hope."

"But you're not there yet?"

"Candidly, no. I've got the desire, but not the conviction, at this point." A pause. "You know, there's a lot of talk about how the traditional media outlets, like newspapers, no longer have the clout they once did. Conservatives blame it on liberal media bias and technology advocates say it's the Internet. I think it's just that people have lost hope. They don't care what's going on in the world. They're just trying to get through the day and deal with their own problems. I know that sounds terribly cynical, but I really think that's what it all comes down to."

"It's hard to argue with," Leah agreed.

"At any rate, let's get on to a lighter topic," Brad suggested. "Why don't you tell me about Leah Warner. Start in the beginning – birthplace, parents, siblings, etc."

As he spoke, Brad again produced his small tape recorder and set it in the middle of the table.

For the next hour, Leah told the story of her life, often pausing to recall forgotten memories. She began with her childhood in Scottsburg, Indiana, a small town on the border with Kentucky, in a region known colloquially as Kentuckiana. Her mother was a high school English teacher and her father was a toolmaker at the massive General Electric appliance plant across the river in Louisville.

The family moved to Michigan when Leah and Sunny were six and one, respectively, so that their father could take a new job at Ford's massive Rouge River complex, which once employed more than 100,000 workers, 5,000 of them just to keep the place clean. The family lived in Romulus, where both of the girls attended public school and their mother was a teacher.

Leah skipped over her adolescent indiscretions, of course. It wasn't just a question of avoiding the embarrassment. In some ways, she had thought to herself after the meeting with William Vaughn, she was almost happy that Helen Luft would be bringing it all out in the open. It would give her a chance to prove that it wasn't who she really was, even if she didn't know it at the time.

When she got to her marriage, she had to stop once to retrieve a tissue from the counter across the room.

"If you don't mind my asking, how did you get by financially when your husband died? Did you go back to work?" Brad inquired.

"No. Greg was a saver and had the foresight to buy extra life insurance. I really wanted to be home with the boys, particularly since they had just lost their father. I knew I'd have to go back to work eventually, but I came up with a budget that would allow me to stay home until they went off to college."

"What about your sister? Does she have a family?"

"No. That's a sad story," Leah answered, going on to explain the gambling addiction and ensuing embezzlement.

"I never did think those casinos were going to be so great for Detroit. I never could understand the logic of putting a potentially addictive recreation in easy access of the poorest people in the region."

"I guess it produces a lot of revenue for the city," Leah noted, happy to have a break from the story of her marriage.

"That's the argument," Brad acknowledged, "City's still broke, though." After a pause, he continued. "What about your parents? Are they still living?"

"Retired and moved to Florida," Leah replied. "Had a few good years, but then they got hit by a car while they were out for an evening walk. The driver was a 90-year-old man who shouldn't have been driving in the first place. They took his license away, but that didn't bring my parents back. Now, it's just me and Sunny and the boys."

"I'm sorry." A pause. "How'd she get the nickname Sunny? I assume it's a nickname."

Leah laughed. "Yeah, her real name is Lisa, which she hates. My father gave her the nickname."

At that moment, Sunny entered the kitchen with the boys.

"Movie over?" asked Leah.

"Yeah," Tyler replied.

"It was cool," Ryan offered enthusiastically.

"What'd you watch?" Brad asked.

"Some Kung Fu thing," Sunny replied. "I don't even know the name of it."

"Well, it's time for you two to go to bed," Leah said, looking at the clock over the sink.

"Yeah, I think we've done enough for one night, too. I'll let you go," Brad offered.

"I'll put 'em down," Sunny interjected. "Then I think I'll watch another movie – something with an actual plot. You guys are free to join me if you want. These people have an incredible DVD collection," she added.

"I'll put the boys down," Leah said. "And then I think I'll go to bed, too." Looking to Brad, she added, "You're welcome to stay and watch a movie with Sunny if you want. I hate to be a party pooper, but they're keeping me pretty busy these days."

"No, that's fine," Brad replied. "Actually, I think I will stay, if you don't mind. I'm kind of a night owl, and since I live alone and work most of the time, it'd be kind of a treat to watch a movie with another human being."

"What's that line from *Splash*?" Sunny posed, "'I'm really a nice guy. If I had friends, you could ask them.'"

"Sunny," Leah said reproachfully. "That's not very nice."

"No," Brad said, laughing. "It's true. No offense taken."

"Good," Sunny replied. "I really was just kidding."

―――

A television talk show entitled, *Behind the Headlines*, airs nightly on WPYD, the Detroit PBS affiliate. It's a roundtable discussion of major local news stories. The host is Elise Thomas and her guests for the last segment on this particular evening were: Pastor Larry Rataj, Senior Pastor of the Carbondale Community Church, in Carbondale, Michigan; Rabbi Micah Krickstein of Temple Beth El in Hanover; and Professor Gazi Kemal, a Professor of Religion and Islamic scholar at the University of Detroit.

"Pastor Rataj," Elise began the segment, "you said before the break that you doubt the veracity of Leah Warner's story. Can you explain?"

"Well, Elise, let me say that I don't doubt that Mrs. Warner believes her story about being a messenger of God. She seems like a very nice person and I don't believe that she's out to fool anyone. Nonetheless, I do not take her story literally."

"Then how do you explain it? Do you think she's simply delusional or that she had a particularly vivid dream?"

"I leave that to her doctors. I can only look at it from a theological perspective; and from that perspective it doesn't align with what I know and believe. There is no biblical notion that, following the crucifixion and resurrection of Jesus Christ, God would communicate with us through a messenger. Christ, who was the human form of God, marked a new covenant between God and humankind. And under that covenant, it is biblically clear that the pathway to God is through Christ and no one else."

"Interesting," Elise said, with great seriousness, as if the answer had been unusually profound.

Looking directly at the camera, Elise continued, "For the benefit of our audience, I should note that the Catholic Church, through the office of Most Reverend John Huntington, a local bishop, offers no official comment on the story, suggesting that while the occurrence of miracles is an integral part of official church history, it has no way of verifying the veracity of Mrs. Warner's claim and that it is unaware of any evidence that Mrs. Warner has otherwise lived the kind of 'saintly' life normally associated with officially recognized heavenly intervention."

Turning to her second guest, Elise asked, "Rabbi Krickstein, what are your thoughts?"

Leaning forward on his forearms, the rabbi said, "Traditional Judaism has long held that a person is born in every generation with the potential to become the Messiah, or Moshiach, if the time is right for the messianic age within that person's lifetime."

"And that person will be the Jewish equivalent of Jesus Christ?" Elise asks.

"No. Jews do not believe that the Moshiach will be divine, or in any way super-natural. He will be a great political and religious leader, but he will be very much a human being." Continuing, he added, "Clearly, Mrs. Warner is not the Moshiach, for a variety of reasons, one of which is that the Moshiach must be a man and a direct descendant of King David and his son, King Soloman. What may or may not be relevant in this case, however, is that there has been no shortage of individuals who, throughout history, have claimed to be the Moshiach."

"Can you give us an example?"

"There have been many," the rabbi explained, "but perhaps the best known is Sabbatai Zevi. He lived in the 17th Century and was the founder of the Donmeh sect, which combined elements of Christianity and Islam, as well as Judaism. It became very popular in the Ottoman Empire."

"And how did *he* prove his claim to be the messiah?"

"A passage from a Jewish mystical text known as the Zohar was thought to suggest that the year 1648 would be the year of Israel's redemption. He revealed himself in that year, at the age of 22. He was never successful, however, in convincing many others of his claim and he ultimately did not fulfill many of the requirements of the true Jewish Moshiach."

"Fascinating," Elise offered with great enthusiasm. Turning to her last guest, she asked, "Professor Kemal, how do Muslims view Leah Warner's claims?"

"Yes. Muhammad, of course, was the last in a long line of messengers and prophets. Muhammad, therefore, was not the founder of Islam in the same sense that Jesus Christ was the founder of Christianity. Muhammad, however, is believed by most Muslims to have been the final messenger and prophet. Like the Jewish Moshiach, Muhammad is not believed to have been divine. He was a man. He was, however, the man to whom God's word was revealed."

"The Qur'an?" Elise interrupted.

"Yes."

"And at the risk of getting off the subject, I've always wondered, is there an ethnic requirement to being considered a Muslim?"

"No, there is no ethnic or racial preclusion," Professor Kemal answered.

"Very interesting," Elise concluded. "Mrs. Warner, of course, has not taken a position as to which of the world's religions is the 'right' one, if you will. She says that during her time with God she learned no more, theologically speaking, than that there is one God and that he loves us, a belief shared by all of the religions represented here tonight." Looking at the camera, she concluded, "That does it for us tonight. I thank each of my distinguished guests for their participation. And, of course, thank you for watching."

———

Leslie called a few days later to report that Donny Hammond, pastor of the Faith Church in Charlotte, North Carolina, had agreed to lend his support to Leah's cause. A large, independent, evangelical church, Faith Church had nearly 10,000 members and Pastor Hammond, the author of three best-selling inspirational Christian books, was a nationally recognized religious leader.

"That's great," Leah responded. "Does he believe me?"

"Who knows," Leslie replied. "Could be just looking to get in on the ground floor and enhance his own reputation, but he's certainly not going to tell us that. We'll just have to take him at his word."

"But you think this will help," Leah noted.

"This will really make a big difference among churchgoers. I think people will be more willing to disagree with their own clergy if they know that a credible religious leader of Hammond's reputation has taken your side."

"So, how's it going to work?"

"He wants you to come to Charlotte this weekend and appear on stage with him. He wants to discuss you in his lesson and then bring you out and let you tell your story."

"I'm not much of a public speaker," Leah noted.

"That's good. That will give you credibility. Most people aren't good public speakers, so people will relate to you."

"How big will the audience be?"

"Well, he's got nearly 10,000 members who attend over five services – two Saturday evening and three Sunday morning. And one of the Sunday morning services is carried nationally by CBS affiliates."

"Oh my." A pause. "Will you be making the arrangements, Leslie?"

"Yes. And I'll be going with you. Would you like Sunny to go, or will she stay home with the boys? And what about Gail? I think it would be great to take her along, too."

"Let's assume Sunny no, Gail yes. She's here now, so I'll talk to her."

"Good. By the way, the first tv spots roll out in Charlotte starting Friday, so people will know your face by the time you get up on stage. The timing has worked out perfectly, for once."

"We were just watching the finished videos. I think they turned out well."

"They did," Leslie concurred. "I watched them earlier. Listen, I'll make these arrangements as soon as we hang up and get back to you with details."

"Okay, that's great," Leah replied.

"Here we go, Leah. Get ready for the ride of your life!"

CHAPTER 11

After a contemporary gospel song was performed by the 100-member Faith Church choir, Donny Hammond strolled onto the massive stage, clapping enthusiastically in appreciation of the performance as he went.

Other than the choir, a simple podium, and loads of fresh cut flowers, the stage was empty. There was no altar and few of the religious artifacts that you would normally find in a traditional house of worship. The massive auditorium, in fact, which sat 2,500 people between the main floor and balcony, looked more like a modern concert hall than a church.

Pastor Hammond took his place behind the podium and the audience immediately quieted down, anxious to hear his message. He was young and handsome, and had a dynamic presence that marveled his audiences and gave him the aura of a spiritual rock star. He was dressed, on this occasion, in a conservative suit and a crisp white shirt adorned with a red silk tie.

"The title of my lesson this morning," he began, "is, 'Let us Listen to God.' I've talked many times on this stage about the importance of carrying on a constant and fervent communication with God. He hears us. And we can hear him, if we listen."

Coming out from behind the podium, he said quickly and with conviction, "So why should we be surprised if God communicates with a woman from Michigan and gives her a message of love to share with the world?" There was a collective gasp in the auditorium as spouses and friends turned to exchange looks of surprise with each other.

"That's right, I'm talking about Mrs. Leah Warner, the Michigan woman who suffered terrible injuries at the hands of a drunk driver and who, after being miraculously cured, awoke from a coma to report that she had been with God and that he wished her to convey a message of love to the world.

"Why is that so hard to believe?" he asked, gesturing dramatically as he leaned forward toward the audience. "Why is that so hard to believe?

"Some of my fellow church leaders note that the Bible makes no mention of God sending a messenger in the 21st Century." A pause. "And that's true." Another pause. "But who ever said that the Bible would be God's last word?

"Some people have asked why God would bother to warn us about our behavior. But God made a pact with Noah after the flood that destroyed the earth. He said that he would never flood the earth and destroy all of mankind again. So why wouldn't he warn us if we were pursuing a way of life that would ultimately bring us sorrow and damnation?

"And this is a message of love. Does anyone in this auditorium not believe that God loves them? If so, you might be in the wrong place."

Scattered laughter.

"And isn't Christian love a selfless love, a love of serving others in a compassionate and selfless way?" He paused, holding his hands out to the side, palms up.

Turning to pace in the other direction, he said, "And what about 'the Christ problem,' as it were? Do you know what I'm talkin' about? I'm talking about the argument that some Christians have made that God communicating directly with a woman from Michigan is an insult to our Savior, Jesus Christ." A pause. "Why?" he asked emphatically.

"Jesus Christ is the way to God. The Bible makes that clear. But the trinity of God, Jesus Christ, and the Holy Spirit are the three faces of one God. How is it an insult to that God to believe that he communicated with one of us?

"We should be thrilled!" he exclaimed.

There were several shouts of "hallelujah" from the audience.

"Amen," he answered. "That our kind and benevolent and almighty God talked directly to one of us and asked that individual to tell the world that he loved us should be cause for great celebration, not a cause for hand-wringing and doubt.

"I have to admit," he went on, pacing more slowly for effect, "that I was cautioned by many not to deliver this message today. 'It will undermine the church,' I was told. 'It will undermine your leadership.'

"You know what I say to that?"

The auditorium was silent.

"I say," he whispered, "that this ain't about me."

A deafening cheer arose from the auditorium as the audience sprang to its feet, clapping intently.

After the audience had stopped clapping and sat down, he went on. "And, at the end of the day, this ain't about this church. This," he said, sweeping his hand from side to side, "is a house of worship. The sole purpose of this building is to allow us to come together in Christian community to praise our Holy Father and to know his grace.

"We are an evangelical church. That means that we believe that we have an obligation to spread God's word for the benefit of all mankind. How can we, therefore, not support God's message of love?

"Some have said that if God were to want to speak with us that he would communicate through a religious leader or a member of the clergy. But I've thought a lot about that and I think the fact that God did not communicate through a member of the clergy is one more example of just how benevolent and kind and loving our God is. Where is the hope for the average man and woman if God speaks only to the ordained clergy?"

"Amen," someone shouted from the balcony.

"We are all equal in God's eyes. It doesn't matter if you've got some slip of paper that says that you graduated from some seminary somewhere or if you work in a factory trying to put food on the table for your family. We should be ecstatic, our souls bursting with joy, that God has delivered his message of love to someone who has led the kind of life that most people lead.

"Leah Warner is not a movie star or a powerful politician. She's not a world-renowned theologian or a great scholar. In her own words, she is a simple woman with a simple message. And that, to my way of thinking, is the strongest proof possible that she was, in fact, held at the bosom of God and that he did miraculously heal her so that she could deliver a message of hope to the world."

More applause.

"And to let you hear that simple message from the lips of the woman delivering it, I have asked Leah to join us this morning."

Again, there were gasps throughout the auditorium.

"Leah, would you please come out here and join me."

As Leah walked across the stage, dressed in a simple dark pants suit, the audience once again rose to its feet and cheered and clapped enthusiastically. When she got to where Donny Hammond was waiting with outstretched arms, he hugged her with great enthusiasm. Finally, he stepped back and motioned for her to take the podium.

Leah told her story and shared God's message in simple words presented in a sincere, humble tone. At first, her voice cracked with obvious anxiety. By the end, however, she appeared calm and confident. While not a riveting, polished speaker, she came off as very genuine. Leslie was very pleased.

At one point in her talk, she recognized Gail, who was sitting off to the side in the front row of the audience with Leslie and Donny Hammond's pretty wife. When, at Leah's request, she stood, the audience once again rose and cheered in support.

When she finished, no one clapped more enthusiastically than Pastor Hammond, who once again hugged her, as nearly every eye in the auditorium, including Leah's, filled with tears of joy. She was, she thought proudly to herself, as she waved modestly to the crowd, rising to the challenge that God had given her. She was finally standing up.

———

Portions of the video of Leah's speech at Faith Church were shown on the nightly newscasts of all the major networks. The church, as a result, was inundated with literally thousands of requests for copies of the tape and the networks received tens of thousands of e-mails begging them to run the entire event.

The website set up by A.A.F. was shut down for more than four hours due to overwhelming traffic, forcing the technicians at A.A.F. headquarters to scramble to find more servers and install an automated response system to explain to mailers that the volume of messages Leah was receiving would preclude an individual response.

On Tuesday, ABC called Leslie and asked if celebrity interviewer, Amy Cabot, could interview Leah for an hour-long primetime special. Leslie, of course, agreed, and, after negotiating a few ground rules, scheduled the interview for the following evening, at Leah's new home.

Amy Cabot was very petite, but enjoyed a larger than life confidence. Only 32, she had gained a reputation for asking tough questions and getting the celebrities she interviewed to uncharacteristically answer them.

She had little to say to Leah ahead of the interview. She was having an intense discussion with her producer, which she repeatedly interrupted to answer her cell phone.

As the cameramen set up, Leah had makeup applied and her hair combed by the professionals with the filming crew. Leslie, once again, had chosen her wardrobe - a simple pink silk shirt with navy pants and mules.

Finally, Leah and Amy were positioned in large leather chairs that had been arranged in front of the fireplace. A gas-fueled fire was burning warmly at the suggestion of Leslie.

"Mrs. Warner, for the sake of our viewers, why don't you tell us your amazing story in your own words," began Amy Cabot.

Leah once again recounted her story, which, in fact, ninety-nine percent of the television audience already knew.

"And when you say you were with God, what do you mean, exactly?"

"Well, it's difficult to describe. It's not like I was sitting there having a conversation with someone. But I did hear a voice, and although I couldn't see him personally, I could see. Most of all, I just sensed that he was there. I felt a presence."

"A sensation on your skin?"

"No. No. It wasn't like that. It was like a sensation throughout my whole body; throughout my whole being. As I say, it's hard to describe."

"But you didn't actually see God. What did you see?"

"Light, mostly. It was a different kind of light than I've ever seen, however. It wasn't too bright. It wasn't too soft. It was like it was perfect."

"And God said that he loved you?"

"Yes. Over and over again."

"In a soothing voice that was neither a man nor a woman. Is that right?"

"Yes."

"And you've voiced your belief that God embodies both a man and a woman. And that's gotten you into some hot water with some conservative religious leaders, has it not?"

"Some have certainly taken exception with it. They believe that the Bible makes it clear that God is a man."

"That God made Eve from Adam's rib in order to provide companionship."

"That's right. One of the frustrations I've had, frankly, has been being constantly drawn into a debate over theology. I'm not a biblical scholar. I don't pretend to be. And I don't pretend to be a prophet or a saint, or anything else. I'm just a woman – a very human woman – who God chose, for his own reasons, to deliver a message of love. He loves us, each of us, and he wants us to love him and each other in the same way."

"Which he defined as selfless and humble."

"Yes. He specifically said that we are too pre-occupied with acquisition and achievement."

"Which precludes us from being selfless and humble?"

"Yes."

"But why can't we be both. Can't someone be successful and humble at the same time?"

"Conceptually, sure, if you consider humble to be the opposite of arrogant. I wonder if God doesn't use the word in a more basic sense, however."

"How so?"

"It seems that we've diluted the meaning of so many words through overuse. We've lowered the standards of qualification, if you will. *Webster's*, for example, defines humble as 'not proud or arrogant; modest.' I believe, however, based on research that I've done, that the word comes from the Latin word humus, which means earth. To be like the earth, or to be one with the earth, or on par with the earth is, to me, more demanding than simply being modest."

"Can you elaborate?"

"I'll try," Leah replied, leaning away as she laughed. "I think it's a matter of degree. There are a lot of successful people who are genuinely modest. How many, however, put themselves on par with the earth itself? How many devote themselves to all that is of the earth?" A pause. "I think people are generally nice. I really do. But how nice? Are they as nice as they could be? Are they nice to the standard that God is nice to us? I'm not so sure."

"But God isn't always nice to us," Amy noted, cocking her head slightly.

"Is it that God is not nice to us or is it that this life he has given us comes with a certain amount of pain? Would our lives really be better if we never experienced pain? Would life be so precious? Despite all of the pain and suffering that goes with life, how many of us welcome death? On balance, I think most people would agree, the life that God has given us is pretty wonderful."

"Does the same standard apply to charity, do you think? Does it matter that wealthy people give a lot if they could give more?"

"Some would say that I'm not qualified to answer that because I'm not wealthy. And, unfortunately, that discussion inevitably gets into a political debate, which I make every attempt to avoid. Let me just say this; I think we could all live simpler lives, myself included."

"But this home," Amy challenged, "where you now live, is anything but simple. This is pretty lavish," she added, as she made an exaggerated effort to look around the room.

"Yes, it is. And I know that that makes me seem hypocritical. It is not my home and I don't expect to live here for very long. When this all started, however, I was besieged by people who wanted to touch me, or pray with me, or ask me questions about God and heaven. It was impractical for me to think that I was going to return to my home and live the quiet life that I had been leading. People just weren't going to let that happen. So when a nonprofit religious organization offered to help me and to provide security, I took them up on it. I wish I didn't have to, but I really had no choice."

"So, they're paying for the house?"

"Yes. The security company they hired thought it would be too difficult to secure my own home. Plus there wasn't enough room for the security company personnel to stay or have a place to go."

"And what's the name of the organization?" Amy asked.

"It's called the Association for the Advancement of Faith."

"Based in Washington, correct?"

"Yes," replied Leah.

"The same organization that some have accused of being a right wing political organization masquerading as a non-profit religious organization," Amy said accusingly.

"I don't know what people you're referring to, but I have not seen nor heard anything that would support that claim. They told me from the beginning that they had no agenda other than to help me get my message out and, to date, they've been true to their word."

"But this is a very wealthy organization that is spending a lot of money on your cause. The advertising alone has to be costing tens of millions of dollars."

"I don't know the precise number, but it's obviously costing them a lot."

"And that doesn't make you feel compromised? That doesn't make you feel a bit like a pawn?"

"No," Leah replied firmly, meeting and holding Amy's accusatory stare. "They haven't been the only ones to offer financial assistance."

"Who else has," Amy interrupted.

"I'd rather not name names. I'm not out to fight with anyone or to push any political platform. I will only say that A.A.F. is the only organization that hasn't tried to influence my message, so whether they've got a lot of money or not, I believe their intentions are honorable."

"Are they paying you?"

"You mean, like a salary? No," Leah replied, somewhat offended by the implication. "They pay my expenses; they provide my security; they paid for my travel to Charlotte; and they pay for the advertising and the publicity services."

"And you'd like us to believe that they expect nothing in return," Amy concluded snidely.

Leah sat quietly for a few moments collecting her thoughts and her composure. "Look," she finally said, "did you ever see the movie *My Blue Heaven*?"

"Not that I remember,"

"It was a comedy in which Steve Martin played an ex-gangster who was ratting out his boss and was in the witness protection program. When he goes to court to testify, the defense lawyer starts bringing up the fact that the government's paying him money to live. So Martin's character says something to the effect that, 'If you're saying that I'm testifying just so the government will take care of me, you make a good point. But the truth is still the truth.' A.A.F. is spending a lot of money. They, however, had nothing to do with my medical recovery or with God's request for me to communicate his message to the world."

"Let me change gears," Amy retorted, obviously skeptical of Leah's veracity. "Why do you suppose God chose you?"

"I honestly don't know. I am not a special person in any way. Frankly, I am dismayed by the number of people who have come to think of me as holy or divine. I'm not. God had to choose someone. He chose me. I'm quite confident, however, that whomever he chose, there would be controversy."

"You have to admit, however, that you are a particularly improbable choice. By your own admission, you weren't a religious person before this all happened. And you haven't exactly lived a saintly life, from what we read in the papers. Arrested for shoplifting and drug possession; and a reputation for sleeping around. You have to admit that that doesn't sound like the kind of person God would choose for a messenger."

Leah took a deep breath. "I can't tell you," she said slowly, lowering her chin toward her chest, "how difficult it has been to have some of my poor decisions of the past paraded out by those who wish to discredit me for their own purposes. I can only say that I have made mistakes. Everyone has. In the end, I know, God will judge me. I leave that to Him. I do know, however, that he will judge me both for what I've done and what I haven't done. First and foremost, I believe he will judge me by how much I've learned to love. If I have, I believe he will forgive my mistakes. That, ultimately, is God's message of hope."

"And how do you respond to those people who say that they're just fine the way they are; that they don't need hope; that you're just trying to force your religious beliefs down their throats?"

"I am a middle-aged, Midwestern, stay-at-home mom. I am incapable of forcing anything on anyone. I am sharing a message. I believe it is a message that all of us would want to believe; a message that each of us would welcome. What greater news can there be than that there is a God and that he loves us in the most selfless way possible? Why does it matter who the messenger is? Why does it matter that I'm not a religious leader or that I've made mistakes in the past or that I'm not a man? Why?"

When the interview was over, Amy Cabot removed her microphone and walked out without so much as saying goodbye to Leah.

"Don't take it personally," one of the cameramen said as he began to dissemble his equipment. "She treats everybody like crap."

"Why is she so angry?"

"Who knows? I can tell you that you did great, however. I think she's probably upset because she couldn't break you," he laughed. "She prefers to make her guests cry."

———

Returning late one afternoon from a checkup with Dr. Marcus, Leah was walking up the front steps as Sunny emerged from the house. There was drizzle in the air, so Leah was under a red umbrella. She collapsed it once she was under the protection of the roof over the entranceway and shook it gently to get the excess rain off.

"Where you off to?" Leah asked.

"Dinner and a movie, but I thought I'd do a little shopping first," Sunny replied.

"By yourself?"

"No, I'm meeting Brad," Sunny responded in an attempt to be nonchalant.

"Really? You're dating your sister's biographer?" Leah asked, laughing.

"He's nice." Sunny retorted.

"He is that," Leah agreed. "Have fun. But no talking about me," she added, grinning broadly.

"Don't worry," Sunny replied in playful sarcasm, as she opened her own umbrella and headed to her car parked off to the side of the house. While the offer of fulltime security had recently been extended to Sunny, she had steadfastly refused. She would take her chances, she said repeatedly, not wanting to give up that degree of independence.

Leah entered the house and went looking for the boys, who were in the den watching television.

"Hi guys. How about a hug?"

Both boys were sitting on the floor with their backs against the couch. They pushed themselves to their feet and ambled over to give their mother a hug.

"Do you mind if I turn this off for a minute?" she asked, gesturing toward the tv. "We haven't had a chance to talk in a while and I'd like to catch up."

"Okay," Ryan agreed. Tyler, as usual, simply shrugged.

Picking the remote up from an end table, Leah turned off the television and sat down in one of the stuffed recliners, removing her shoes and bringing her feet up under her. The boys resumed their positions on the floor.

"So, there's been a lot going on," Leah began. "What do you guys think about all this?"

"You're famous," Ryan said excitedly.

"Well-known, perhaps," Leah responded. "I don't know about famous. I don't feel very famous. I just feel like your mom, which is all I've ever wanted to be."

"How come we have to have the guards take us to school? Why can't we just ride the bus like everybody else?" Tyler asked, looking up.

"I wish you could," Leah replied. "But it's for your own safety. You see, there are some people who are angry at your mother for saying what she's saying and I don't want to take the chance that one of those people is going to get so angry that they take their anger out on you because you're my sons."

"So why are you saying those things?" Tyler asked.

"God asked me to, sweetie. Don't you believe that?"

"I don't know," Tyler responded in obvious confusion.

"Well, God is a pretty tough concept for a 13-year-old. Heck, it's a tough concept for a 38-year-old. But I know now that there is a God. And I know that he loves you. And I know that he asked me to deliver his message to the world."

"Why couldn't he just tell everybody himself?" Tyler wondered.

Leah laughed. "That's a good question. And I've thought a lot about it. I don't know that I have an answer." A long pause. "Who's the meanest bully you know at school?" she ultimately asked.

"Easy. Harold Berkley," Tyler responded with a note of disgust.

"And does Harold get kids to do things that he wants them to do?"

"Yeah."

"But do they do it because they like Harold, or because they don't want Harold to bully them?"

"Everybody hates him."

"Well, you see, God doesn't need us to do anything for him. He's God. He can do anything. But he does want us to like him – to love him. And he knows that we can only love him if we choose to. If he makes us love him, then it isn't really love, is it?"

"Harold Berkley is God?" Ryan asked in bewilderment.

"No," Leah laughed. "Harold Berkley is just a kid who probably doesn't have much self-esteem and needs to bully other kids so that he can feel good about himself. God, on the other hand, is the creator of the universe. He doesn't need to bully us, but he does want us to love him – and each other."

"I still don't understand why he has to have you speak for him," Tyler noted.

"Well," Leah sighed. "I think God is very careful not to do anything that will seem like he's bullying people to love him. He wants them to choose to love him. So he does things in indirect ways, so that people can still make their own choice whether to believe or not."

"Did you see Dad when you were in heaven?" Ryan asked innocently.

"No," Leah replied in a tone of sad empathy for her son. "I wish I had. But I'm not even sure that I was in heaven. I'm sure he's there, though."

The three of them sat in silence for several minutes.

"You miss your dad, don't you? I do, too. More than I can put into words. We just have to remember that he's with God. He's waiting for us. We'll be together again. And when we are, we'll be together forever and ever."

"Are you going to get married again?" Tyler asked out of the blue.

"I'm not planning on it, sweetie. I'm not sure who'd have me. But I'll tell you what; I won't get married unless you approve. Fair enough? Now come here, both of you, and give me another hug."

Leah and her two children sat embraced in the big recliner for several more minutes. Finally, Tyler asked sheepishly, without looking up at his mother, "Is it true what they're saying about you?"

"That I did some bad things when I was young?"

"Yeah."

"Well, here's the thing," Leah replied. "I can lie to you and say that none of that ever happened. Or I can tell you that I made some very, very bad mistakes when I was younger – long before you were born and long before I met your father – and ask you to forgive me. What do you think I should do?"

"You always say not to lie," Ryan noted, looking up at his mother's face.

"That's right. And that's still what I say."

"Did you go to jail?" asked Tyler.

"No. I did have to go to court, though."

"Did Dad know about it?" Ryan asked.

"I had a criminal record. It was hard to hide," Leah explained.

"Was he mad?"

"Mad? Your father didn't get mad much. He was disappointed, I'm sure. But I think he also knew that I've always had trouble standing up for myself and sometimes that got me into trouble." A pause. "Look, guys, we all make mistakes. You will too. That's not an excuse. But it is the truth. That's why it's so important that God loves us. He loves us even when we mess up."

"Do you love us even when we mess up?" Ryan asked innocently.

Leah laughed. "You don't mess up very often. You're pretty good kids. But, yes, I love you even when you mess up. I will always love you."

At that moment, the phone rang. It was Leslie, asking to see Leah that evening.

———

Leah was sitting at the kitchen table with Gail when Leslie arrived.

"Leah," Leslie began, "I've learned that they're organizing a major rally here in Oakville for this weekend. They're expecting all of the networks to show up."

"Rally for what?" asked Leah.

"A rally against you, I'm afraid," Leslie replied. "They're not calling it a rally against Leah Warner, of course. They're billing it as a rally to promote religious freedom and tolerance."

"I'm all for that," Leah noted.

"Not as they see it," Leslie replied. "They want the right to be secularists and atheists and not made to feel guilty about it."

"I don't get it," Leah said with a sigh.

"You threaten people. You scare them. You jeopardize the status quo," Leslie explained.

"Isn't that a good thing?" Leah asked in confusion.

"For some people, yeah. And most of those people are embracing your story. You've offered them hope. For some people, however, change is not a good thing. They have something to lose. Or, more likely, they're just afraid."

Leah got up to get a bottle of water from the refrigerator.

"Anybody want anything?" she asked.

"No thanks," Leslie replied.

"I'll take a bottle of water," Gail said.

Leah returned to the table with two bottles of water and handed one across the table to Gail.

"You know," Leah offered, "I can understand why some people don't believe me. I don't understand, however, why anyone would want to protest against me. I understand the whole status quo thing. And I understand where the churches are coming from. But I can't understand why they can't just not believe and let it go at that."

"They're too scared," Gail suggested.

"Of me?"

"No. Of God," Gail answered in a soft monotone that enhanced the impact of her statement. Both Leslie and Leah immediately looked at Gail, as if she had uttered something unexpected and startling.

"Think about it," Gail continued. "You've led a life of sin and now you learn that there is a God. That's a big uh-oh for a lot of people. Very few people have been making much of an attempt to abide by the Ten Commandments of late."

"But he's a God who loves us," Leah pointed out.

"Nonetheless, a God who will hold us accountable. You said yourself that he was warning us."

"Gail makes a good point," Leslie agreed. "Consciously or not, people have got to realize that there is a downside to your message of hope. They are expected to behave in a certain way and they will ultimately have to answer for their lives. It would make it easier to sell the story if there was a way around that."

Leah took a long sip of water.

"God will forgive them," she said, after setting her bottle down.

"If they're willing to change," Gail noted. "Many people aren't. God made sin way too inviting for a lot of people to resist. At times, I've been one of them."

"Yeah, why do you suppose that is? It does seem that if God wanted us to lead a moral life that he could have made it a little easier," Leslie chortled.

"When things come too easily they're not as rewarding," Leah observed. "I think God wants us to have rich, rewarding lives. That requires a lot of work on our part. If there's no effort involved, rewards aren't very rewarding."

"So sin is an opportunity?" Leslie asked quizzically.

"In a way," Leah responded. "It gives us the choice not to sin, which in turn gives us the opportunity to be rewarded with God's grace and blessing."

"Makes sense to me," Gail responded.

The three women sat in silence for several more minutes.

Finally, the phone rang.

"I'll get it, Leslie offered."

After answering, she offered the phone to Leah. "It's William Vaughn," she mouthed, her hand over the mouthpiece.

"Yes, Mr. Vaughn."

"Good evening. I'm sorry to bother you, but the office just called with some information that I feel obligated to share with you."

"Yes?"

"We've received a death threat via e-mail. It came through about an hour ago."

"A threat against me?" Leah asked, incredulous.

"Yes. I don't believe there's anything to worry about. I've contacted the security company and they, in turn, have contacted the local police and the FBI. Everybody's on alert. Frankly, I'm not too surprised. I would normally dismiss this kind of thing as a prank, but the e-mail specifically mentions your address. The e-mailer obviously knows where you are. While we haven't kept that a big secret, we haven't gone out of our way to advertise it either."

Leah was silent.

Finally, Mr. Vaughn said, "Are you still there?"

"Yes, I'm still here," Leah replied.

"As I say, I don't think you should worry. You're in very capable hands. I did, however, feel obligated to tell you."

"Yes, I appreciate that." A pause. "I guess," she said quietly to herself as she hung up the phone.

———

The protest rally took place on Saturday as planned. It was held on a large parcel of private property on the outskirts of town that had been rented by the organizers. Michigan was enjoying an Indian summer. The day was warm and dry and the sky was blue and cloudless.

About 75,000 people showed up, bringing traffic to a standstill and angering many Oakville residents who couldn't easily get to or from their homes. The attendees purported to represent a large number of diverse groups, including those that had been at the hospital upon Leah's departure. The man in the devil costume was also there, doing his little dance and laughing demonically.

The speakers had very little in common with each other even though each cited the need for religious tolerance, including, many noted, the right not to believe. Leah Warner, one speaker argued, was a symbol of ignorance and oppression. Another argued that she was just a shill for religious conservatives who wanted to oppress women.

One speaker, dressed as a Roman Catholic priest, turned out not to be a priest at all. He was an anarchist who advocated the overthrow of the government through armed revolution. Organizers ultimately turned the microphone off before he finished his militant diatribe.

Helen Luft was not there, but A.S.P. was represented and anonymously helped to fund the rally. Helen did spend two days on the phone beforehand, however, reminding her media contacts of Leah's youthful mistakes in an effort to make sure that they were mentioned in any reporting on the rally.

The rally lasted for four hours. In addition to the speeches, there was a lot of chanting and waving of signs, but no violence. Several motorists driving by on the adjacent road did, however, honk their horns and wave their fists out the window. A few yelled vulgar epithets and one young man leaned out the window and shouted, "You'll all burn in Hell!"

CHAPTER 12

"How did the rally go?" Howard Dreyfus asked, once again seated at the head of the conference table for a meeting of A.S.P.'s senior staff.

"Okay," Helen replied. "A couple of wackos showed up, but for the most part it was a pretty credible group."

"I was there, actually," offered a young woman sitting opposite Helen. "It was quite well organized. And the news coverage was phenomenal."

"Any clashes?" Howard asked.

"No," the young woman replied. "A few motorists yelled as they drove by, and local residents, as usual, didn't appreciate the traffic, but it went pretty smoothly, all told."

"Good. So, where are we?"

"Hard to say," Helen answered. "Both sides are making an awful lot of noise. Right to choose advocacy groups and gay rights lobbies have really stepped up their attacks on Warner, but they're doing more to heighten emotions than to influence opinions."

"Both political parties are still on the sidelines, with a few exceptions," a young man at the table observed. "Too much uncertainty."

"I have to admit," Howard offered, "that I'm more than a little surprised that the churches haven't ultimately gotten on the Warner bandwagon."

"Their members are putting a lot of pressure on them," Helen noted. "So far, however, most have said that while it's alright if their members accept Leah's story at a personal level, it would be imprudent for the church to accept her story as a matter of doctrine."

171

"So, no one has yet answered my question. Where are we? Is Mrs. Warner making progress or not?"

Not looking at Howard, Leah replied, "It would be hard to argue that she isn't. We've still got a long way to go."

"I'm sure you have a plan to change that, Helen. What is it?"

Helen looked at Howard. "The more people who believe her, the greater the chance that the economy will head south. We can pin it on her."

"How so?"

"She's telling people not to spend money. That may or may not be what God wants, but it's going to put a lot of people out of work. We just need to convince people that they might be next and that Leah Warner is to blame," Helen explained.

"Could work," Howard noted while mulling Helen's idea.

"There are no shortage of economists who would be willing to paint a picture of doom and gloom. Most of them don't care if they're right; they just want to get on television," Helen suggested, causing snickers around the room.

"And," Helen continued, "we can come up with some carefully worded polling questions that will suggest, by implication, that most people believe that Warner is more interested in Warner than the economy. People like to be in the majority in their opinions. If they think others believe that Warner is going to put them out of work, they'll be inclined to blame her."

"It always comes back to the economy, doesn't it, and our personal sense of financial well being," Howard observed, speaking more to himself than his staff.

Helen just raised her eyebrows and compressed her lips.

"Anything else?" Howard asked.

"She received a death threat," Helen offered. "Via e-mail. I understand it was pretty specific and shook her up a bit."

"No doubt."

"If anyone wants Leah Warner to go away," the young woman offered, "the last they thing they should do is make her a martyr."

Helen looked at Howard, then at the woman. "I suspect they're just trying to scare her," she noted.

"Vaughn probably sent it in order to raise sympathy," Howard noted wryly, causing the room to erupt in laughter.

"Doubtful," Helen noted. "She's his golden egg. According to his IRS filings, he's never had so much money coming in."

"Mrs. Warner, I must say, has been good for us, too," Howard responded.

"We still need to get her off the front page," Helen pointed out. "Unfortunately, there's not much news competing with her at the moment."

"Maybe we should start a war someplace," Howard offered, eliciting more laughter.

"I'm not sure she isn't already starting one," Helen observed. "People are getting pretty heated on both sides. It won't take much to spark violence between them."

———

On the heels of the Oakville rally, other rallies were organized around the country. The A.S.P. had a hand in most of them and they grew enormously in size.

Leah's supporters, however, also began to organize marches, rallies, and vigils, and they, too, attracted more and more people over time. At one two day rally in Washington, at which Leah and Gail both appeared and spoke, nearly 800,000 people attended.

The country, in short, became increasingly divided and acrimonious and Leah was the fault line. When competing rallies were held, there were, as Helen Luft predicted, physical skirmishes between the groups on more and more occasions. In several, police dressed in riot gear had to intervene.

The debate, as might also have been predicted, ultimately became far broader than the debate over whether or not to believe Leah's story. Her supporters became increasingly aggressive in pushing for social and political change. Legislators were pressured to pass laws that were friendly to religion and provided funding for religious initiatives. Judges were pressured to ease the restrictions they had imposed in recent years on the separation of church and state. And entertainment providers were pressured to clean up the movies and music they sold.

Critics of Leah Warner and her message, naturally, strongly resisted such change, arguing that it would undo decades of social progress. There were constant allusions to back-alley abortions, the roll back of civil and women's rights, and the McCarthy-style climate that excessive censorship was sure to lead to.

While the opposition was formidable and enjoyed the overwhelming support of the mainstream media, however, most objective observers believed that Leah was gaining ground with her message. She was a credible advocate and found sympathy among mainstream Americans, particularly in the heartland.

As Leah's popularity grew, however, so did the threats against her. Pinnacle, at the request of the A.A.F., added more security guards to its detail and the Michigan State Police added round the clock patrols of Forest Glen. A special unit of the FBI tracked down and arrested many of the threatening e-mailers, in places as far away as Indonesia and the Sudan. It was a formidable task, however, just to keep up.

On the home front, Leah decided to pull Tyler and Ryan out of the public school and, with Sunny's help, who had taken a leave of absence from her teaching job when the new school year began, school them at home. And Gail, who devoted virtually all of her waking hours to helping Leah, had quit her job and finally conceded to Leah's request to move into the house in order to insure her safety.

Sunny, on the other hand, increasingly spent the night with Brad. The "love birds," as Leah referred to them, were two peas in a pod, and Leah was pleased to see her sister finally fall in love again.

Brad, for his part, continued to work diligently on the book, *The Life and Message of Leah Warner*. While the A.A.F. had planned to pay for the publishing of the book out of its own pocket if necessary, Leah's swelling popularity, or infamy, depending on which side of her story you came down on, motivated several New York publishers to compete for rights to the book. Leah offered to give all royalties to A.A.F. to offset their substantial spending on her behalf, but William Vaughn refused, again suggesting the fundraising was at record levels due to the intense interest in Leah's cause.

Corporate America, unfortunately, was not faring as well. Supporters took Leah's admonishment against excessive acquisition to heart and sharply reduced their personal spending. While savings rates soared, to the benefit of the financial services industry, the sale of automobiles and other consumer products plummeted.

The trend was guaranteed to push the economy into a severe recession and economists were agonizing on the nightly news about the potential for crippling deflation. Unemployment rose steadily and despite the amount of money flowing into the financial markets, stock prices dropped precipitously.

Helen's strategy, as it turned out, was an effective one. Armed with polling data provided by A.S.P., newscasters and journalists successfully associated economic despair and Leah Warner in the minds of more and more Americans.

———

"This woman is single-handedly crippling the U.S. economy with her rhetoric," Hank Glasgow, senior research analyst at one of New York's big investment banks, said angrily on the set of *Financial Fracas*, a nightly network free-for-all among guest financial experts and the host, Gloria Copp, an attractive young English woman with a Harvard MBA.

"What rhetoric?" asked Jane Haley, financial reporter, and another guest on the show. "She's delivering a message from God."

"Yeah. A message that says stop spending money or you'll go to hell," Hank retorted.

"That's a bit of an exaggeration, Frank," Gloria suggested.

"That's how people are taking it," Frank replied, holding his hands, palms up, in front of him, while shrugging his shoulders.

"There's no question that retail sales have hit the skids," Gloria noted. "The big box retailers are reporting monthly same store sales are down anywhere from fifteen to thirty-five percent. Unemployment broke 10% last month, and orders for machine tools are off by more than half. But, is Leah Warner the one to blame? Jim, what do you think?"

"Well," replied Jim Benson, a prominent hedge fund manager, as he leaned forward in his chair and rested his arms on the table in front of him, "I doubt she's getting a lot of pats on the back from her neighbors in Michigan. The domestic automotive companies will surely be forced into bankruptcy if current trends continue, although some analysts think they can't – cars and trucks wear out and have to be replaced at some point. Nonetheless, there were problems in the domestic automotive industry long before Leah Warner came along, so it's hard to lay all of its trouble at her feet."

"She may have accelerated the process, but there's little question that there had to be a fundamental re-structuring of that industry anyway," Jane interjected. "I agree with Jim."

"It could, however, have been a controlled re-structuring," offered Greta Freeburn, a bond fund manager for Haggerty Thompson, the huge mutual fund company. "Even if she's just accelerating the process, she is inflicting an awful lot of damage that might otherwise have been avoided."

"Look," Frank suggested, "there's no question that the economy's been on a long uptick and at some point it was going to have to cool off. The Fed has kept interest rates at unsustainably low levels and consumers have been getting in over their heads. There's also no question, however, that Mrs. Warner is forcing the economy into a tailspin that corporate America may not be able to pull out of, even with the benefit of increased savings rates."

"That's financial fear-mongering, Frank," Jane said in an acidic tone. "I really don't think this is all bad. I don't think anyone can argue that consumerism has been getting out of control in recent years. We've all got way too much stuff. With a strong savings rate we're going to have the capital wherewithal to re-direct that excessive consumer spending into economic and physical infrastructure. It might be painful in the short term, but we'll probably be better off as a society in the long term."

"Do you believe in blood-letting, too?" Frank asked sarcastically.

"Okay, so what has to happen?" Gloria asked the panel.

"Somebody's got to shut her up," Frank immediately replied.

"She's got a right to speak," Jane noted. "She's not forcing anyone to listen."

"Can the government do anything?" Gloria asked, putting her pencil down on the table in front of her and crossing her arms. "Greta?"

"Well, they can loosen the money supply further, which they're doing. And they're talking about a massive public works bill as a way to put some of that savings back into the economy quickly. Having said that, however, my sense is that politicians are running scared on the Warner issue. I don't see them doing much of anything to slow her down."

"Jim?"

"Well, I think that's right. You've got two big ole freight trains barreling down parallel tracks side by side," Jim continued, gesturing to reinforce his verbal analogy. "One is Leah Warner. The other is the forces aligned against Leah Warner. No politician is going to step out in front of either one of 'em until he or she knows which one is going to arrive at the station first."

"There is a deafening silence coming out of Washington," Jane added. "I don't see any political leader coming out against her, although if the economy continues to slide like this, they're all going to lose their jobs in next year's elections anyway; particularly the president."

"For once, I agree completely," Frank interjected. "So I think they'd better get off the sidelines and start asking people to keep this thing in perspective. It's not goin' to matter if there is a God or not if no one's got a job."

———

Leah, Gail, Sunny, Brad, and Dr. Marcus were having a late dinner in the dining room to celebrate Brad's completion of the book. The final manuscript had been mailed to the publisher earlier in the day and would be on bookshelves in less than 30 days. The boys had eaten earlier and were in their rooms studying.

"You must be glad to have that behind you," Leah noted as she lifted a fork full of meat loaf off her plate.

"Yeah, in a way," Brad responded. "I enjoyed it, though. You've got an interesting story."

"And have we made any progress in convincing you that it's true?" Leah asked.

Brad paused, put his fork on his plate, and clasped his hands in front of himself, his elbows resting on the arms of the ornate wooden chair he was seated in.

"Yeah. I can honestly say that I'm a believer."

"And what got you over the hump?" Leah probed.

"Lots of things, really. I never seriously believed that you were making it up. You just aren't the type. And if it was a dream, or a delusion, or whatever, it seems to me that at some level of consciousness you would have started to question yourself by now, particularly given the ferocity of your detractors. From what I can see, that hasn't happened."

"It hasn't," Leah responded.

"Well, it shows," Brad observed, causing the group to laugh warmly together.

"I also have to give a lot of the credit for my conversion, if you will, to Dr. Marcus," Brad continued, gesturing toward the doctor. He's taught me that the key to religious faith is the willingness to believe."

Dr. Marcus smiled. "Or the willingness to accept your belief," he noted. "As my friend, Professor Bradshaw is fond of saying, a lot more people believe in God than are willing to accept that they do. Denial is a fairly basic human emotion. We use it to protect ourselves from change, the unknown, and the inexplicable."

"Well, at any rate," Brad continued, "once I slowly started to lower my guard, it became obvious to me that God does exist. The world's too beautiful to have just happened."

"Spoken like a man in love," Gail teased.

"Well, there's no doubt that the lovely Sunny played a role," Brad replied, turning to Sunny and smiling warmly.

"Miss skeptical, you mean?" Leah asked jokingly, causing Sunny to make a funny face and stick her tongue out at Leah.

"Well, there is that, I have to admit," Brad agreed in jest. "But more than that, I'd have to say is how she makes me feel. This is a little embarrassing for a guy to say, but Gail is right. I don't think you can explain love without God."

"Ahhh, that's sweet," Gail offered.

Sunny looked at Brad and squinted her eyes tightly while smiling.

"That is," Leah agreed. "How about the other people at the paper? What's your sense of the general reaction?"

"Well, I'm not involved in any of the day to day reporting on you. They took me off that assignment, of course, when I agreed to write the book. It does come up at the daily editorial meeting, however. I don't think there's a day goes by that there isn't something about you in the paper." A pause. "I'd say people at the paper are pretty much like people everywhere. They're pretty divided. And people on both sides are pretty emotional about their beliefs."

"Didn't you say that you thought that Harry Snyder had turned into a believer," Sunny said to Brad.

"Yeah. Crotchety ole Harry."

"Who's that?" Dr. Marcus asked.

"Metropolitan editor," Brad replied. "He's the editor who's handling Leah's story. He'd never come out and say that he believes. I think he enjoys his reputation as a cynic too much," Brad chuckled. "I have, on several occasions, however, seen him force reporters covering your case to revise their stories in order to provide a slant that's more favorable to you."

"What about Granger?" Sunny asked.

"Oh, Granger only cares about selling newspapers, and we've never sold so many. Circulation is way up. Having said that, however, I have heard him moan and groan about the economy of late. Doesn't matter how many copies you sell if your advertisers all go out of business," Brad concluded.

"That is the one thing that really bothers me about all this," Leah noted, putting her fork down on her plate as she spoke. "I wish we could change our ways without so many people losing their jobs. I really do feel personally responsible."

"You're doing what God told you to do," Dr. Marcus reminded her. "You didn't make them begin their conspicuous consumption to begin with."

"Yeah, I know," Leah replied. "Still."

"I also think they could do a lot better job of sharing the pain," Brad added. "It's the factory workers who are taking all the hits. Some of these high-priced executives should start feeling the pain, too. I never did buy into this 'we're only paying our executives what the market demands we pay them' baloney."

"It does seem to have gotten out of control," Sunny agreed.

"Market value is what you can buy a comparable product or service for. That's not how they determine what to pay these guys. They pay them what other greedy executives have convinced their companies to pay them. I find it hard to believe that there isn't anyone qualified to run these big companies who wouldn't do it for less than the millions they're paying the current guys."

At that moment, two sharp sounds came from the front of the house.

"That's gunfire," Brad exclaimed.

"The boys," Leah shrieked in alarm, leaping instinctively from her chair and running toward the main stairway at the front of the house.

As Leah approached the grand entranceway in a frantic sprint, there was a terrific explosion that blew the front door and entranceway inward, hurling Leah backward several feet, where she landed on the hard marble floor and was immediately covered with shattered glass and debris.

"Leah," Sunny cried. She had followed her sister from the dining room and was also stopped by the blast, although she hadn't been close enough to be hurt by the flying rubble.

Gail, Brad, and Dr. Marcus had themselves followed Sunny and arrived as she was attempting to clear the wreckage on top of Leah.

"Let me see to her," Dr. Marcus shouted. "Sunny, you and Brad go check on the boys. Gail can help me here."

Sunny and Brad obeyed and ran up the stairs two at a time.

Gail and Dr. Marcus quickly uncovered Leah, but she was unconscious and bleeding heavily.

"I'll get some towels from the kitchen," Gail offered.

Jim Roberts ran up the front steps and stopped at what had been the front door. He turned, his gun drawn, and crouched, rapidly scanning the yard in front of him. "Is everyone okay?" he yelled over his shoulder.

"Leah's hurt," Dr. Marcus answered. "Don't know the extent yet."

"An ambulance is on the way."

"Good."

"Where are the boys?"

"Upstairs with Sunny and Brad."

Gail returned with an armful of dishtowels and a roll of paper towels.

"Back is clear," came a voice over Jim's radio.

"Ditto for the west," came another.

"And the east," came a third.

"Carl, go in the back door and up the back stairs and check on the boys," Jim said hurriedly into his microphone. "They should be with Sunny and Brad."

"Mark," he continued, "check the front gate."

"Jose, are you on? Jose?"

The state police car on patrol in the neighborhood was the first to respond. It sped down the street with lights flashing and siren blaring, skidding to a stop at the front gate. Mark, the security guard who had been sent to check the gate had found it intact and opened it to allow the police cruiser to enter. Soon, several other police cars and an ambulance could be heard off in the distance racing toward the scene.

Sunny and Brad found the boys in their rooms unharmed. The four of them were huddling in Tyler's room when the security guard entered.

Within fifteen minutes the house and its surroundings were eerily lit by the flashing colored lights from the dozen or more police and emergency vehicles, and the air was filled with the cackle of radios and people scurrying about shouting directives.

A fire truck had been called in, but was not immediately needed, so it parked off to the side. The firemen milled about outside in their boots and bibs, conjecturing among themselves about what had happened.

Unfortunately, no intruder was found and an all-points bulletin failed to immediately snare anyone suspicious in the area. Whoever had detonated the bomb had vanished into thin air.

Sadly, Jose was discovered by Jim lying dead about forty yards from the front porch. He was shot twice in the chest, just an inch above his protective vest.

Leah remained unconscious, but Dr. Marcus and Gail had stopped the worst bleeding by the time the paramedics arrived. After confirming that she was breathing and that her blood pressure remained strong, they loaded her onto the stretcher and into the ambulance. Sunny had left the boys upstairs with the security guard and Brad and returned to check on Leah, so she, Dr. Marcus, and two security guards jumped in with her and the ambulance sped away.

Brad walked up to Jim, who was standing near the front steps, surveying the damage with one of the state policeman.

"What do you think?" Brad asked.

"Definitely professionals," Jim answered instantly. "Nobody puts two shots just above your body armor with luck. And that was no household-variety Molotov cocktail. I guarantee they'll find residue of plastique explosive. It's not something you're going to mix in your garage."

"How'd they get in here?"

"It appears they jumped the wall," Jim answered without turning away from his assessment of the scene. "Jose obviously challenged them."

"Were there two of them?" Brad asked.

"Don't know yet," Jim replied. "It doesn't look like it, judging from the angle of entry, but we'll have to wait for the ballistics tests."

Jim leaned over toward the police officer and pointed to a spot off to the side of where the front door had been. The officer nodded, but didn't say anything.

Turning to Brad, Jim said, "One of the sheriff's deputies knows a builder who agreed to send a crew out right away to close this off. I don't think it will be necessary to move the boys to a hotel. I've called in all my men and we'll keep a guard just inside the house, in addition to keeping a full perimeter watch."

"I'll stay with Gail and the boys," Brad said.

"Good. I'll let my guys know. We don't need any more shooting tonight."

CHAPTER 13

"Leah Warner," began Professor Bradshaw, immediately walking out from behind the podium at Davis Lecture Hall and walking slowly, but deliberately, across the floor. "While she was in a coma following a head-on collision, Mrs. Warner claims God revealed himself to her and asked her to share a message of self-less love with the world." A pause. "The argument from revelation. Can anyone tell me how this argument, which wraps up our series and our semester, differs from all of the other arguments we have discussed so far?"

"It's phony," called out a young man off to the side, eliciting laughter from the filled auditorium.

"Think Socrates, my friend," admonished the professor. "We don't know nothin' about nothin'."

"It's not an argument based on reason," a young female offered.

"It's experiential," agreed Dr. Bradshaw. "It is the only argument that flows from the senses rather than the intellect. Mrs. Warner has not reasoned God's existence. She knows it because she has experienced it. For that reason, it is, to Mrs. Warner, at least, an argument without flaw or any element of doubt. Not everyone, however, accepts her experience at face value. Why?"

The young Asian woman with the heavy accent raised her hand.

"Yes"

"We are naturally skeptical of the personal experiences of others if they are not supported by reason or corroborated."

"Yes. The irony of the argument from revelation is that while it is often the most powerful argument for the one to whom God's existence and his wishes are revealed, it is generally the least convincing for everyone else. Whether or not it's accepted by others, in fact, turns not on the revelation itself, but what?"

"The credibility of the one to whom the revelation came," said a young woman in the front row.

"Exactly. And, in this case, that credibility is fairly high, but not a slam dunk."

Professor Bradshaw lowered his head and bit his lip before going on. After a pause of several moments, he looked up and asked, "Does anyone doubt that we are here in this hall or that I am standing before you?"

A student in the back started to make spooky sounds, causing scattered laughter.

"We know because our senses tell us it's true. Our eyes see that we are here and our brains accept what the eyes tell them. But how do we know – for a fact – that it's true?"

"What other explanation could there be?" a young woman asked in bewilderment.

"Perhaps the images we see have been planted in our minds. It's a fairly common scenario in science fiction literature."

"But that's fiction," someone suggested.

"Yes. But my point is this: We rely on precedent to affirm our perceptual experiences, by which I mean the representation of what we perceive. We perceive our senses to be telling us the truth because they have before. That belief, however, as I said earlier, is inductively reasoned. Just because our senses have been accurate before does not guarantee that they are now." A pause, while the professor turned and began to walk back across the floor. "Yet we commonly accept, as Mrs. Warner has, our own perceptual experiences to be valid. If we see something, or we touch it, or we hear it, feel it, or taste it, we accept its truth without a lot of question, even though an experiential argument, in the end, has no more likelihood of being valid, and perhaps less likelihood, than a reasoned argument." A pause. "Having said that, however, the mystical revelation, which is the kind Mrs. Warner had, is not the type of experience around which the argument from revelation is typically framed. Can anyone tell me what is?"

Several hands went up.

"Yes," the professor said, pointing to a young man in the back.

"The most common form of revelation is the revelation associated with holy texts."

"Yes. God, the argument goes, has revealed himself and his wishes through holy texts. Each religion, of course, has its own sacred texts. Christians have the Bible; Jews have the Tanakh, the Jewish Holy Scriptures; and Muslims have the Qur'an. In all three cases, people of faith believe that God has used those texts to reveal himself and his desires for humankind."

A young woman wearing a black beret raised her hand.

"Yes."

"Doesn't that require faith to begin with?" she asked.

"Therein, of course," the professor continued, "lays the catch. You have to have faith, or at least openness to faith, to discern the revelation. It's a classic Catch-22, the term that originated with Joseph Keller's 1961 book of the same name. As an aside, does anyone know what the original name of Keller's book was?"

No hands went up.

"*Catch-18.* The publisher asked him to change it because Leon Uris had just published *Mila-18* and the publisher didn't want the two books to be confused. A little trivia for you."

After pausing and raising his pointer finger to his lips, the professor continued. "In the case of holy texts, however, many have argued that the argument itself is not entirely experiential; that there is an element of deductive reasoning. Islamic scholars, for example, argue that the pure literary grace of the Qur'an is itself evidence of its divine origin. Christians, similarly, point to the timelessness of the Bible and its continued relevance to the modern world. What mortal author, it is argued, could have accomplished this?"

The Asian woman raised her hand.

"Yes"

"But all of these texts have been translated from their original languages. Isn't the evidentiary case weakened by that?"

"Excellent point. Each of these texts was originally written in a language, or a form thereof, that few people can read today. The Old Testament and the Tanakh were originally written in Biblical Hebrew, with a few passages in Aramaic. The New Testament was written in Koine Greek, although some scholars now believe that the Greek version was an early translation from Hebrew. Either way, none of it was written in English, giving rise to literally dozens, if not hundreds, of different English Bibles. And even though the Qur'an was originally written in a form of classical Arabic that has been maintained as a literary language to this day, it is not the same Arabic as that spoken by modern day Arabs. In fact, the Qur'an itself contributed to the dilution and adaptation of classic Arabic. With the rapid expansion of Islam after the death of Muhammad, Arab rulers found themselves having to communicate with millions of foreign subjects. To accommodate this need, spoken Arabic was greatly simplified, losing some of its nuance along with its complexity."

A young man of Middle Eastern descent raised his hand.

"Yes"

"Muslims, however, consider only the original text to be the real Qur'an," he noted.

"Yes, that's true. While there are translations available, they are not considered to convey the direct word of God. And in that sense, Muslims, to their credit, have formally recognized the pitfalls of translation."

———

Leah re-gained consciousness on the way to the hospital.

"Where are my boys?" she immediately asked.

"They're with Brad," Sunny answered. She was crouched over Leah, holding her hand. "They're fine," she added soothingly.

"Do you have any intense pain anywhere?" asked Dr. Marcus. "Do you feel like you might have any broken bones?"

Leah concentrated. "No," she replied. "I just feel sore all over."

"You took a pretty severe blast," the doctor noted. "You're going to feel sore for awhile, I'm afraid. Does your breathing feel constrained in any way?"

"No."

"Any headache?"

"It feels like I have a big bump on the back of my head."

"That's where your head hit the marble floor. It doesn't appear to have cracked the skull, but they'll do x-rays at the hospital."

"Five minutes," the driver announced through the intercom.

"What about the gun shots? Did someone get hurt?" Leah asked with great concern.

Sunny looked up at Dr. Marcus.

"Sunny?" Leah repeated.

Finally, Sunny looked back at Leah and said, "Jose was killed, Leah."

"Oh my God," she shrieked as she began to sob. In a short time her sobs were uncontrollable. "What have I done?" she cried in grief and anguish.

The two guards exchanged looks, while Sunny squeezed her sister's hand more tightly as she, too, began to cry.

"It wasn't your fault, Leah," Dr. Marcus said, in a futile attempt to comfort her.

Fortunately, Leah's wounds weren't serious and she had no broken bones. There was no damage to the skull, as Dr. Marcus had predicted, but the E.R. physician was concerned about concussion, so she admitted Leah to the hospital for the night for observation. The two guards and Sunny remained with her throughout the night.

The next morning, after one final exam, Leah was released. The word of what happened had missed the evening news, so people were just learning of the bombing and Leah's hospitalization. As they exited the hospital for the black Suburban, therefore, there was no more than the usual amount of hospital activity.

When they arrived at the house, a work crew was already busy re-building the entranceway. They had come out the previous night to prepare a makeshift plywood cover over the opening to get Brad, Gail, and the boys through the cool October night.

The Suburban pulled around back and Leah and Sunny entered through the back door. When they entered the kitchen, where Brad, Gail, and the boys were having a late breakfast, the boys jumped up and ran to greet their mother.

"Whoa," Leah said quickly, raising her hand. "Your mother is a little sore. Hug gently please."

Both boys gave her a careful hug and she proceeded to the kitchen table where she tenderly took a seat.

"You look like you got in a fight," Ryan observed.

"I did," Leah chortled.

"How do you feel this morning?" Brad asked.

"Very sore. And very lucky," Leah replied.

"It was quite a blast," Brad noted.

"And you took the brunt of it," Sunny added.

"The guard died," Tyler said without emotion.

Tears immediately welled up in Leah's eyes. "I know, honey. I can't tell you how sorry I am," she said, sniffling.

Brad looked at Sunny inquisitively, but she made no attempt to answer.

The group sat silently for several moments as Leah re-gained her composure. Finally, Brad suggested, "Why don't you guys and I go out back and we'll toss the football around. I'm sure your mother needs to rest."

As Brad and the boys rose and headed for the back door, Leah reached out and touched Brad's arm warmly in thanks.

"What do you think I should do?" Leah asked when they heard the back door close.

"About what?" Sunny asked.

"About all of this. I'm putting my family – and my friends - in extreme danger," Leah said with some exasperation.

"Well, as far as Brad and me, we're putting ourselves in danger," Sunny replied.

"That goes for me, too," Gail interjected.

"What about the boys?" Leah posed.

"They love their mother," Sunny answered.

"Should I move them?"

"To where? They're safer here than they're going to be anywhere else," Sunny stated.

"It's not for me to decide for you," Gail added, "but I think it would be very hard on the boys not to be with their mother with everything that's going on. At least you're a family."

Leah nodded and looked down at the table.

There was a knock on the door jamb of the entranceway which connected the dining room and the kitchen. It was Jim Roberts.

"Am I interrupting?" he asked before entering.

"No, that's fine," Sunny replied.

Jim entered and walked purposefully across the room, taking Brad's open seat at the table.

"How do you feel?" Jim asked Leah.

"Like I just killed somebody," Leah replied solemnly, not looking up.

Jim looked at Sunny and then Gail. Finally, he said, "I know it won't make you feel any better, but every one of us knows what the risks are. Jose was no different. He put himself in harm's way by choice. It was who he was."

"He has a wife."

"Who also knew what the risks were," Jim replied.

"Who no longer has a husband," Leah retorted.

Wishing to change the subject, Sunny asked, "Any word from the police on what happened?"

"No," Jim answered. "They got nothing with their dragnet, so they shut down their roadblocks early this morning. Whoever it was is probably long gone by now."

"And who was it?" Gail asked. "Do they have any clues?"

"Not a one," Jim said, shaking his head.

"What do you think?" Sunny asked.

"Well," Jim began, "I think it was one guy and that he was an experienced professional. I think he climbed over the fence, Jose confronted him, he shot, ran to the porch and detonated his bomb, and got out of here."

"Why?" Leah asked, finally looking up.

"Well, that's the part that concerns me," Jim answered. "Professionals don't do this kind of thing because they don't like somebody or they disagree with their politics. They do if for one reason only – the money. They're paid to do it."

"So somebody hired him," Sunny confirmed.

"Somebody very powerful," Jim replied. "Those guys aren't listed in the Yellow Pages and they don't come cheap." After a long pause, he said, "The good news, if there is any, is that I really don't think they were trying to kill you, or even hurt you. I think they just wanted to scare you. If a pro had wanted to harm you, it's doubtful that he would have failed."

"Just wanted to scare me *this* time," Leah observed in a soft voice.

———

"As of today, we have a presidential election exactly one year away," television political commentator, Eliot France, said into the camera. "The campaign, of course, has been well underway for some time now. One issue, nonetheless, has not been addressed by any of the leading contenders. That issue is Leah Warner and her claim to have a message of love from God. What impact, if any, will she have on the election? And which candidate, if any, will gain the most from her presence on the national stage? For answers, let's turn to our panel of political experts."

The camera panned to each of the three panelists as the host introduced them.

"Eric Hightower, political pollster."

"Candice Rubach," political reporter for the Washington Daily.

"And Jack Brandt, syndicated political columnist."

"Eric, what do you think? How does Leah Warner fit into this election?" Eliot began.

"Not very neatly, I must say. She continues to suck the air out of the room when it comes to national public interest. Frankly, I think the biggest challenge that she will present to any candidate is getting his or her message out through all the noise."

"Candice. Agree?"

"Absolutely," Candice responded immediately. "She represents a huge distraction to both parties. And if the electorate was split three years ago, it is downright split apart right now. And the two sides are fractious to say the least."

"What about the politicians. They're universally mum on the subject," Eliot pointed out.

"Oh, they've all decided," Jack responded, sitting in his chair with his arms crossed in front of him. "They're just not telling anyone *what* they've decided."

"Why not?" Eliot asked. "It seems, at this point, that every politician must know where the majority of his or her constituents stand. Why not pick sides?"

"Well," Eric jumped in, "as Candice pointed out, the people who have made up their minds are making a heck of a lot of noise. There is a sizeable group, however, which remains largely undecided. On any given day, these undecideds may waffle one way or the other based on the day's events, but they might well change their minds the following day. I don't think anyone can say for sure where that split is going to lie a year from now when election time rolls around."

"And, from the people I've talked with," Jack added, "I think there is some genuine concern about some big surprise between now and the election."

"Like what?"

"Well, if she is a messenger from God, perhaps she pulls off some kind of miracle. Or, if she's not, maybe somebody digs up some evidence that she's made the whole thing up. There is no shortage of people looking for it."

"Or maybe she just goes away," Candice offered. "Maybe she decides that she's accomplished what she wanted to do and backs off."

"Or gets pushed off," Jack added.

"Literally?" Eliot asked, as if shocked by the comment.

"Why not?" Jack replied. "They still haven't found Jimmy Hoffa. And someone did kill one of her guards and blow the front off her house, sending her to the hospital."

"Although most experts don't believe that was a murder plot," Eliot pointed out. "Whoever it was, they suggest, only wanted to scare her, although that obviously can't be said for the guard."

"It was a pretty extreme scare job," Jack suggested. "Look, all I know is that emotions are running pretty high. There's an awful lot at stake."

"There's no question about that," Eric chimed in. "The supporters of Leah Warner are no longer content just to believe. They've turned that belief into a pretty far-reaching political agenda."

"But isn't that true of the other side as well?" Eliot asked.

"Absolutely," agreed Candice. "Both sides are attempting to take what has historically been considered a private personal matter and put it on the political center stage."

"What is it that they want, Jack?" Eliot posed.

"Well," Jack began, uncrossing his arms and leaning forward on the table, "I think it really comes down to the role that religion is going to play in American politics and society. Warner's supporters want to see religion front and center, both symbolically and literally. Those on the other side of the issue want to essentially push religion out of public view."

"It almost seems like there's more than an agenda at stake, though," Eric added.

"How so?" Eliot responded.

"It almost seems that what both sides want, more than anything else, is to force the other side into submission. It's really gotten personal. Neither side appears willing to peacefully co-exist."

"So there's no turning back, in other words," Eliot suggested.

"I don't think so," Eric replied. "I dare say it's going to be a fight to the death."

"Candice, what do you think?"

"I think Eric's probably right. There are, however, some specific issues on the table. Warner's most extreme supporters, for example, want to turn the Ten Commandments into formal law, although it's unclear how that would work since even the faithful agree that we're all prone to sin."

"And," Jack interrupted, "the extremists on the other side want to, among other things, strip churches of their non-profit status. As much as the politicians might secretly love to get their hands on that money, I don't seriously think that will ever happen. I think the churchgoers of this country would storm Washington."

"And what about the constitutional amendments that each side is pushing?" Eliot inquired.

"Well," answered Eric, "I think it really gets back to what I said earlier. The faithful want an amendment that formalizes God's authority over the nation. The other side wants to reinforce the separation of church and state and formally recognize the right to atheism. Both are fairly symbolic gestures."

"I disagree," Jack offered brusquely. "I think we're talking nothing short of re-inventing the nation."

"And do you agree with Eric?" Eliot probed. "Is it a fight to the death?"

"No question," Jack replied with certainty. "Neither side is going to take any prisoners."

"So who's left standing?" Eliot put forward. "Candice?"

"I have to admit," Candice replied, shifting her weight, "that I support the basic idea of what Warner says. What's not to like, really? I think the idea that we should be nice to each other, whether you call it love or not, is right on the money. Now, do I believe that she got this message directly from God? I don't know. It strikes me as a little far-fetched."

"At the end of the day," Eric offered, "one side is promoting change, while one side is resisting that change. History, I believe, ultimately supports the resistors. The agents for change may make some progress in the short term, whatever that is, but things eventually have a way of returning to normal."

"Déjà vu all over again," Eliot replied, citing the famous Yogi Berra prognostication. "Jack, what about you?"

Jack sighed before speaking. "Frankly, I'm not sure either side is left standing in this one."

"Mutual assured destruction, to use an old Cold War term?" Eliot asked.

"I think so," Jack answered, clasping his hands behind his head.

"Look," Candice observed, "this is clearly not going to be a run of the mill election. I think we can expect record voter turnout, assuming the candidates are eventually forced to take sides, which I can't see them avoiding."

"So what does this all mean for the sitting president, who is obviously hoping to re-elected? How does all of this affect his bid for a second term?" Eliot queried.

"Given his political base," Jack noted, bringing his hands down to the table, "I honestly can't see him coming out in support of Warner, unless, of course, virtually all of those undecideds come down on her side between now and the election."

"Frankly," Eric said, "I think Warner is almost a secondary, although clearly related, issue for him. I think his chances all come down to the economy. Second term presidential elections are a referendum on the president. And what most people judge his performance by, when all is said and done, is their personal financial condition. If large numbers of people are out of work, or fear they soon will be, he's got no chance of getting the nod for another four years."

"And there's little question that will be the case," Jack added. "The economy's in a tailspin, and while a whole lot of people are trying to pin the blame on Warner, the president has to be tainted by it at some point."

"I think there's another risk," Candice quickly interjected. "And it's one that nobody's talking about."

"And that is?"

"That the violence and the unrest that now seems to accompany this debate wherever it goes continues to escalate. I would think the president's going to have to step in and uphold the peace. I don't know what he does, but it seems likely that neither side will be happy with it."

"I think that may be another reason that he and other politicians aren't publicly taking sides," Jack added. "They don't want to fan the flames any higher than they already are. I think they realize the dangers of this thing getting out of control."

"Any chance that Leah Warner throws her weight behind one candidate or the other?" Eliot asked, holding his arms out to the side before crossing them across his chest.

"I think it's very unlikely," Eric replied. "I just don't see what she's got to gain."

"I don't think so," Candice agreed. "Whether you believe her or not, she seems like a pretty straight shooter. She's said repeatedly that she will not be drawn into the political debate and I think we can take her at her word."

"I agree," Jack concurred. "Let me say this, however. If she does throw her weight into the political ring, every politician in America will be on record for or against her within twenty-four hours."

————

Leah's wounds healed quickly and she was back giving interviews within two weeks. Most of the questions she was asked had been asked many times before. She was, however, increasingly asked about the upcoming election and the attack on her home.

Regarding the attack, she repeatedly voiced her grief over the loss of Jose and her sympathy for his wife. She also shared her ongoing disbelief that anyone would want to harm her. As she said many times, she was only sharing a message of love from God. How could anyone feel threatened by that?

On the issue of the election, Leah always declined to comment, reaffirming her lack of interest in acquiring any kind of political power and her desire not to have her message overshadowed or discredited in any way by a perceived political bias. Most interviewers, nonetheless, refused to leave it at that and went on to badger her for some kind of comment.

One television network, on one of its evening political talk shows, went so far as to bring in a panel of jury consultants and psychologists to analyze video of various interviews Leah had done in an effort to decipher her political leanings from her body language. Needless to say, there was no consensus among the panelists.

The economy, for its part, continued to slide. There were daily announcements of major layoffs and corporate bankruptcies. The automotive industry, in particular, was in tatters. What few consumers were in the market for new vehicles were overwhelmingly drawn to the generally less expensive and more modest looking models produced by the foreign automakers.

As a result, emotions in Oakville were running particularly high. When Leah's black Suburban, now widely recognized, made its way through the streets of town, pedestrians and motorists inevitably shouted epithets and made obscene gestures toward the vehicle.

When in Oakville, therefore, Leah spent nearly all of her time confined to her secure compound. She desperately wanted to avoid any kind of confrontation that might result in harm to one of her security guards. Jose's death continued to weigh heavily upon her.

Leah did, however, maintain a heavy speaking schedule, traveling around the country to appear at rallies and other events. This was greatly enhanced by the growing number of churches and other houses of worship that slowly began to follow Donny Hammond's lead and embrace Leah's cause.

The Carbondale Community Church was one of them, and the process by which they shifted their position was fairly typical. Pastor Rataj, for his part, continued to remain skeptical of Leah's claim. He was under increasing pressure, however, from his congregation and, as a result, his board of elders.

In a private meeting between the pastor and his chief elder, Ron Laetner, the latter said, "Look, Larry, I understand you're concerns about the theological implications of the Warner issue. The reality is, however, that she has gained strong support within our congregation and our unwillingness to come out in support of Mrs. Warner is starting to be seen as more than a little self-serving."

"It's an issue of church doctrine," replied Pastor Rataj. "Every one of our members knows exactly what that doctrine is. That's why we go to such great lengths to educate our members before we accept their applications to join."

"That's true," Ron conceded. "They've all heard it. That's not to say, however, that they all live it. You have to accept that people are simply not that doctrinaire."

"Are you suggesting that we have members that weren't entirely truthful when they said that they accepted the church's doctrine and beliefs?"

"That's an over-simplification." A pause. "But yes. We have, I believe, a large number of members who do not live, or even accept, some part of our official doctrine. I don't think that they're intentionally rejecting any specific doctrine. I just don't think that they give it that much thought. I think they want to be active Christians and they found a church where they felt comfortable and they joined. I just don't think new members to any church sit down beforehand and carefully analyze competing church doctrine."

"I guess I have to agree with you there," Larry conceded.

"Look. How many copies of *The Purpose-Driven Life* did Rick Warren sell?" Ron asked.

"Zillions."

"Exactly. And how many of those readers do you think took everything that he said literally and incorporated it into their daily lives?"

"I'm afraid I don't see your point," Larry responded.

"My point is that millions of people thought it was a great book. And it was. If you look at what Rick wrote, however, and how those readers continue to live today, there's a pretty big dis-connect. That doesn't mean, however, that the book didn't have any impact. It did. But the change was incremental."

"So you think I should stop being so dogmatic. Is that it?"

"No," Ron replied. "I think that a lead pastor should be dogmatic. A church, however, needs to be a little pragmatic. If our members want to support Mrs. Warner, and it doesn't represent a gross violation of church doctrine, which I don't think it does, then I think we, as a church, should support her too."

"Well, if we want to be pragmatic, what about all the people around here who have lost their jobs and hold her partly responsible?" Larry asked.

"In that case I think we have to be dogmatic," Ron laughed.

"How so?" Larry asked quizzically.

"Don't you think Christ would be appalled at our modern materialism?" Ron asked rhetorically.

"No doubt," Larry agreed.

"At the end of the day, Mrs. Warner's message is perfectly aligned with Christian doctrine. There are dozens of biblical passages that deliver the exact same message. The message isn't the doctrinal issue; the messenger is. And that, to my way of thinking, is the far less important of the two."

"I guess I have to agree with you there," Pastor Rataj conceded.

———

"You can go in now, Dr. Marcus," Helen Luft's young assistant informed him after setting the phone back in its cradle.

Upon entering, Dr. Marcus closed the door behind him and walked deliberately toward the desk where Helen was sitting. She rose to greet him and shake his hand, but did not come out from behind the desk.

"Please, have a seat," she said motioning to one of two chairs placed facing Helen's contemporary, but modest, glass-topped desk.

"Thank you for seeing me, Ms. Luft," the doctor began after sitting. "I won't take much of your time."

"You said on the phone that you are working with Leah Warner. In what capacity?" she asked brusquely.

"Well, as you may know, I was the attending physician for Leah when she was in the hospital," he began.

"Yes, I know that," Helen interrupted. "But what is your role now?"

"Nothing official. I'd like to think of myself as a friend who supports the idea of a more caring society."

"If that's all this was about, I'd be at your side," Helen replied sharply. "But it's not, is it?"

"Some people have certainly tried to make it into something more than that; on both sides, I might add. At the end of the day, however, the message is really a very simple one. How you get there, to my way of thinking, is really a secondary issue."

"But it isn't, Dr. Marcus. How you get there is, indeed, *the* issue. Leah Warner's supporters have made it the issue. When someone argues for a constitutional amendment to formally recognize God, I'd say that's making God, not love, the issue."

"I understand," the doctor replied, nodding his head slightly. "Leah, however, cannot control how the message is interpreted, or what it leads to. And she has made no attempt to. She has not publicly supported any of the initiatives that have been wrapped in her message."

"So she has no agenda. Is that what you're asking me to believe?"

"Yes," Dr. Marcus confirmed. "She really doesn't."

"Everyone has an agenda, doctor. You're asking me to believe that Leah Warner is more pure of thought than the rest of us. I say she's human. And that means she has an agenda, whether she's willing to admit it or not."

"What she has, Ms. Luft, is a desire to take control of her life; to be a better person." The doctor leaned forward slightly before continuing. "You see, I never knew Leah before she came under my care. I believe, however, that she has long struggled to acquire self-respect. It's not easy to do, frankly. Genuine self-respect, that is. A lot of people pretend to have it, or even think they do. In the dead of night, however, most of us struggle to admire the people we are. At any rate, this experience has given Leah the opportunity to take control of her life and to believe in herself. I really think that's her real motivation."

"Are you telling me that she doesn't believe her own story?"

"No, no. I don't mean it that way. Oh, I'm sure there are times when doubt creeps into her mind. That's to be expected. On balance, however, I believe she has accepted her story as truth. My only point is that her motivation is a very personal one. She's not out to do any more than share her message. What people do with it will be up to them."

Helen exhaled deeply and leaned forward on her desk with her hands clasped. "Dr. Marcus," she asked politely, "why are you here? Does Leah know that you're here?"

"No," he replied, shaking his head vigorously. "I came on my own. As to why, I just wanted to try and explain." After pausing, the doctor looked directly at Helen and said, "I'm sure you know that there was an attack on Leah's home. She might have been killed. I don't know who did it and I'm not accusing you of being behind it. But things are escalating out of control and, well, I'm told that your organization has been behind some of it."

"Told by William Vaughn?" Helen said calmly.

"Yes," the doctor answered after a long hesitation.

Leaning back in her chair again, Helen asked, "How well do you know Mr. Vaughn, doctor?"

"We've been friends for many years. I'm a member of A.A.F."

"So, you've known him in his capacity of managing director."

"Yes."

Helen stood up from her desk and walked toward the window behind her. When she arrived, she turned around and leaned against it, crossing her arms and her ankles.

"My mother, doctor, was a very religious woman. She went to church three times a week at a minimum. To hear her talk, you'd think she was shooting for sainthood." A pause. "She and my father divorced when I was eight. He remarried and lived about 20 miles away. For the next ten years, however, my mother and father would, with some frequency, meet at a motel and have sex. It may have gone on longer than that for all I know. I was kicked out of the house. My mother found some marijuana in my room. That, of course, made me the consummate sinner in her eyes."

Helen returned to her chair. "Well, my mother, of course, being the pious hypocrite that she was, couldn't live under the same roof with a dirty, filthy sinner. I threatened her self-proclaimed purity. So she sent me off to Phoenix to live with her sister who, my mother didn't know, was a closet lesbian. She, however, lived a double life because she had to. She was, as a person, the most caring, loving, and selfless person I had or have ever been around."

"What are you suggesting?" Dr. Marcus asked quizzically.

"I'm merely suggesting that people aren't always the people they would have you believe they are."

"And that applies to William Vaughn?"

"That," Helen replied, leaning forward on her desk, "applies to all of us."

Sitting back again, Helen continued. "You see, Dr. Marcus, I am neither evil nor hateful. I have no ill will toward Mrs. Warner. And I certainly don't wish to see her harmed. In the end, this really isn't about Leah Warner. Frankly, I would be personally elated if her story were true. And, in fact, between you and me, I haven't ruled out that possibility in my own mind."

"Then why have you done what you've done?"

Helen clasped her hands, her elbows resting on the arms of her chair. "Leah Warner is trying to deliver a message of love. Is that correct?"

"Yes."

"Selfless love. Correct?"

The doctor nodded in agreement.

"And how many of the people who purport to believe her, do you think, are really willing to live the message? How many people are really willing to live humbly and selflessly and lovingly in the way that God really desires?" A pause. "You see, doctor, if this were all about putting her message into practice, and nothing more, then I'd be out there standing at her side. And for a few, like yourself, it may well be that simple. For many, however, whether they're willing to admit it or not, it's not about real selflessness. It's about using selflessness to promote themselves. And William Vaughn, I submit to you, is one of the latter rather than the former."

———

Leah's living room was once again filled to capacity with people. William Vaughn had brought his extensive entourage to Michigan to review the status of efforts on Leah's behalf and to make future plans.

"Leslie, you've done a magnificent job on the publicity front. Congratulations," Vaughn said.

"Thank you," Leslie replied.

"And where are we on the advertising campaign?" Vaughn continued.

A young man leaned forward in his chair and reported, "Pretty much wrapping up the current cycle. We estimate close to a billion ad impressions in total, about four for every man, woman, and child in the country." A pause. "We've still got a little time, but we will need to commit to the next cycle, if we decide to do one, fairly quickly. That puts us into the holidays and space is going fast."

"What do think, people?" Vaughn asked. "Do we need to continue?"

The room was momentarily silent. Finally, Leslie suggested, "It seems like we've gotten the message out there. I'm not sure more advertising buys are going to give us much incremental exposure. I'm thinking we should concentrate on enhancing credibility. We need to make sure that everyone who has heard the story really believes it."

"That's a good point," Vaughn agreed. "How do we do that?"

A middle-aged man in a suit raised his hand and said, "The interviews are certainly our most productive tool. Leah is very convincing in person."

"So, too, is Gail," Leslie interrupted. "Medical professionals, in general, enjoy very high public trust ratings, but Gail's sacrifice on Leah's behalf really moves people."

"I agree. You've been a great addition to the team, Gail," Vaughn said, looking at Gail, who was seated next to Leah.

"Thank you," she replied, smiling proudly.

"How about the rallies?" Vaughn asked.

"They work," the man in the suit responded, "for the same reasons the interviews do. People are more likely to believe the story when they hear Leah tell it herself. Security, however, is getting to be a bigger and bigger challenge. I'm really afraid we're going to have a major problem at some point."

"And the other side gets as much, if not more, media coverage than we do," added a young woman sitting to the side of Vaughn.

"True," Vaughn replied. "Our friends at A.S.P. are working their media contacts pretty hard. And they may well be behind some of the violence, although they'll never admit it, and we'll never prove it."

"Another thing," the man in the suit said, raising his pointer finger in the air. "We're becoming persona non grata in more and more places. Permits are going to be tougher to come by because of the security issue."

"I certainly hope we wouldn't knowingly put Leah in danger," Dr. Marcus said pleadingly.

"No, of course not," William Vaughn quickly replied.

"I don't want to see any more security people getting hurt, either," Leah added.

"Of course," Vaughn agreed. A pause. "We're also coming into the holiday season. Tensions are undoubtedly going to escalate even further, if that's possible."

Vaughn sat back in his chair and tented his hands in front of him, his elbows on the armrests of the large Victorian chair he sat in. Recognizing that he was deep in thought, no one spoke for several moments.

"Okay," he finally said, sitting upright and lowering his hands, "let's forgo the rallies for now. As far as the advertising plan, let's go to a maintenance level. John, you draw it up. What's the date of the book release?"

"Two weeks to the day," a young man furiously taking notes offered.

"Leslie, how are we doing there?" Vaughn asked.

"Great. We're not scheduling any book signings at this point, because of the security issues, but we are doing interviews on all of the major networks."

"And what is the publisher saying about distribution?"

"All the major booksellers have made huge commitments. Most of them will have big dump displays front and center as you walk in, and most of the metropolitan stores are planning special events with special hours and such. A few small independents have refused to carry it for philosophical reasons, but they're a drop in the bucket."

"Online?" A young woman asked.

"Definitely," Leslie responded. "Amazon's got it on their homepage and is already taking pre-orders."

Sunny and Brad were sitting quietly off to the side observing the proceedings. Looking at them, Vaughn asked, "How about Brad? Do we have anything scheduled for him?"

"I've agreed to do several radio talk shows by phone," Brad responded. "I do have another job, of course, so there's a limit to how much time I can devote to it."

"Of course," Vaughn replied. "Well, as I've told you before, we're thrilled with the finished product."

"Thanks. It makes it a lot easier when you believe what you're writing," he offered, smiling at Leah.

"Leah, can you think of anything else we need to discuss?" Vaughn asked.

"No, but I've been wondering if there's anything that can be done for Jose's wife."

"Security guards like those that work at Pinnacle have a hard time getting life insurance, for obvious reasons. Pinnacle, however, has an internal program that is quite generous when there's a death on the job. In addition, we have made arrangements through our contacts for his wife to get a very good job. None of that erases the loss, of course, but I think that she's well taken care of in a practical sense."

"Good, thank you," Leah replied.

"Anything else?"

The young man responsible for the advertising plan raised his hand and asked, "What about related issues? A lot of Leah's supporters are turning her message into a political agenda. Where do we stand on that officially?"

"Good question," Vaughn noted. "That's a sticky wicket. While I'm tempted to weigh in at some level, I think we need to stick to our knitting. Leah's got a mission and our objective is to help her. I think that if we stray from that narrow focus we stand to compromise that mission. Do you agree, Leah?"

"Absolutely," Leah replied emphatically. "God didn't tell me to tell people what to do with the message, or how to act upon it. He only asked me to deliver it. I think it would be presumptuous for me to go beyond that."

"Yes, I agree," Vaughn replied, slapping his knee lightly.

"What about the elections?" asked the young woman seated next to Vaughn.

"What about it?" Vaughn replied.

"Are we going to take sides?"

"No," interjected Leah. "I really want to stay out of it."

"Is that possible?" the young woman asked, looking to Vaughn.

"Leah is going to be an election issue. There' s no question about that," Vaughn replied. "Still, I agree with Leah. We can be dragged in, but we can't be made to participate. I think it would be suicidal for us to jump in."

"Thank you," Leah said, nodding her head.

"You are the boss, Leah," Vaughn said, smiling. "We are just here to help." A pause, as Vaughn canvassed the room. "Okay, people, that's it for today. Thanks for coming."

CHAPTER 14

After returning to the podium for a drink of water, the professor turned to the class and said, "Another problem some critics have with the argument from revelation, where sacred texts are concerned, is that there is considerable evidence that there were and are, in each case, alternative texts. Human religious leaders, in other words, at various points in history, have had to decide which texts, and which versions of those texts, would be official.

"But let's, as we wrap up, get back to Mrs. Warner. There is little question that there are millions of people in this country and around the world who believe her story in the most literal sense. She has, nonetheless, angered millions more; who charge that she is advocating religious intolerance. What is fascinating about Mrs. Warner's case is that she has been shunned, not just by atheists and skeptical agnostics, but by several conservative branches of all the major religions. Why? Anyone know?"

"She's a woman," a young woman shouted.

Everyone, including Professor Bradshaw, laughed.

"Well, there is a great deal of truth to that. Most sacred texts are pretty male-dominated. That's not the answer I was looking for, however. And I will note that the Roman Catholic Church, specifically, has canonized women who claimed to have had mystical experiences with God. Catherine of Siena claimed that she was in a mystical marriage with Christ and that Christ, an infant in her vision, presented her with a wedding ring."

A hand went up, to which the professor pointed.

"Her story was not prophesized?"

"That's true. Again, however, neither were the mystic experiences of many other people who enjoyed the support of the church." A pause. "The real issue, I suspect, is that she does not validate, or even show support for, any specific religion."

The Asian woman raised her hand.

"Yes?"

"Established religion has always shunned religious thought that challenges existing doctrine. Luther was but one example."

"A very good example," agreed the professor. "Luther was arguably the most devout Catholic of his day. His teachings, however, which he believed were true to Catholic tradition, challenged the status quo of the church, leading ultimately to his excommunication." A pause. "And didn't Socrates suffer a similar fate? Wasn't he put on trial for what he believed largely because those beliefs challenged the then current power structure?"

"So nothing's changed," ventured the young woman in the front row.

"Well, one thing that hasn't changed is that the search for truth remains tainted by personal incentive. The status quo remains fortified by the potential for personal loss that change inevitably carries. Which is why Socratic skepticism is essential to the search for knowledge and why the death of Socratic reason, in my opinion, has resulted in the deep political and social divisions that the fight over Mrs. Warner's story has brought to the fore."

"So, do you believe she is telling the truth?" a young man asked.

"She could be," the professor replied. "How do we know she's not?"

Professor Bradshaw stood silently for several seconds.

"I can't believe," another young man offered, "because it doesn't align with what else I believe."

"So you're not willing to give her the benefit of the doubt?"

"Yeah, I guess so."

"But isn't that really your problem, not hers?" the professor continued. "Why should her veracity suffer because of your beliefs?"

"I just don't think it makes any sense," another young woman said. "If God wanted to send a message, why wouldn't he just send it himself?"

"That suggests both that God is logical in the human sense and that you know how he thinks. What if, as many of the great philosophers we've studied believed, God is incomprehensible to our tiny little pea-brained minds?

"Look, let's ask the psychological question: What would motivate her to make this up?"

"She's trying to promote religion."

"She's not religious," the professor answered.

"She wants to make money."

"I'm not aware that she has. Are you?"

"Well, she's living in a big mansion."

"And it is entirely logical that she is living there for security reasons. She obviously needs security. She's already had someone blow up her house.

"No, I've got to believe that Mrs. Warner wishes, in the worst way, at one level anyway, that none of this ever happened. Who, assuming she's not insane, which there appears to be no evidence of, would want to bring what she's had to deal with onto himself or herself?"

"So, you believe her?"

"I believe in what Socrates once said: 'I am the wisest man alive, for I know one thing, and that is that I know nothing,'" the professor concluded with a Cheshire cat grin.

———

Leah, Gail, Sunny, Brad, and the boys spent Thanksgiving together at the house with Dr. Marcus. Leslie went to Tennessee to visit her parents.

The day was cloudy and cold and snow flurries were in the air. Leah and Gail spent the day in the kitchen preparing the meal, while Sunny, Brad, and the boys watched television. Dr. Marcus sat with them, but spent the day reading Dr. Bradshaw's latest book, *The Argument from Alternative – Why God Must Exist.*

"It's hard to believe it's Thanksgiving already," Leah observed as she rolled out the crust for a pumpkin pie at the center island.

"It is," Gail agreed as she peeled potatoes over the kitchen sink. "It's funny, though. Sometimes I feel like our time together has flown by. At other times, however, it's hard to remember a time when we weren't together."

"I know what you mean," Leah replied. "You've been a very good friend to me."

"Well, I can't tell you what working with you has done for me," Gail answered.

A pause.

"Do you ever miss nursing?" Leah asked.

"Yes and no," Gail responded. "It was always a great feeling when you did something to help someone get better or you helped to save a life. Life felt like it really had a purpose. In medicine, however, there are lots of other times, too. Sometimes the patient doesn't get better. And a lot of the work doesn't seem all that important - changing bedpans, making beds, and the like."

"Oh, I think that's important work," Leah interjected. "It's all part of the healing process."

"Yeah. Maybe important is the wrong choice of words. It gets old; let's put it that way. At any rate, now I have the feeling of purpose all the time. When I wake up every morning I feel like I'm going to make a difference in the world. It's very satisfying."

"I feel the same way," Leah noted. "I have to admit, however," she continued, sighing, "that there are times when I wonder if we really are making a difference. I have my moments of doubt."

"You know you are," Gail admonished. "I read some of the letters and the e-mails people send you and I'm amazed at how much you've touched so many lives. There's one word that comes up again and again when people describe themselves before they heard your message – hopeless. You've given them hope. Next to life itself, I can't imagine a greater gift."

"I think I know how they feel," Leah said contemplatively. "You know, before the accident I thought I was pretty happy with my life. I obviously missed Greg terribly, but I really thought I was doing all right, all things considered. I look back now, however, and realize that I've lived my life in constant fear. Now that I've been with God, I feel so safe. I feel like nothing can harm me. Do you know what I mean?"

"I think so." A pause. "I adored my dad. I worshipped the ground he walked on. And part of the reason, I'm sure, is that all of my fears evaporated in his presence. I knew that whatever happened while I was with him, he would take care of it."

Leah smiled. "Unfortunately, I never felt that way about my own father."

"No?" Gail asked, looking up from her peeling.

"I hated him actually. He didn't think much of me, either. Sunny was the sparkle in his eye."

"Were you resentful?"

Leah stopped what she was doing and looked up at the far wall. "No, actually. I was more self-loathing than resentful. You have to have a reasonably healthy ego to be resentful. I didn't."

"Was he the cause?"

Leah hesitated before answering. "He was its face. I'm not sure I know what the cause was."

Both women returned to their work and there was a long lull in the conversation. Finally, Gail looked up from her peeling and said to the window over the sink, "You know, you make me feel just like my father did. I feel very safe and content just being in the same room with you."

"Ahhh," Leah gushed, "I think that's the nicest thing anyone's ever said to me. Thank you."

Both women went back to their work in the deep satisfaction of knowing that each had found the kind of friend you only make one or two of in a lifetime.

After a long pause, Leah asked, "Have you talked to your children lately?"

"I don't hear from Ralph very much. He still thinks I've lost my mind, although, the truth be told, I think his real problem is that I embarrass him."

"That's too bad," Leah offered consolingly.

"Yeah. That's his problem, though, not mine."

"How about Connie?"

"Well, did I tell you that Connie finally found her father?"

"No!" Leah replied in surprise, stopping her work on the pie to look at Gail. "Where is he?"

"San Antonio"

"Really. Does he have a family?"

"Apparently not. I guess the woman he ran away with came to her senses and left him a few years after moving there," Gail explained. "Decided Cecil wasn't so classy after all, I guess."

"Huh. What prompted her to go looking for him?"

"Identity crisis, I think. Said she had to find out who she was."

"I take it you haven't talked with him."

"Are you kidding?" Gail laughed. "I want nothing to do with him."

"God, I suspect," Leah noted, "would suggest forgiveness. I know where you're coming from, however."

Late in the afternoon, after the Lions game was over and Detroit had lost yet again, Leah called everyone into the dining room for the Thanksgiving meal.

"Brad, will you do the honors of carving?" Leah asked, as they prepared to sit down for dinner.

"Be happy to," Brad replied, "although I warn you that I'm a better writer than butcher."

"I thought all men liked to carve things up," Sunny said playfully.

"Just like all women like to submit to their men?"

"You wish," Sunny replied with mock sarcasm, slapping Brad on his backside with the palm of her hand.

Leah sat at the other end of the table opposite Brad, with Dr. Marcus on her left and her boys on her right. Sunny sat to the left of Gail and right of Brad.

They joined hands and Leah asked Tyler to lead them in grace. When he was finished, Leah put her hands in her lap and said, "Before we get started, I just want to give thanks to all of you for your support these past six months or so. I often wonder if I would have been so supportive if the shoe had been on one of your feet. I don't know."

"You would have been," Sunny said confidently.

"There's no doubt in my mind," Gail agreed.

"Well," Leah replied, "I appreciate the sentiment."

Turning to the boys, Leah said, "And you guys have been real troopers. I know you guys didn't ask for any of this. And I know it's been hard on you at times. But you've both been very good to your mother. I'm very proud. And I know your father is, too."

"We love you, Mom," Tyler said, uncharacteristically, causing Leah's eyes to fill with tears.

"Oh, thank you, honey. I love you, too. More than you'll ever know."

"Me, too, Mom," Ryan jumped in enthusiastically.

"Thank you, sweetie. I love you, too," Leah replied, wiping away her tears with her cloth napkin.

"Well," Leah concluded after regaining her composure, "what do you say we eat. It all looks delicious."

The mood was jovial as the dishes made their way around the table.

"So, Dr. Marcus, how are things at Saint Mary's," Leah asked casually.

"No miracles this week," he said, smiling warmly at Leah, who held his gaze. "Frankly," he continued, putting his fork down on his plate, "I'm actually planning to retire at the end of the year. I told the chief of staff yesterday."

"Really," Brad replied, stringing out the word. "What made you decide to do that?"

"Well," the doctor answered, taking a deep breath. "A few reasons actually. I've been taking a lot of time off from my practice to help here and it's very difficult to be a part-time neurologist. I'm afraid that some day one of my patients isn't going to get the care that he or she deserves."

"I'm sorry, Dr. Marcus," Leah said with concern. "I didn't realize we were putting you in that position. As much as your support and your friendship has meant to me, I certainly don't want to be the cause of your having to leave your practice."

"No, no," he assured her, waving his hand back and forth. "I didn't mean to suggest that. To be honest, I'm ready to open a new chapter in my life."

"What will you do?" Leah asked gently.

"Well, with the help of a couple of friends, Steven Bradshaw, the professor I've told you about, and Dr. Heidrich, who you've met, I'd like to start a foundation."

"What kind of foundation?" Brad asked inquisitively.

"One that promotes and supports service to others."

"A religious organization?" Sunny asked.

"Yes and no," Dr. Marcus replied. "Religion won't be part of the official charter. Religion, as we've all learned in the last six months, can be a double-edged sword. Some people, it seems, have a hard time being truly selfless and religious at the same time – from both directions."

"You haven't lost your faith, have you?" Leah asked in a concerned tone.

"No. No. I remain committed to my faith. I've just decided that real faith means rising above faith alone. It's time to let my faith really drive my actions – to put my faith to work."

"So, what kinds of things will your foundation do?" asked Brad.

"Free medical clinics for the poor; drug and alcohol rehab; homeless and battered women shelters; that kind of thing. I like to think of it as the Warner message in action."

"Really," Leah said slowly. "That's wonderful."

"Do you have a name for your foundation?" Gail asked.

Dr. Marcus looked toward Leah. "Actually, with your permission," he answered slowly, "We'd like to call it The Warner Foundation."

Tears again filled Leah's eyes.

———

216

Leah came down with the flu two days after Thanksgiving. She was scheduled to do a remote interview at the studio of ABC's Detroit affiliate on Tuesday morning. On Monday afternoon, however, it was apparent that she wouldn't be up to it, so she called Leslie.

"Hi, Leslie, how was your holiday?"

"Oh, hi Leah. I was just about to call you to talk about tomorrow. Thanksgiving was good," Leslie offered cheerily. "My parents are slowing down, and my mother's memory is fading, but it was nice to see them. How about yours? You sound like you've picked up a cold."

"I know," Leah replied. "The flu actually. I came down with it on Saturday. I spent yesterday and today in bed, but I seem to be getting worse rather than better. I don't think there's any way that I can do that interview tomorrow. I feel like I got hit by a freight train." Holding the phone away from her head, Leah sneezed into the wad of facial tissues that she held in her hand.

"Bless you. Well, you've been pretty busy lately, so I'm sure your immune system isn't up to snuff, if you'll excuse the pun."

"Ha, Ha," Leah replied, in a playful tone.

"This isn't a huge one anyway. I hate to pass up the opportunity, though. What do you think about Sunny or Gail doing it?"

"Sunny's speaking to a women's church group in Grand Rapids tomorrow. Gail, I think, is free. I'll ask her. She's got her nurse's cap back on and is taking care of me. She's downstairs now preparing some soup. I'll ask her when she comes up."

"Great. I'm sure it won't be a problem having her substitute, but I'll call the producer just to let him know."

"Thanks. I really don't think they want me spreading germs all around their studio."

"You need your rest," Leslie said reassuringly. "What about the boys? You want me to come over to be with them since Gail and Sunny will be gone?"

"No. Thanks, but that's not necessary. I'll be here. I think they'll be fine on their own for a few hours."

"Okay, well let me know if you change your mind about the boys. By the way, the book sales are through the roof. The publisher's already scheduled another printing. Seems it's the season's must read."

"That's good as long as people believe what they read," Leah noted.

"I think it's gotta help," Leslie offered.

"Let's hope," Leah concluded.

"I'll let you go. Make sure you get some rest and I'll check in with you late in the day tomorrow."

"Don't worry; I plan to sleep most of the day."

The following day was windy, cold, and dreary, as it often is in Michigan at the end of November. The ground was hard and the grass, now dormant for the winter, looked like it was hunkered down against the wind. The landscape was a monotone of grey and it was hard to tell where the horizon ended and the sky began.

Leah got out of bed long enough to join Gail and the boys for breakfast. Sunny spent the night with Brad and left for Grand Rapids early in the morning.

Gail got into the black Suburban and left for the downtown studio with two security guards at ten o'clock. Leah got the boys set up with study assignments and went back to bed, telling them beforehand that they would have to make their own lunch if Gail wasn't back in time and their mother was asleep.

In fact, with the help of some sleeping medication prescribed by Dr. Marcus, Leah slept hard and long. It was already dusk when she woke with a start. Sunny was sitting next to her, nudging her gently.

"What's wrong?" Leah asked forebodingly. From the look on Sunny's face, however, and the fact that Jim was standing on the other side of the bed, Leah suddenly realized, she immediately knew the answer.

"What's happened to Gail?" she asked in a panic.

Sunny looked up at Jim, tears streaming down her cheeks.

Jim cleared his throat nervously. "I'm afraid she's been shot. On the way into the studio."

Leah sat up abruptly, pushing the covers back with her feet, as if she were about to jump out of bed.

"Is she alive?"

Jim lowered his chin and shook his head. "I'm sorry."

Leah looked straight ahead in shock.

"When did it happen? Why didn't you wake me?" she demanded.

"Just after they arrived," Jim replied.

"Jim called me on my cell phone and I begged him not to disturb you until I got here. There wasn't anything you could do, Leah."

"They had just pulled up to the curb," Jim explained. "Jack and Norm were with her. Jack jumped out and surveyed the scene carefully. Everything looked clear, but there was a lot of pedestrian traffic and everybody was bundled up against the cold. As soon as Jack opened the door to let Gail out, a guy walking by in a trench coat pulled out a gun and shot before Gail had even turned to get out. Jack went for the guy, but he was already out of reach. According to procedure, Jack went back to help Gail. Norm jumped out and gave chase, but the guy had gone around the corner and disappeared. He obviously planned the whole thing pretty carefully. I suspect it was another professional."

"Jack and Norm are both okay," Sunny added.

Leah couldn't speak. She sat on her bed, staring directly ahead, her eyes open wide. Sunny began to sob as she put her arms around Leah and attempted to lower her to the bed. Leah didn't resist, but continued to stare straight ahead as if in a trance. Sunny pulled the covers up over Leah and, still sobbing, lay down on the bed beside her, wrapping her arms around her devastated sister.

"I know it doesn't matter, but I'm sure she didn't feel any pain. She died instantly," Jim offered. He then turned and, head bowed, left the room.

Leah and Sunny lay embraced, but motionless, for several hours, while Leah continued to stare wide-eyed at the ceiling. She was in too much shock to even cry."

Later that evening, the house shrouded in deep November darkness, Leah spoke for the first time.

"Do the boys know?"

"No," Sunny replied, still embracing Leah on the bed. "I called Brad as soon as I heard and he came over to take care of them, but we agreed that you needed to decide how to tell them. I'm sure Brad's downstairs with them now."

"I'll tell them," Leah said in a voice devoid of emotion or inflection.

Leah rose silently and, moving slowly, retrieved her bathrobe from the chair next to the window. Wrapping the sash carefully around her waist, she left the darkened bedroom and headed downstairs. Sunny followed quietly behind.

The sisters found the boys with Brad and Dr. Marcus in the den watching television.

"Hi, Mom," Ryan exclaimed as they entered. "How you feelin?"

Without responding, Leah sat down in one of the empty chairs next to the couch on which Tyler and Ryan were sitting. Sunny quietly asked Brad and Dr. Marcus if they would help her with something in the kitchen and the three of them left.

"Tyler," Leah directed, "would you please turn off the tv."

Tyler picked up the remote that was lying next to him on the couch and did as she requested. "What's wrong?" he asked, a note of alarm in his voice.

"I don't know how to tell you this," Leah began, "so I'm just going to say it. Gail has been killed. A man shot her this morning while she was entering the tv studio to do an interview. She's with God now."

"Why?" Tyler asked in distress, moving to the edge of the couch.

Leah hesitated. "He thought she was me," Leah replied without emotion. "I was the one who was supposed to be doing the interview."

"Someone wants to kill you?" Ryan shrieked in panic.

"I'm so sorry," Leah said as she finally broke down in uncontrollable sobs. Both boys moved instinctively to her and embraced her as her pain and her grief poured forth in tsunamic waves of sorrow, regret, and guilt.

After several minutes, Leah's sobs subsided, her body and soul emptied of emotion. Pulling a wad of tissues from the pocket of her robe, she collected herself as the boys backed away and returned to the couch, a combination of sorrow and terror in their eyes.

"What are you going to do now?" Tyler asked cautiously.

"I don't know," Leah replied, shaking her head from side to side. "I really don't know."

"Why did God let her die?" Ryan asked innocently.

Leah looked up at Ryan and said, "I don't know that either, honey."

"Are you going to be safe?" Tyler continued hesitantly.

"I'll do whatever I have to do to be safe," Leah replied. "I'm not going to leave you guys. I promise," she concluded, immediately wondering if that was a promise she would be able to keep.

"What would happen to us?" Tyler went on.

"Well," Leah sighed, "you'd live with Sunny, I guess. But that's not going to happen. Mommy's going to be very, very careful."

"Are you going to stop telling people about God?" Tyler asked pointedly.

Looking him in the eye, Leah answered, "Maybe I will."

———

For the next several days, Leah went numbly through the motions of living. At night she prayed fervently to God for guidance and to Gail for forgiveness.

The killer was never apprehended. Unfortunately, not even Jack could provide enough of a description of the man for a police artist to create a composite drawing. He had used the wind and bitter cold to skillfully disguise himself. He wore a hat pulled low, the collar of his trench coat turned up, and his face turned down, his chin buried in a bulky woolen scarf that he wore around his neck. Despite a massive manhunt and search effort, neither the man nor his weapon was found.

The people on all sides of the debate over God's existence and the role of religion in society took pause over the shooting. How, sensible people wondered, could the affirmation of God's existence and his love be perverted into murder?

The funeral was held at the house several days after the shooting. Gail's son, Ralph, did not attend, citing some unavoidable conflict. Connie, however, did attend, albeit without her family.

There were several of Gail's close friends from the hospital in atten-dance, including Valerie Noosum, who wept throughout the short service. Leah had cried all of the tears she had in her by then. She stood motionless between Sunny and Dr. Marcus with her head bowed, looking old and tired. Sunny held her hand and gently rubbed her back. The boys stood solemnly just in front of Leah, thinking about their father, and secretly wondering if their mother would, in fact, keep her promise not to leave them.

Donny Hammond flew in with his wife to conduct the private service. William Vaughn was also in attendance, as were several of the A.A.F. staff with whom Gail had worked.

The security staff was scattered around the house and grounds, anx-iously searching for any sign of trouble. Several off-duty policemen and sheriff's deputies were also brought in for the service and a bevy of police cars from various local and state agencies lined the road outside the gate.

When the service was over, the casket was loaded into the hearse for the ride through the sea of cameras and reporters to the internment. While the timing had been kept a secret, a steady vigil had been kept outside the gates and calls had gone out when the hearse arrived. By the time it left, a media circus had erupted.

As the mourners followed the casket out of the house, Leah stood inside the door, staring at the floor in front of her. Members of the somber procession stopped to once again offer their condolences to Leah, but few words were exchanged. Most just reached out to touch her gently. Donny Hammond, for his part, reminded Leah that Gail was now at God's side, knowing the love that Leah herself had felt in his presence. After smiling briefly, however, the grief returned to Leah's face.

Connie did not follow the casket out, but waited for the house to empty before making her departure. As she did, she stopped in front of Leah and stood silently for several moments. "Thank you, Mrs. Warner. You've really been a great help to my family," she finally said, her anger and bitterness bursting forth from its confinement.

Leah's face didn't change and her body didn't move. She lifted her blank gaze, however, and looked directly into Connie's eyes. Sunny, still standing next to Leah, started to open her mouth, but Leah gently put her hand on Sunny's arm.

"I'm sorry, Connie," Leah said softly. "I can't tell you how sorry I am. I loved your mother."

Connie, however, made no response. She turned on her heel and walked briskly out.

————

"What do I do, Sunny?" Leah asked pleadingly as the two sisters sat at the kitchen table with Brad and Dr. Marcus one dark, rainy evening in the middle of December.

"I wish I knew," Sunny answered despondently.

"I guess I've got to give it up at some point. Maybe now's the time," Leah said in a tone of resignation.

"How long is the lease on the house?" Brad asked.

"A year, I think," Leah replied. "Vaughn's never said that he's going to keep me here that long, though. I've always assumed that I'd be on my own at some point."

"He can't pull the plug on you now, given what's happened," Sunny said emphatically.

"The William Vaughn that I know would not do that," Dr. Marcus noted.

"Perhaps not," Leah replied. "But this is all costing A.A.F. a lot of money, and I think there has to be an end to it sometime."

"What will you do?" Sunny asked anxiously.

"I don't know," Leah answered with a sigh. "I guess I'll have to see where things are at the time. Something tells me I won't be going back to Grover Street, however."

"Will you move out of the area?" Brad asked.

"I'd rather not, for the sake of the boys," Leah answered. "But who knows. One thing I've learned throughout all of this is not to think too far ahead."

After a long pause, during which each of them contemplated the incredible events which had engulfed them all, Brad said, "You know, I was wondering the other day if God had any idea how this would all turn out."

"You mean how divided and angry people would be?" Sunny wondered.

"Yeah. I mean, you almost have to assume that he did. After all, God knows everything, so why not this?"

"Good point," agreed Dr. Marcus.

"But, what is your point?" Sunny prodded.

"Well, this whole thing has grown into something far bigger than God, on the surface, seemed to intend. It appears that he simply intended to send the world a very simple message of love. It's created, however, these warring factions with very broad and far-ranging ambitions to more or less re-wire society. The original message has really been lost, despite Leah's best efforts to keep everyone focused."

"The law of unintended consequences," Dr. Marcus suggested.

"Yeah, but this is God. We have to assume they weren't unintended or unexpected. So maybe his intent was bigger than we, at least I, have been assuming."

"You're being way too subtle for me," Sunny observed.

"Did you ever hear of Marshall McLuhan, the guy who said, 'The medium is the message,' perhaps the most widely misunderstood statement of the 20th Century?"

"I've heard of him," Dr. Marcus answered, intrigued by the conversation.

"Ditto," Sunny nodded.

"Sorry," Leah said, smiling falsely.

"Well, McLuhan, who was a Christian, by the way, wasn't talking about the news media, as most people assume. He defined a medium as an extension of ourselves. A hammer, for example, is an extension of our arm. An automobile, in a sense, is an extension of our feet. And a message, by his definition, encompasses all of the things, like inventions and innovations, which impact our lives. Essentially, McLuhan argued that every advancement, particularly technological ones, come with a lot of baggage that isn't altogether obvious at first, but which becomes apparent when the medium becomes over-extended. The automobile, for example, in addition to giving us mobility, ultimately brought us air pollution, traffic fatalities, and an increasingly overweight population."

"Okay?" Sunny said in mock sarcasm.

"My point is that maybe God knew that this is how it would all unfold. Maybe he knew that the vast majority of us wouldn't get it. Maybe he knew that he couldn't stop the social processes that divide us so bitterly. His only choice was to accelerate the process by enflaming the underlying drivers."

"Which are?" Sunny asked inquisitively.

"Self-absorption, for one. Maybe he knew that if he pushed us far enough, our self-absorption would push us to the verge of social collapse and we'd all have to look in the mirror and wonder how things had gotten so far out of control. Maybe he wanted us all to see how silly we've all been acting by making us act so silly that even we can't overlook it."

"How in the world does that help Leah decide where to go from here?" Sunny asked in joking exasperation.

"Maybe she's already accomplished what he really wanted her to do. Maybe it's up to everyone else now. Maybe you just let the two sides fight it out until everyone realizes how over the top this whole thing has become."

"So maybe I should just put out a message that I'm going off the air," Leah wondered aloud. "Maybe I just tell everybody that I stand by my story and now it's up to them."

"Something like that," Brad agreed. "No admission of defeat. More an unwillingness to fight."

"But how will that not be taken as an admission of defeat?" asked Sunny.

"Maybe that's the point," Dr. Marcus noted. "People have taken a simple message from God and turned it into a contest in which they seek to acquire victory. Maybe trying to win the battle over whether or not Leah is telling the truth, and what it means for the world if she is, is no different than trying to acquire wealth or status or popularity."

"Maybe we're all missing the real point of the message," Leah said contemplatively. "We're all fighting over a message of self-less love."

"Instead of laying down our arms," Brad added, "we're building up our arsenals. We were headed there anyway, but this has certainly accelerated the process to the point that we now stand on the brink of outright civil war, at least in the figurative sense."

"He knew we wouldn't listen," Dr. Marcus said absently to the bottle of water he was holding in both hands.

"People usually do have to learn from their mistakes," Sunny observed.

"Exactly," Brad agreed. "At the end of the day, people just don't listen." A pause. "Actually, I take that back. They don't hear. The words fill their ears, but their meaning never gets to the brain."

"But will people ever look in the mirror and really see their true reflection?" Leah pondered.

"That's the question," Brad acknowledged.

———

Several nights later, Leah was sitting in the kitchen with Dr. Marcus. Sunny and Brad had gone to a movie and the boys were in the den watching television.

"How are things going with the new foundation?" Leah asked.

"Well, actually. We put out our first press release today, announcing its formation."

"Great. How are the new offices?"

"They're adequate. I haven't moved in yet. I'm still closing down my practice. We have, however, hired our first staff member. We thought that if we were going to promote service to others we ought to at least have a live human being to answer the phone," he laughed.

"That's wonderful. I'm very happy for you," Leah said warmly.

After a pause, Dr. Marcus looked up and asked, "And how about you? How are you getting along?"

Leah sighed audibly. "I'd like to say great, but you know me better than that."

"I'd be worried if you said it and actually believed it. You've been through a great deal of trauma. It's a long healing process."

"Well, I'm trying to get back into a routine, for the boys as much as me."

"And how are they doing?" Dr. Marcus queried.

"It's hard to say. I've had trouble getting them to talk about it."

"Don't give up," he counseled. "They'll talk when they're ready."

"I won't," Leah replied.

"At the risk of being too forward, Leah, perhaps it might do you some good to talk to Dr. Heidrich. I know he'd be happy to come out and sit with you. He's a very good listener and he understands the grieving process. It might be helpful to get his perspective."

Leah and Dr. Marcus exchanged a long glance.

"Okay," Leah said softly.

Dr. Marcus uncharacteristically fidgeted in his chair.

Finally, Leah spoke. "Dr. Marcus." A long pause. "You're always afraid of being too forward. I was, too, once. That's why I suddenly have a strong suspicion that something is being left unsaid between us."

Dr. Marcus continued to stare at his hands on the table in front of him and swallowed hard.

"What is it?" Leah asked pleadingly.

"I don't know," he replied softly, clearing his throat. He stood up and went to the kitchen sink, gripping it tightly with both hands and staring off into the December darkness.

Leah followed slowly, standing silently behind him for several seconds before slowly and gently raising her hand and putting it on his back. "There's nothing to be afraid of. And certainly nothing to be ashamed of. I've thought about our relationship many times over the last months."

"And?" he asked softly.

"And I've thought that I'm being very, very silly. There's no way that a wonderful man like you would ever feel in any way romantic toward me."

"I'm afraid I don't know how to feel romantic, Leah," the doctor replied, still staring out into the darkness. "My life has been my work and my faith. I've never had a real relationship before. I'm not even sure how to go about it."

Leah began to rub his back gently.

"All I know," Dr. Marcus continued, "is that I feel like I know you at a level that I've never known anyone before. I've watched this tremendous transformation of someone who was, like most of us, more or less just living life. And now you're defining it. You've risen above your fear and your trepidation and you've released the goodness within you. I have great admiration for that."

"Thank you," Leah replied softly.

Dr. Marcus turned around and faced Leah, the heels of his hands on the kitchen counter. There was only six inches between them.

"You humble me, Leah. You make me feel insignificant. At the same time, however, you fortify me. I've been trying to put it into words. And I keep coming back to intimacy. In your presence I feel the same kind of intimacy with life that you say you felt in God's presence. It's an intimacy that is both soothing and liberating at the same time."

Leah looked down. Dr. Marcus then slowly removed his hands from the counter and put them around Leah. At the same time, she put her arms around him, pulling herself into the warmth of his embrace, her head on his chest, tears streaming down her cheeks.

They stayed that way for several minutes, embraced against the pain of loss and controversy.

Finally, Leah spoke. "So where do we go from here?" she asked softly.

"I don't know," he replied. "I guess we see what happens."

"Okay," Leah replied, strengthening her embrace even further.

"Maybe you could at least start calling me David," he said, laughing lightly.

"Okay," Leah replied softly, pulling her head back from his shoulder and kissing him tenderly on the lips.

———

Leah and Dr. Heidrich met two days later, on another cold, damp December Michigan evening. They sat in the living room next to the fire. The boys were in their rooms completing homework assignments and Sunny and Brad were out Christmas shopping.

""It's silly of me to ask how you're doing," Dr. Heidrich began, "but human communication is too primitive for me to avoid it. So how are you doing?"

"I'm surviving."

"That's a start," he noted.

"Beyond that, how I'm doing depends on when you ask me. Sometimes I'm angry; sometimes I'm fearful; sometimes I feel guilty; I'm always sad."

"All normal reactions, I'm afraid. Tell me about the guilt. Do you feel guilt because you believe that you were the intended target?"

"I think it's pretty certain that I was," Leah answered.

"Do you think Gail would hold you responsible?"

"No. But only because she's Gail. She was a very special person. That doesn't mean she shouldn't, though."

There was a long pause in the conversation. Leah was sitting on the edge of her chair, her legs turned to the side, and her hands clasped in her lap. Dr. Heidrich was slouched back in his chair, his right hand holding his chin.

"Guilt," he finally offered, leaning forward in his chair and putting his elbows on his knees, "is a prerequisite of a functional society. If you think about it, if no one felt any guilt, lawlessness would abound. In a very real sense, therefore, a sense of healthy guilt is the sign of a moral person."

"But it should have been me in that car. I asked her to take my place," Leah replied.

"I understand. But where is the immorality in that? You certainly didn't know that a killer would be waiting outside of the studio. And you were sick. You asked a trusted friend and associate to fill in for you. That certainly wasn't an immoral request."

Leah sat silently, looking down at her clasped hands, while Dr. Heidrich sat back in his chair once again.

"Gail came to you and asked to help," Dr. Heidrich finally said. "Is that correct?"

Leah nodded.

"And what if you had turned her down on the basis of not wanting to be responsible for her? Would that have made you feel guilty?"

"Probably," Leah admitted.

"Why? Because you would have been denying Gail something that she wished for herself?"

"I guess," Leah replied tentatively.

"But isn't that the pertinent point? Gail wanted to be a part of your mission. And unless you believe that Gail was somehow mentally inferior, which I know you don't, you have to assume that she knew as much about the risks involved as you did."

"So I'm being arrogant by feeling guilty about what happened?"

"No, arrogance is a pro-active emotion. Guilt is a reactive one. Just as remorse and grief are. This is why guilt and remorse often become all balled up into one in bereavement. It's almost unavoidable. In this case, however, I think that if you can mentally separate the grief and the guilt you will more clearly see that you have absolutely nothing to feel guilty about."

Once again, there was a long pause in the conversation.

"There have been numerous attempts to map the process of bereavement. Depending on the author, it's been broken down into anywhere from four to a dozen or more distinct steps. To date, however, no one has really come up with a single, universally accepted model. And the reason for that is that grief, and the appropriate way to deal with grief, is very personal. We're all different."

After a pause, Dr. Heidrich continued. "Grief is the process by which we separate ourselves from the person we lost and get on with our lives. And since every relationship is a little different, so, too, is the process by which we deal with the loss. Freud called it 'grief work,' which is literally appropriate, and broke it down into four tasks. The first is to recognize and accept the loss. The second is to mourn the loss. The third is to understand how the loss will change our own lives. And the fourth is to look to a new future. The process is not always an orderly one and even Freud, later in life, agreed that there is no universal timetable."

"The middle of the night is usually the hardest," Leah noted. "And some nights are harder than others."

"That's a function of biology as much as psychology," Dr. Heidrich pointed out. "In the middle of the night we are the most disconnected from the world around us. It's the coldest part of the day, and when we awake in the middle of the night we often do so in response to our nightly attempts to work through the unresolved conflicts of the day through our dreams. That's why most heart attacks occur during the night. Two-thirty in the morning, to be exact."

"I didn't know that." Leah noted absently.

"Yes. Unfortunately, your current living arrangement disconnects you from the world in much the same way that we are disconnected while we sleep. That, I suspect, will make the process of working through your grief that much harder."

"I don't really have much choice," Leah lamented. "I do feel increasingly like a prisoner here. It's very isolating."

"Indeed. And I'm not suggesting that you should give up the security you have here. Someone obviously means you harm. I think it is helpful, however, to recognize your disconnection from the world and to do what you can to overcome it. Read the newspaper; stay up with current events; watch television."

"And get really depressed, you mean?" she replied, smiling for the first time.

He laughed. "The content of the news can be very uninspiring, to say the least. Nonetheless, being informed is a way to feel more connected. It might also help to start a journal. A lot of people find that a very good way to work through grief. It causes you to focus on the object of your bereavement in a methodical and objective way. Perhaps take a little time each day to carefully recall some aspect of your relationship with Gail. It will help to reinforce your memories and it's a way to paint a clearer and more accurate picture of what you've lost. In bereavement we have a tendency to put the person we've lost, and the relationship we've lost with them, on a very high pedestal. It's a natural mechanism for avoiding the guilt of thinking ill of someone when they're no longer here. While that's a kind and considerate thing to do, however, it tends to make the hole in our life that much bigger. The challenge of defining a future around that void, therefore, becomes that much greater. By taking the time to recall specific events and specific shared moments, we tend to minimize the potential exaggeration and to paint in our minds a more realistic understanding of what we've lost without having to intentionally think bad thoughts or in any way disparage the one we grieve. In turn, that gives us a more realistic and attainable plan for our alternative future."

The two sat silently for several moments, while Leah looked at the floor and Dr. Heidrich scrutinized her face. "Call it a shrink's intuition," he finally said, "but I sense there's more running through your head than grief. Care to share it?"

Leah didn't look up.

"A relationship perhaps?"

Leah nodded slowly. "Dr. Marcus."

"Really? And has this relationship blossomed, or is it still germinating?"

Leah laughed nervously. "I'm not even sure it's planted yet."

"But words have been exchanged."

Leah nodded. "At this point, I think we're both just confused. It was unexpected for both of us."

"Why confused? You're both available. You share a common interest. What are you worried about; the difference in your ages?"

"No, that doesn't bother me," Leah replied.

Dr. Heidrich remained silent.

Tears welled in Leah's eyes. "I'm not worthy of a man like Dr. Marcus."

"Isn't that for him to decide?"

"Only if he has all the facts," Leah noted.

"Oh, so you have a past? Is this the past that everyone, including Dr. Marcus, has been told about, or is there more?"

Leah shook her head.

"Do you not think that Dr. Marcus has a past?"

"I'm just not worthy," Leah said softly.

"God seems to think you are," Dr. Heidrich noted. Sighing, he continued. "David Marcus is a very good friend of mine. And because of that I know that he, like the rest of us, carries a lot of personal doubt around. Don't be fooled by the fact that he's a famous neurologist. Physicians are very good at hiding their feelings. They have the impenetrable wall of medicine to hide behind. My point is not to say he's anything different than what he appears to be. My point is that you shouldn't deny him the chance to be human. If he lets you in, you will be doing him no favors by convincing yourself that you're not worthy to enter."

The two again sat silently for several moments.

"The fact that David has retired from his practice and started the foundation is a very big move. I'm not sure either one of us can comprehend how big. What I do know, however, is that David is growing in a way that he has long yearned for. And you, I presume, are partly responsible."

Leah looked up at the doctor and smiled faintly.

CHAPTER 15

The following editorial appeared in the *Detroit Dispatch* just ten days prior to Christmas.

It is the Christmas season. It is the season of Hanukah. It is the season of Kwanzaa. And it is the season of irony.

Just six months ago, Leah Warner, in a turn of events that no doctor can yet explain, was miraculously cured of all of the injuries she had incurred in a terrible head-on collision just three weeks prior. Warner emerged from her coma, removed the ventilator that had been necessary for her to breathe, and was immediately alert and lucid.

Just as miraculously, she announced that she had been with God and that he – or she - had given her a message to deliver to the world. He said to tell us that he loves us all and that he wants us to love each other in the same selfless and caring way. He also cautioned us against our current pre-occupation with acquisition and achievement.

And how have we reacted? Have we come together as a nation – or a world – and embraced the ideal of self-less love and sacrifice? Have we eschewed our excessive consumerism? Have we collectively reconsidered the standards by which society defines success?

With few exceptions, one would have to answer each question with a resounding no. Oh yes, Christmas spending is expected to be down significantly this year. The economy is in the tank. And the domestic automotive industry's demise, already underway before Mrs. Warner's arrival on the scene, appears to be accelerating.

We must, however, gauge these results against where we started. Our national savings rate was essentially at zero. Christmas spending, by nearly everyone's agreement, was at obscene levels. And most of us were driving vehicles that, in a different time and place, we probably couldn't afford.

The fact is that suburban lawns are still littered with blow-molded play structures and toys. Few of us will get a bag of coal for Christmas. And most families continue to have more cars than they do garage space.

Mrs. Warner does have her supporters. But she also has her detractors. The country has largely separated itself into two warring factions, each intent on pushing the other aside in its attempt to grab political power and further its own social, economic, and political agendas.

Political pundits and talking heads constantly conjecture about what impact "the Warner issue," as it has come to be called, will have on next year's elections. Economists and Wall Street types fret daily over what Mrs. Warner is doing to the economy, as if she somehow got into the economy's master control room and locked the door. She's also been blamed, by various special interests, for promoting racism, McCarthyism, censorship, the invasion of privacy, and the creation of an American Iran.

The battle, in other words, has gotten personal. Mrs. Warner has been both vilified and exalted. She has been both praised and blamed. She has been assigned both divinity and evil intent.

Throughout all of this, however, Mrs. Warner has constantly reminded us that she is nothing more than a Midwestern homemaker with a simple message from God. She has sought no political power, she has pushed no political agenda, and other than accepting the offer to live in a nice home in which she is now a prisoner, she has sought no financial reward.

For these reasons and more, not the least of which is that she is simply a credible person, I have come to accept Mrs. Warner's story as *true. Coming from a crotchety ole' previously-agnostic newspaper editor, that's quite an admission. It is, nonetheless, quite irrelevant.*

Why does it really matter if Mrs. Warner's story is true or not? Whether you believe her or not, isn't hers the message we all need to hear? Isn't the truth still the truth no matter what its origins?

Could it be that we are so pre-occupied with what this means to each of us personally that we have overlooked what it means to us as a human family? Could it be that we haven't really listened to what Mrs. Warner has to say? Could it be that we are viewing this whole episode through the lens of self-absorption?

As we finish out the year and the holiday season, perhaps we should all agree to stop arguing about Leah Warner. Let us not, however, stop talking about the need for more compassion in the world. Let us not stop challenging our priorities and our pre-occupations. Let us not stop pausing in our achievement long enough – dare I say it – to love our neighbors as we love ourselves.

Harry Snyder
Metropolitan Editor

Despite Harry Snyder's plea, spontaneous protests broke out in major cities around the country in the final days leading up to Christmas. In each case, the police worked diligently to keep the two sides separated, but frequently failed. In Houston, Philadelphia, and Boston the National Guard was ordered in by the respective state governors in an effort to re-gain control after massive protests and riots cast the cities into near anarchy. Hundreds of people were injured and millions of dollars in property damage was sustained.

Leah watched the tragic events unfold on her television screen. Increasingly appalled and horrified, she anxiously considered what to do next. The world seemed to be falling apart in front of her very eyes; her message of selfless love in tatters.

Despite the growing firestorm that surrounded them, Leah and Dr. Marcus continued to explore their relationship and their confusion. Within a short time, their relationship seemed very natural, as if it had been going on forever.

Christmas morning arrived on an Arctic wind filled with snow. Leah, Dr. Marcus – who she now called David – Sunny, Brad, and the boys all sat in front of a roaring fire in the living room to exchange gifts. By prior agreement, the adults limited their reciprocal giving to one gift each.

"I dare say this is the first Christmas present I've ever given," David said jovially as he handed Leah a small package wrapped in bright blue paper. "Which, as I think about it, is ironic given what it is."

Leah carefully opened the package to find a small, thin decorative case several inches in length. It was made of wood and sterling silver and very ornately decorated.

"It's a mezuzah," David offered. "It goes on the doorpost. There's a scroll inside with short passages from the Torah written on it."

"It's beautiful," Leah offered. "And what is its significance?"

"Jews put them on their doorposts to fulfill a biblical command in which Moses commands the Israelites to love God with all their heart, strength, and soul. It serves as a reminder of God's laws and presence. Some Jews also think of it as a protective amulet or lucky charm."

"Thank you. That's very sweet," Leah gushed as she leaned over from her chair to kiss David on the cheek.

As they were cleaning up and getting ready for a late breakfast, the phone rang. Sunny answered. It was Leslie, who was spending the holidays at home in Washington with her cat, which had spent most of the last six months in the care of Leslie's neighbor and friend. After exchanging Christmas greetings and wishes, Sunny handed the phone to Leah.

"Merry Christmas," Leah said cheerily.

"Merry Christmas to you," Leslie replied. "Have you opened gifts?"

"Just finished."

"Good. Well, I won't keep you, but I wanted to wish you a Merry Christmas and thank you for the lovely sterling pendant. I'm wearing it now."

"You're welcome. And thank you for the beautiful picture and frame. It will go on my bedside table."

"I'm glad you like it," Leslie replied. "I wasn't sure you needed any more reminders of what happened, but I thought it was a wonderful picture of you and Gail together during a happy moment."

"I love it. Thank you," Leah assured her.

"Besides," Leslie said teasingly, "how do you buy for someone who's been with God?"

Leah smiled warmly.

"So how are things in Washington? Have you seen Mr. Vaughn?" Leah inquired.

"A couple of days ago," Leslie responded. "Frankly, he seemed a bit anxious to me. Nothing to do with us, I'm sure. But he just seemed a little on edge. You know how unflappable he normally is."

"Not big on the holidays, perhaps," Leah offered.

"Yeah. And as far as Washington," Leslie continued, "it's pretty empty. The government's shut down and all the politicians have left. It's actually a pleasant time to be here. You can actually get into the better restaurants."

"Good. Well, I hope you're relaxing and catching up with old friends."

"I am. It's been fun," Leslie admitted. "Listen, I hate to bring up business today, but I do have to tell you that I have run into a few political aides I know and they tell me that the politicians are in an absolute tizzy about this upcoming election."

"Oh? Nothing to do with me I hope," Leah noted.

"Everything to do with you from what I'm told. It seems there's a general fear that your support will continue to grow."

"And why is that a problem for politicians?" Leah asked innocently. "I have no political agenda."

"You don't, but many of your supporters and detractors do, and they're trying to force their candidates to endorse their position. That's typically not a problem in districts where the voters are politically extreme one way or the other. There's still a large mass of people who haven't quite made up their minds, however, and no one's quite sure which way they'll ultimately turn. And then, of course, there's the whole issue of the economy and how that will play out. All told, politicians, particularly incumbent politicians, don't like uncertainty, and they're facing a whole lot of it right now."

———

The number of protests and rallies had fallen off sharply with the arrival of Christmas. The private debate surrounding Leah remained heated and vitriolic, however.

It didn't help to quell the country's pugnacity when several major cities, including New York, decided to cancel their public New Year's Eve celebrations in response to growing concerns over security and dwindling tax receipts.

And, as many analysts had feared, the holiday season never arrived for many retailers. During a period when many retailers make nearly all of their annual profits, most stores reported sharp declines in same store sales, the yardstick of retail financial health. Only craft retailers, due to a greatly enhanced interest in handmade gifts, reported increases for the period. Many luxury retailers, reported declines as high as 75%, forcing a record number into immediate bankruptcy.

Leah was slowly recovering from the loss of Gail. With added encouragement from David, she took Dr. Heidrich's advice and started to keep a journal of her memories of their short, but deep-felt friendship. As he predicted, she gradually learned to live with her loss and could now envision an alternative future that was not shrouded in black.

The practice was so successful, in fact, that Leah had the boys start their own journals, which the three of them worked on during their lessons each day. The therapeutic value of the exercise, in fact, became all encompassing. It prompted the boys to talk more openly about their emotions relating to the feared loss of their mother, the loss of their father, and their social isolation.

Leslie remained in Washington after the holidays. Leah had requested more time off from the hectic pace of the fall's schedule of interviews and rallies. They agreed, therefore, with the consent of William Vaughn, to meet at the end of January to make future plans and renew their effort. In the meantime, Leah would focus on her well-being, her family, and her growing relationship with David Marcus.

David, for his part, was engrossed in both his relationship and his new foundation. Donations had already exceeded $10 million, about half of which had come from his friend, Professor Bradshaw, who joked that he finally found something other than his Charger worthy of spending his inheritance on.

He was sitting in his office at foundation headquarters sorting through a pile of grant requests when his assistant informed him that a woman by the name of Helen Luft, claiming to be an old friend, was on the phone.

"She's hardly an old friend," he noted, "but I'll take the call."

Picking the phone up from its cradle, he said, in a calm, confident voice, "Yes, Ms. Luft. How may I help you?"

"Dr. Marcus, thank you for taking my call. And congratulations on your new foundation. Yours is a worthy mission and I wish you all the best."

"Thank you."

"Dr. Marcus," she continued immediately, "I'd like you to reciprocate my willingness to meet with you last fall. I would like to meet privately with you and Mrs. Warner."

"May I ask why?" he asked cautiously.

"I have some information that will be of great interest to you, but I'd rather share it in person."

Dr. Marcus hesitated before responding. "Why do I get the sense that you have some terrible secret to share regarding William Vaughn?"

Helen laughed. "Well, it does have to do with William Vaughn, but I'd hardly call it a secret. It won't be anyway."

After a slight hesitation, he asked, "When and where did you want to meet?"

"Next Tuesday. Let's say 7 o'clock in the evening. I'll come there, to Mrs. Warner's home."

"I can't accept on Leah's behalf," the doctor noted.

"I understand. You can call me back with her decision. My cell is 255-397-8465.""I'll talk with her this evening."

———

"I take it that things have worked between the two of you, then. Congratulations."

"I'm sorry," Dr. Marcus replied in bewilderment.

Helen laughed. "Oh come, Doctor. Despite what William Vaughn might say, I am a woman. I knew the minute you walked into my office that Leah Warner was more than a patient and friend."

"I'm afraid I'm at a loss for words," Dr. Marcus said after a long pause.

"Don't be embarrassed, Doctor. I hope it works out for the both of you." A pause. "Can I assume, then, that Leah is aware of our visit?"

"Yes, she is," Dr. Marcus replied hesitantly.

———

At 7:00 p.m. the following Tuesday, David and Leah sat anxiously on the sofa in Leah's living room awaiting the arrival of Helen Luft. At Leah's insistence, Sunny and Brad were also in the room.

Helen arrived promptly at seven and was ushered into the room by one of the security guards. She was dressed in a long African print skirt nearly identical to the one she had worn during her first meeting with Leah in the hospital. She now wore a heavy black sweater that appeared several sizes too big, however, beneath a bulky wool coat that looked almost as heavy as Helen herself. A long black wool scarf was wrapped around her neck and a matching wool sailor's cap sat atop her head. Whatever footwear she had been wearing had apparently been left at the front door. She was now wearing only heavy grey socks on her feet.

There was no attempt at formalities. Helen quietly removed her coat, hat, and scarf, piling them on the plush rug next to one of the open chairs facing David and Leah.

Sitting down in the chair, Helen pushed her hair back over the top of her head with her hand and said, hurriedly, "Thank you for seeing me. And congratulations on your relationship. You're both absolutely glowing."

"Thank you," Leah replied, smiling nervously.

"I'll be brief," Helen continued. She then reached into the same large and over-stuffed hobo bag that she had brought into Leah's hospital room and retrieved a yellow envelope large enough to hold documents without having to fold them. She passed it to Leah.

"You need to read this," she said.

"What is it?" Leah asked.

"It's self-explanatory."

Leah slowly lifted the envelope flap and removed the single piece of paper inside. It was a letter, on A.A.F. letterhead, addressed to an individual whose name wasn't familiar to Leah, although David, reading over Leah's shoulder, recognized it to be a member of the board of directors of A.A.F. It was dated just a few days after Leah's miraculous recovery and read as follows:

Dear Frank:

I appreciate your reservations about our plan to offer support to Leah Warner. Although I do believe, based on my meeting with her, that she is either lying or delusional, she appears, nonetheless, to be pretty convincing. Believe me, I put her through her paces.

I admit, therefore, that this is a risky move. If Mrs. Warner ever decides to change her story, or if the truth is eventually uncovered, we will have made a considerable investment in a losing cause and suffer significant embarrassment. If she is successful, however, we will have greatly furthered our agenda to promote a religious society here in America and, more importantly, stopped the secularists in their tracks.

After careful consideration, therefore, I recommended to the board that we commit to supporting Mrs. Warner. As you know, while each member shares your reservations, as do I, each, other than yourself, voted in favor of the resolution. While that provides sufficient authority for me to move ahead, I would, nonetheless, prefer to have unanimous consent before the vote is formally entered into the record.

To that end, I would be extremely appreciative if you would re-consider your vote. As I said, I think it's important to have board unanimity in the record should our actions ever be subject to scrutiny.

If you wish to discuss the matter with me or the other board members, please don't hesitate to contact me or them. In the meantime, I hope you will give my request to support this decision careful consideration. I will call in a few days to discuss it further.

Sincerely yours,

William Vaughn
Executive Director

Finishing the letter, Leah looked up in horror.

"This is a forgery," she said accusingly to Helen. "What do you think you're doing?"

"It's not a forgery," Helen responded calmly. "That's Vaughn's signature."

"That can easily be forged on a computer, Ms. Luft," Dr. Marcus retorted. "This cannot possibly be legitimate."

Leah looked again at the signature. "Where did you get it?"

"From Vaughn," Helen replied.

"You stole it?"

"No. He handed it to us."

"I assume you're being sarcastic," Leah responded harshly.

"No. I'm not. He literally handed it to us. We didn't even ask for it. We didn't know it existed."

Leah looked to David, and then to Sunny and Brad, her mouth still agape. "Can I see it?" Sunny asked, reaching out tentatively.

Leah didn't respond, but handed her the letter as she looked back at Helen.

As Leah sat back on the couch there was a soft knock at the door. It opened and William Vaughn entered the room.

"You're having a party and I wasn't invited," Vaughn said in mock disappointment. Walking across the room, he removed his coat and set it on the table in the middle of the room. As usual, he was immaculately dressed in a double-breasted suit.

Straightening his suit coat and tie, he assumed the seat next to Helen, casually crossing his legs and leaning back in the over-sized chair. He smiled aloofly, but didn't speak.

"I had a suspicion I'd run into you here," Helen noted. "Let me guess. You get a copy of the security register."

"Of course," Vaughn replied curtly, inspecting the finely manicured nails on his right hand.

David and Leah looked inquisitively at each other. Finally, Dr. Marcus looked to William Vaughn and said, "William, Ms. Luft has just shown us a rather startling memo that she attributes to you."

"Did she?" Vaughn replied nonchalantly. "And why would you do a think like that, Helen?"

"I thought they had a right to know about the deal that you and Howard struck on Tortola over the weekend," Helen said forcefully.

"And why's that?" Vaughn added as he continued to inspect his manicure.

"I want to help them," Helen replied.

Vaughn looked up from his manicure abruptly. "Will wonders never cease," Vaughn exclaimed sarcastically. "What on earth for?"

"I believe in what they're doing," Helen answered, in no way intimidated by Vaughn's arrogance.

Leaning forward to hand the letter back to Leah, Sunny spoke for the first time. "Will someone please explain what's going on here. There's obviously an inside joke that I don't get."

"Yes," added Dr. Marcus. "William, I'm quite distressed by the flippancy of your attitude at the moment. What's going on?"

"I'm sorry to offend your sensibilities, Doctor," Vaughn replied, sitting upright in his chair, "but this is a side of the business you haven't been exposed to before. I have no doubt you will find it distasteful."

"What business? What side?" David asked in bewilderment.

"The business of power," Helen interjected.

Vaughn remained silent.

"You've been too successful," Helen explained. "Not even William thought you'd get this far in delivering your message."

"I don't understand," Leah replied, looking intently at William Vaughn. "I thought you were on our side."

"I was," Vaughn replied.

"Then what are we missing," David asked.

"David," Vaughn began, "Helen and I, and others like us, are arms dealers, figuratively speaking, of course. Arms dealers, in the end, make their money from conflict, not resolution. They want to see intense, epic battles, but they don't want to see either side emerge overwhelmingly victorious."

"How does the letter fit in?" Brad asked, speaking for the first time.

"Under the deal cut between William and Howard, I'm to leak it to my press contacts. William obviously can't just release it or the media will be suspicious. So we'll leak it for him. Our press contacts will assume that we stole it or that someone inside A.A.F. leaked it to us."

"Why?" Leah asked softly.

"To slow you down," Helen replied. "It's an election year. You've created too much uncertainty. You're too much of a threat to the incumbent politicians who have given each of us a seat at the table of power. By taking you out of the picture, A.A.F. assures that most of their political supporters get re-elected and they get the added bonus of having them even more indebted to them for doing so."

"If Leah's being so successful, why wouldn't you use this as an opportunity to gain political support by knocking off some of the opposition incumbents?" Brad challenged.

"As I told Leah and Sunny at our very first meeting," replied Vaughn, "no one in Washington is who they appear to be. Your question presumes an ability to distinguish between friend and foe."

"In reality," Helen added, "most politicians are both friend and foe to both of us. It's a little game they play to protect their incumbency. You see, there are two political parties in the U.S., but they're not the Republicans and the Democrats. They're the incumbents and the challengers. It's a very tight little club. When it comes to protecting their respective incumbency, the club locks arms. Even the fiercest political enemies become the staunchest of allies — behind the scenes, of course."

"Does the board of directors know you're doing this, William?" David asked.

"Of course. They're the ones taking the brunt of the pressure."

"But you've spent millions of dollars to get to this point," Sunny observed. "You're throwing that all away."

"What we've spent," Vaughn replied curtly, "is a drop in the bucket compared to the time and money it took to gain the level of influence in Washington that we currently enjoy. We don't relish the idea of having to start over with a large class of successful challengers."

"But this is immoral, if not illegal," David noted in exasperation. "It goes against everything the A.A.F. stands for."

"Does it?" Vaughn snapped. "You give your fellow members too much credit."

"We'll see," David retorted. "I have every intention of making all of this public."

"That's a battle you won't win, David, I assure you."

"Are you threatening me?" David said accusingly.

"I'm protecting you from your rather droll naiveté."

The two men, jaws clenched, scowled at each other with growing resentment and outrage. Leah reached out and rubbed David's arm to calm and reassure him.

"A lab would be able to date this letter," Brad offered in an attempt to ease the rising tensions.

"That's true," Vaughn acknowledged.

"So we can prove that it's not authentic. You just wrote it," Sunny added with a spark of optimism.

Vaughn laughed. "Please," he spat sarcastically. "I am not stupid."

"The letter is authentic," Helen offered. "It's dated accurately."

"And, as our records will clearly show, my personal printer was replaced the following week, making the letter rather easy to date."

"I suspect," Helen said matter-of-factly while staring at Vaughn, "that you'll find that Mr. Henry, the director to whom the letter is addressed, was in on the whole thing. He initially voted as he did just so this letter could be written and filed."

Vaughn smiled. "Oh Helen, you're an admirer after all. I'm tingly all over."

Dr. Marcus leaned forward and said, rather indignantly, "William, I feel cheated and betrayed. I cannot believe that you would stoop to this level. I will make the truth known to the board of directors."

"And what is the truth, David?" Vaughn shot back, his own anger rising. "That letter is the truth. That letter was written. It is real. If you suggest that this was all a pre-meditated setup, it will be your word against mine."

"They know that I have no reason to lie about all this," Dr. Marcus said forcefully.

"Oh no? You don't think the fact that you have become romantically involved with God's messenger won't be taken into consideration."

Dr. Marcus jumped to his feet. Seething with anger, he spat, "You son of a bitch."

"Sit down, David," Vaughn said dismissively.

Leah reached up to put her hand on David's arm. "Don't stoop to his level, David."

Dr. Marcus sat down.

"You must understand the problem," Vaughn began to calmly explain. "We have created an issue on which there is no middle ground that allows politicians to stand on both sides of the issue. Taking sides is what outsiders do. Incumbency is all about not taking sides, or, more to the point, taking them all at once."

"Do you know what a mugwump is?" Helen asked Leah.

"It's derived from an Algonquin word," Brad answered for her. "It originally meant 'great chief' but has come to denote a person sitting on a fence, his mug on one side and his wump on the other."

"Exactly. A person who can't, or won't, make up his mind. Or, in the case of politicians, a person who won't disclose how he's made up his mind for fear of becoming embroiled in controversy. Politicians hate controversy, particularly in an election year." A pause, as Helen leaned forward. "You see, most politicians are mugwumps when it comes to real controversy. As the battle between your supporters and your detractors intensifies, however, it's become increasingly more difficult to sit on the fence without running the risk of falling off."

"There are no ideologues in Washington, Mrs. Warner," Vaughn interjected. "There are only politicians who hide their self-absorption behind their ideology."

Silence fell over the room momentarily.

"Mr. Vaughn," Leah finally asked, "Have you never believed my story from the beginning?"

Vaughn licked his lips. "I've never cared one way or the other. It never really mattered one way or the other. I'm a careful man. If you were telling the truth, great. If not, and the word got out, I had the letter to distance myself."

"So why didn't you just come out and say she was lying? Why hedge the accusation?" Brad asked.

Vaughn laughed. "I don't want to annihilate the other side. I, however, do not want them to annihilate me either. Wiggle room is good for all of us. I don't want to destroy all that Leah has done any more than Helen does."

"What if you get caught for having leaked the letter?" Sunny asked Helen.

"First amendment. Our media contacts will go to jail before they release their sources. They know it would be the end of their careers if they did."

Leah sighed deeply. "So why are you sharing this with me, Helen? I still don't get it."

"The memo will be released next Monday," Helen began to explain. "You'll lose your funding from A.A.F. shortly after that."

All eyes turned to Vaughn, who made a gesture to suggest that the decision was inevitable.

"You'll lose your security," Helen went on.

"Surely you would have warned us, Mr. Vaughn," Leah asserted.

"No, he wouldn't have," Helen explained. "He couldn't. If he warned you beforehand, the plot would be blown. You could have gone to the press and told them that he had warned you. That would have made them suspicious."

"But we still can," Leah noted.

"But he hasn't told you," Helen quickly replied. "I did. He's only here because he saw my name on the security register."

"But you can set them straight," Sunny observed.

Helen looked down at the floor before answering.

"I'm sorry; I can't. We'd go down with him."

Vaughn smiled fiendishly.

"I think you should consider leaving town for awhile," Helen continued. "I fear that things could get ugly here once Pinnacle is gone. A lot of people are going to feel cheated. They won't be happy. Somebody's already tried to kill you."

"What do you know about that?" Sunny asked accusingly.

Helen stared at Sunny. "Nothing. It wasn't us. I have no idea who was behind it. Frankly, I'm not sure it was someone on our side. It was a stupid move, if it was. If they had succeeded in killing her, they would have made her a martyr."

After a long pause, Helen continued. "When this comes out, I don't think it's going to be the professionals you have to worry about anyway. People that hire professionals don't do it for personal reasons. When you disappear, whoever hired them will have their problem – whatever problem that is - solved. They won't pursue it any further.

"That said, however," Helen continued, "Your cause has been deeply personal for those you have given hope, many of whom previously led lives of desperation. Some of them will feel like their legs have been cut out from under them. There's bound to be a couple of kooks among them who won't react rationally."

As she spoke, Helen leaned over and picked up her bag. From it she withdrew what appeared to be a check. With the bag still on her lap, she said, "You won't have to stay underground forever. And when you come up, you can work to support the Warner foundation. I'd even like to help."

Holding the check out to David, Helen continued, "Here's a down payment."

Hesitantly, David reached out to take the check from her. After looking at it, he appeared bewildered and said absently, "It's for a million dollars."

Leah gasped. "Where did the money come from?"

"The Sisyphus Foundation," Helen replied. "It's a little foundation I started with the help of friends. Most of them would rather not make their participation public, but it's all perfectly legal. In fact, we'd like a receipt. You can send it to my office."

"Sisyphus," Brad noted, "is a character from Greek mythology. The gods condemned him to roll a large rock up a hill. When he finally got it to the top, however, it rolled down again, making the task never-ending."

"Very good," Helen offered in legitimate praise. "The story of life, don't you think?

"A rather cynical perspective, I'd say," Brad replied.

Helen shrugged.

"And to get you through your temporary exile," Helen continued, turning to Leah while lifting her large hobo bag from her lap, "I brought you a little cash." She turned her bag over and dumped its contents on the floor. It created a large pile of bundles of 100-dollar bills, neatly stacked and banded. "Banking transactions are easily traced. And bank clerks don't make a lot of money. Some of them are easily compromised."

David and Leah exchanged looks of shock and bewilderment.

"Helen, you're a romantic," Vaughn exclaimed. "Who knew? Perhaps I should meet with you on Tortola next time."

"Don't get your hopes up."

"Too bad," Vaughn replied, feigning deep disappointment.

The group sat in silence. Finally, Vaughn slapped the arms of his chair lightly and began to stand. "Well," he said, "it looks like everyone is happy now. I think it's time for me to get back to Washington. Helen, dear, there's room on my jet if you'd care to join me. We can sip champagne and share some more titillating secrets."

"My, you are in a jolly mood," Helen replied. Turning to Leah, she smiled and said, "I work in Washington. I have no pride or ethics."

"Not that you want anyone to know about, anyway," Leah replied calmly.

Vaughn helped Helen with her coat and then went to the table to retrieve his own. As he put it on, Leah turned once again to Helen, who was in the process of putting on her wool hat.

"I still don't understand why you did this, Helen. Why do you care what happens to me?"

Helen finished putting on her hat and thrust her hands deep into the pockets of her coat. "Consider it my Pascal Wager."

Leah cocked her head quizzically.

"Blaise Pascal was a 17th Century French mathematician and philosopher," David explained. "He argued that it was logical to believe in God because if there was no God, you weren't out anything in the end. And if it turns out that there is a God, you're covered."

"Bingo, Dr. Marcus," Helen replied, breaking into a smile.

Reaching down to pick up her hobo bag, Helen reached out to shake hands with Leah. Leah stood and accepted her hand.

"Thank you, Helen," Leah said, warmly covering their clasped right hands with her left. "Not just for the warning and the money."

It was Helen's turn to look puzzled.

"Thank you for reminding me that it's a mistake to stand in judgment of others."

"You're welcome, Leah," Helen replied, her face grave with sincerity. "Good luck." A pause. "And God bless."

After shaking hands with David, Sunny, and Brad, Helen then walked to the door to the living room, where Vaughn was standing alone, holding the door open. "Good bye," was all he offered as Helen walked through the open door.

"Mr. Vaughn," Leah called out suddenly. Both Vaughn and Helen stopped and looked back into the room.

"Did you have anything to do with Gail's death, Mr. Vaughn?" Leah asked boldly.

Vaughn raised his free hand and rubbed his forehead. He then turned back around to face Leah without letting go of the door handle. "No," he said shaking his head.

"If you want to know who killed your friend, Mrs. Warner, I suggest you follow the money. Who have you cost the most money? Tax receipts suffer in a bad economy, but the government can always raise taxes or print more money. Corporate America - and the mob - don't have that luxury. One of them, I suspect, wanted you silenced at any cost."

With that, Vaughn turned, gestured for Helen to proceed, and the two Washington power-brokers departed.

EPILOGUE

Leah, Sunny, Tyler, Ryan, and Brad quietly re-located to Winter Park, Colorado, a mountain resort town that sits at 9,100 feet above sea level at the western base of the Continental Divide. They stayed in a secluded mountain home with an advanced security system owned by Professor Bradshaw.

David Marcus remained in Michigan to further the work of the Warner Foundation. He made frequent trips to Winter Park, however, during which he and Leah continued to pursue what ultimately became an unmistakably romantic relationship.

A.S.P. released the letter provided by William Vaughn as planned. As expected, it ignited a firestorm of accusation, denial, and speculation. Vaughn, for his part, declined comment, other than to say that A.A.F. was withdrawing its support. He refused to clarify the skeptical comments made in the letter, insisting that the validity of the A.A.F. mission did not rest on the veracity of one person. The message, he maintained, transcended the messenger.

While secularists and other detractors cheered the release of the A.A.F. memo, most of Leah's supporters did not desert her. They refused to give up the hope that she had given them. Many chose to ignore the memo as outdated opinion and clung to Leah's irrefutable medical recovery. Others dismissed it as a forgery. Some even conjectured that Leah herself had written it to test the faith of the purported faithful.

Some of Leah's supporters did desert her, however, feeling scammed and betrayed. A few were bitter and filled with rage. Others simply shook their head at what they considered to be the reaffirmation of humankind's propensity for deceit and betrayal.

Over time, the media dropped the Leah Warner story and focused instead on the upcoming elections. The politicians and their back room power-brokers breathed a collective sigh of relief. More than 80% of the incumbents standing for re-election, including the president, were re-elected. Although the economy remained in a deep recession, he was able to deflect personal blame.

In December, Leah quietly emerged from her self-imposed exile. She and the boys returned to Michigan, where she became Leah Marcus – with the support of her children - and worked, largely in anonymity, in support of the Warner Foundation.

In the end, the status quo once again showed its formidable resistance to change, even for a messenger of God. Ultimately, however, people did look in the mirror at the society they had collectively created and realized that there had to be a better way.

The cultural excesses of the late 20th Century were ultimately, albeit slowly, reined in. Charitable giving rose greatly. And the political establishment, collectively realizing that a bullet had been dodged, finally got serious about attacking poverty, inequity, and prejudice.

Society, in total, became just a little more civil. People greeted each other in public. Neighbors lent a hand to neighbors. And drivers were just a little more courteous on the road.

More than anything else, Leah Warner caused the world to think, to look at itself in a more critical light. People began to challenge perceptions and motivations. Fewer truths were accepted as a matter of dogma or doctrine. Prejudices and pre-conceptions were dragged into the light of objective scrutiny. In short, a humble Midwestern homemaker with a message of God's selfless love gave new life to a long dead philosopher, Socrates.

And the world was better for it.